PHULE'S PARADISE

PHULE'S PARADISE

Robert Asprin

LEGEND

A Legend Book

Published by Arrow Books Limited
20 Vauxhall Bridge Road, London SW1V 2SA

An imprint of the Random Century Group

London Melbourne Sydney Auckland
Johannesburg and agencies throughout
the world

Century/Legend edition 1992
This Arrow/Legend edition 1992

3 5 7 9 10 8 6 4 2

Printed and bound in Great Britain by
Cox & Wyman Ltd, Reading, Berkshire

ISBN 0 09 992450 1

Prologue

The view from General Blitzkrieg's window was uninspired to say the most, surveying a cramped parking lot and a blank wall badly in need of repainting or tearing down. In some ways, however, it typified the status of the Space Legion, or lack thereof. Perpetually strapped for funding, even the space for its headquarters was rented, and the area was very low rent indeed. That Blitzkrieg's office had a window at all was a sign of his lofty standing in that organization.

'Excuse me, sir?'

The general turned from staring out the window to find an aide poised in the door of his office.

'Yes?'

'You asked to be notified as soon as Colonel Battleax left on her vacation,' the aide said without formality. Salutes, like views, were optional in the Legion, and therefore very rare indeed.

'You're sure she's gone? You saw her take off yourself?'

'Well, sir, I saw her shuttle lift off and then return without her. The ship she had reservations on has left orbit, so I assume that she's on it.'

'Good, good,' the general said, almost to himself, a rare smile flickering across his face. 'And she'll be on vacation for several months, at least.'

Due to the time necessary for space travel, even aided by faster-than-light travel, vacations tended to be long, so the aide found nothing unusual about the length of Battleax's sabbatical, especially considering she had been accumulating time for several years. The aide was, however, puzzled by the general's attitude and interest in it. It was surprising that Blitzkrieg as one of the three directors of the Space Legion, would take such a concern in the long-overdue vacation of a lowly colonel.

'She'll certainly be missed,' the aide commented, fishing for more information.

'She'll be missed more by some than others,' Blitzkrieg said darkly, his smile tightening a bit.

'Sir?'

'The colonel is a fine officer and administrator,' the general said, 'as fine as you'd find in the Regular Army. Still, she's human – and a woman at that – and tends to form attachments to certain individuals and units under her command. It's only natural that she use her position to campaign in their behalf here at Headquarters, as well as sheltering them when they foul up.'

'I suppose so, sir,' the aide said, suddenly uneasy about commenting on the performance of a senior officer.

'Well, that's about to change,' the general declared, sinking into the chair behind his desk. 'While she's on vacation most of her duties will be absorbed by other officers here at Headquarters, but I've set it up so that one unit in particular will report directly to me in her absence.'

'Which unit is that, sir?'

Blitzkrieg's eyes fixed on a spot on the far wall like he was a hungry toad tracking a fly.

'I'm talking about Captain Jester and that Omega Mob of his.'

Suddenly the aide could see the situation clearly.

It was well known around Headquarters that General Blitzkrieg had recently had his heart set on court-martialing Captain Jester for his actions upon taking over an Omega company – a company specifically formed to handle military misfits unsuited for even the Legion's loose standards and guidelines. Exact details were unknown, but the renegade captain had emerged from the incident not only unscathed but with a commendation for himself and his entire unit. Speculation as to how this was accomplished ran high, though many suspected that it had something to do with the fact that before enlisting and taking the name 'Jester', the captain had been one Willard Phule, one of the universe's youngest megamillionaires and heir apparent to the vast Phule-Proof Munitions empire. This latter piece of

6

information became known when Jester ignored the Legion's tradition of anonymity through pseudonym and exposed his true identity and origins to the media, thereby focusing unprecedented public attention on himself, his unit, and the Legion as a whole. The media loved it, but apparently the general didn't.

'Pass the word to communications,' Blitzkrieg said, never changing his tone or his smile. 'I want them to get Captain Jester on the horn for me. I have a new assignment for him and that ragtag gang of his.'

'Yes, sir,' the aide snapped, and quickly retreated from the office.

Several things troubled the aide as he headed for the communications room to carry out the general's order.

First, he had been thinking of requesting a transfer to Jester's company himself, and had been merely waiting for the right time to submit the necessary paperwork. As it was, however, it occurred to him that this was not the proper time for such a move, either from the viewpoint of the general's mood or from the fact that it looked like he had something unpleasant in store for that unit and its commander.

Second, he wondered if Captain Jester was aware of the general's animosity toward him, and even if he was, if he would be able to handle or avoid whatever unpleasantness was currently being aimed at him.

Finally, something occurred to the aide that had apparently escaped the general's mind – that if the Omega Mob was reporting directly to the general in Colonel Battleax's absence, then ultimately Blitzkrieg would be responsible for whatever they did on this new assignment they were being given.

All in all, the aide decided that the best place to be for a while would be on the sidelines as an observer and *not* anywhere near the actual action and/or repercussions.

Chapter One

Journal #171

Contrary to whatever impression might have been created by the first volume of these notes, butlers, even those seasoned by years of experience such as myself, are neither omnipresent nor all-knowing.

To support this assertion, I will acknowledge that I was not present when the call came in from Space Legion Headquarters signaling the start of a new chapter in my employer's career with that organization. In fact, I was not even at 'The Club,' which is how his current charges refer to the remodeled compound. Rather, it being my day off, I was in the settlement, or, as the Legionnaires call it, 'townside.' Even in my wildest flights of ego, however, I cannot claim that my absence had any bearing on the timing of the call, Headquarters being unaware of my exact role in relation to my employer, and totally ignorant of my work schedule. It was, at best, an unfortunate happenstance.

Of course, merely being absent is no excuse for someone of my position to lose track of his gentleman. I am the only civilian privileged to wear one of the wrist communicators which have become the trademark of the company under my employer's command, and have gone to great lengths to establish a close rapport with the terminally shy Legionnaire (known affectionately to one and all as 'Mother') who oversees all communications. Consequently I was alerted to the call's existence as soon as it was patched through.

Needless to say, I brought my off-duty pastimes

*to an immediate halt and returned to the club
with all haste, only to find the company in total
turmoil.*

The Legionnaires under the command of Captain Jester,
known more widely courtesy of his media exposure as Willard Phule, had become passable, and in some cases excellent, marksmen. This was in no small way due to the fact
that the design of the country-club-like barracks centered
around a wet bar/swimming pool/firing range, which was
the troop's favorite hangout during off-duty hours. As they
rarely stood duty more than once a week, this meant con-
siderable time was spent lounging about alternately sipping
drinks, dipping in the pool, and pumping rounds downrange
for practice, fun, or friendly wagers.

Today, however, the main subject of conversation among
the assemblage was not who could shoot better or faster,
or even who was ahead on the betting, but rather the
unscheduled holo call from Legion Headquarters.

Military units, even more than corporate offices, are vulnerable to rumors, and the Omega Mob was no exception.
The fact that no one knew for sure what had been said in the
call only added to, rather than dampened, the speculation.

Some thought their commander was being court-
martialed . . . again. Of course, there had been no new
activity which would trigger such an action, but there *were*
aspects of their *normal* modus operandi which would be
vulnerable to various degrees of legal discouragement were
they known to the authorities, either civil or Legion.

Yet another faction was guessing that their commander
was about to be transferred to another unit – a thought
which generated a certain amount of terror among those
Legionnaires willing to consider the possibility seriously.
While the company was now a cohesive unit, and the individuals within it genuinely cared for each other, there was
no doubt in any of their minds that their captain was the

one who first brought them together and they feared for the repercussions if he were lost to them.

'Do you really think they'll send the captain to another unit?' one of the Legionnaires fretted, idly splintering chips off his now-empty plastic glass.

His companion grimaced, dangling his feet in the pool. 'Sure they will. They assigned him to us as punishment, didn't they? Well, not that things are getting turned around, they're bound to pull him for another assignment.'

'Not a chance,' someone put in from one of the poolside tables. 'Did you see the general's face when he got back on the shuttle? The captain's still in the doghouse as far as Headquarters is concerned.'

'I don't know.' The original questioner scowled. 'Hey, Top! What do *you* think's going on?'

Brandy, the unit's Amazonian top sergeant, was sprawled at one of the poolside tables, filling the seat and her swimming suit more than amply. She was holding a drink in her right hand and a sidearm in her left, her favourite pose these days, and loosed an occasional shot downrange from where she sat, abandoning neither her seat nor her drinking for the exercise.

'Why ask me?' She shrugged, one strap of her suit slipping from its precarious hold on her shoulder. 'Stripes or no, I'm just a grunt like you. Nobody tell me nothin' until it comes to passing out orders. Why don't you ask our fearless leaders?'

The Legionnaire who had asked the question shot a glance at Rembrandt and Armstrong, the company's two lieutenants, but those notables were engrossed in a conversation of their own at the far end of the pool, so he simply shrugged and returned to his original discussion.

One table away, a massive figure bent forward to confer with the figure barely half his size sharing the table with him.

'Gnat. You think the captain will accept transfer?'

Super Gnat, the company's smallest member, turned her attention to her Voltron partner. It was only recently that Tusk-anini had started taking part in the poolside gatherings, as the bright sun hurt his marblelike, nocturnal eyes and the odor given off from his hairy chest, back, arms, and head when wet was, politely put, less than pleasant even to himself. However, by steering clear of the water and utilizing a pair of jury-rigged sun goggles, he was now able to join in on the more social pastimes of the company.

'What's that, Tusk? Oh. No, I don't think he would . . . if they give him a choice, that is. Sorry. I'm a little worried about the Top. Is it me, or is she drinking more lately?'

'Brandy?' Tusk-anini cranked his huge warthoglike head around to glance at the top sergeant. 'I think she worried about the captain. She love him, you know.'

'She does?' his diminutive partner said, giving him her full attention. 'I didn't know that.'

Though she had long since grown used to the Voltron's nonhuman appearance, his broken-English speech made it easy to forget that he was easily one of the most intelligent Legionnaires in the company, not to mention one of the most perceptive. Still, when she was reminded of that fact, as she was now, she had a healthy respect for his observations.

'That all right,' Tusk-anini said, twisting his features into one of his rare smiles. 'Captain not know, either.'

Before Super Gnat could pursue the subject further, however, there was a sudden clamor from one side of the pool.

'Hey! Here's the man who can tell us!'

'Beeker!'

'Hey, Beek! Got a sec?'

The commander's butler, Beeker, had just stepped through the entrance, taking the common shortcut across the pool/firing range area to the captain's quarters. Unfortunately this might not have been the wisest move. Though the butler was notoriously closemouthed about the confidences shared with him by his employer, the crew was still quick to seize on any chance of information and swarmed to him like locust after the last ear of corn on the planet.

11

'What's the word, Beeker?'

'Is HQ after the captain again?'

'Is he being transferred?'

Beeker was on the verge of getting backed against a wall when Brandy, quick despite her size, materialized between him and the advancing horde.

'*As you were! All of you!*'

This last was directed, along with a glare, at the two lieutenants, who had started to join the throng, but now sheepishly resumed their seats.

'Leave the man alone! He doesn't know anything more than we do . . . and if he did he couldn't tell us. You know the rules. Official Legion business comes through channels, *not* from Beeker! Now, back off and let the man do his job!'

The assemblage grumbled and cursed under their breath, but gave ground, reshuffling their groups as they went back to their original speculations.

'Thank you, Brandy,' the butler murmured softly. 'It was starting to get a bit ugly there for a minute.'

The company's top sergeant barely acknowledged the thanks, continuing to glare at the retreating Legionnaires. When she spoke, she did it without moving her lips or looking directly at Beeker.

'*Have* you heard anything, Beek? Anything you can tell us?'

The butler hesitated, then relented.

'Only that a call came in from Legion Headquarters,' he said. 'I'm here looking for more information myself.'

'Well, you might remind our Fearless Leader that he's got some folks out here who are a little curious about what's happening.'

'I'll do my best . . . and Brandy? Thanks again.'

Of course, Brandy had been correct. Beeker was not in the Legion chain of command, being privately employed by Phule, and was therefore doubly constrained from relaying information . . . both by military procedure and by his professional ethic as a butler. His position did, however, allow him one privilege not accessible to the Legionnaires, that

12

of entering the commander's private quarters without being specifically summoned, and he freely exercised that privilege now, pausing only briefly after knocking before opening the door.

'Oh. Hi, Beeker. Come on in. I want your opinion on something.'

Willard Phule was sprawled in a chair, his lanky form the picture of casual relaxation. To the butler, however, this pose conveyed the exact opposite message. Normally Phule was the embodiment of nervous energy during the day, constantly pacing and fidgeting as he tried to do or consider a dozen things at once. For him to sit still, as he was doing now, required a crisis of monumental proportions, one which would put all other worries and tasks on a back burner while he weighed and considered the immediate problem. In short, anytime he seemed relaxed physically, it meant that he was racing about mentally.

'Is there a problem, sir?' Beeker prompted, pointedly closing the door behind him.

'You might say that. I just got a call from Headquarters giving us a new assignment, and – '

'Is that a new assignment for the entire company, or just for the two of us?' the butler interrupted.

'What? Oh. For the entire company. Why?'

'You might want to announce that to your command as soon as possible, sir. They seemed quite anxious when I passed through the pool area just now.'

'I don't know,' Phule said, rubbing his chin thoughtfully. 'I was planning to wait until I had a better fix on this new assignment before announcing it. It's always nice to have the information clear yourself before opening the floor to questions and answers.'

'If you'll forgive my saying so, sir, I *really* think you should say something to quiet their minds. They're aware that a call has come in from Headquarters, and many of them are concerned that you are being removed from the command of this unit.'

'I see. Well, I'll put a stop to that right now.'

As he spoke, Phule raised his wrist communicator to his mouth and pressed a button.

'Mother?'

'Yes, Captain,' came the immediate response without any of that Legionnaire's usual banter.

'Is everyone in range for a general broadcast?'

'That's a big affirmative. Truth to tell, they're all hangin' so close you could probably just raise your voice and save the batteries.'

A brief smile flitted across Phule's face.

'I think I'll follow normal procedure, anyway . . . just for practice. Give me a broadcast channel.'

'You got it, Big Daddy. We're all ears.'

Without thinking, Phule dropped into a deeper, formal voice as he began his announcement.

'If I could have your attention for a moment . . . I have been told that some of you are worried about the recent call from Legion Headquarters. All I can tell you at the moment is that we are being reassigned. I repeat, we are being reassigned . . . That's the entire unit. Details will be provided at a formal briefing tonight at twenty hundred hours. Officers, please stand by. Your presence will soon be required for a strategy session. That is all.'

He clicked off his com unit and leaned back, winking at his butler.

'There, I think that should do it.'

'Quite. Thank you, sir.'

'Okay, now that that's taken care of, I have something I want you to see.'

Phule waved Beeker toward a chair as he rose and fiddled with the holo unit which occupied the better part of one wall of his quarters. He had purchased and installed this unit as a supplement to the one issued the company specifically to ease the reception of calls from Headquarters. Of course, unlike the issued model, this one also had a record and playback capacity.

'This is a replay of the call I just received,' he said. 'I want to know what you think of it.'

As he spoke, the image of General Blitzkrieg materialized

in the room, seated at his desk, leaning forward on his elbows, his hands clasped in front of him.

'Good morning, Captain Jester.' The image smiled. 'Sorry to wake you so early.'

'Actually,' came Phule's phantom voice, 'it's afternoon here, sir.'

While interstellar communications were now commonplace, the problem of coordinating days, much less hours, between widely separated settlements still remained.

'Whatever.' The general shrugged. 'I have some good news for you, Captain. You and your company are being reassigned to a new duty. Orders are being cut, which will be sent to you along with the detailed briefing material, but I thought I should call you personally to let you know what's going on.'

'That's good of you, sir. What is the new assignment?'

'It's a really sweet job.' The general smiled. 'Basic security guard work, actually. The nice part is that you'll be guarding the Fat Chance – the newest, biggest casino on Lorelei. Easy duty in paradise, if you ask me. What do you say to that?'

'My first reaction would have to be "Why us?" . . . sir.'

The general's smile tightened a little.

'Mostly because the owner specifically requested you and your outfit, Captain. I guess all that showboating you've been doing for the media is finally paying dividends.'

'What I meant, sir, was why turn to the Space Legion at all? Our fees are significantly higher than any number of normal uniformed security services. Who is the owner, anyway?'

'I have it right here,' the general said, referring to a sheet of paper on the desk before him. 'Yes. Here it is. The contracting party is Gunther Rafael.'

'I find that hard to believe.'

'What was that, Captain?'

'There are two things wrong with that, General,' Phule said, hurriedly. 'First of all, while I've never met Mr. Rafael, I'm familiar with his reputation, and he's always been dead set against gambling of any form. Consequently it's hard for me to believe that he owns a casino.'

'I see.' The general frowned. 'And the other?'

'The other thing is that Gunther Rafael died nearly a year ago.'

'He did?' Blitzkrieg was scowling now, examining the paper again. 'Ah! Here's the problem. My mistake, Captain. It's Gunther Rafael, *Junior*, that's hiring you. Apparently the son doesn't share his father's dislike of gambling. Does that answer your question?'

'Not my first question: Why us?'

'Maybe he thinks hiring you will generate some publicity. You'll have to ask Mr. Rafael that,' the general said. 'But let me warn you, Captain, it's not the Legion policy to try to *discourage* clients from hiring us. Get my drift?'

'Yes, sir.'

'Very well. As I said, your orders will be forthcoming. Another Legion company has been dispatched to take over your current assignment. You and your company are to leave for Lorelei as soon as they arrive. Is that clear?'

'Yes, sir.'

'All right. Enjoy your new assignment, Captain Jester. Blitzkrieg out.'

Phule turned off the holo unit and sank into a chair.

'All right, Beeker,' he said. 'What's wrong with this picture?'

The butler pursed his lips thoughtfully.

'Well,' he said, 'aside from the obvious questions raised by your getting your assignment directly from General Blitzkrieg as opposed to Colonel Battleax, who is your immediate superior in the so-called chain of command, I guess my feelings could be summed up in one question: Why is this man smiling?'

The commander made little beckoning circles with his hand.

'Elaborate.'

'It has been my distinct impression,' the butler continued, 'that the general holds you in something less than highest esteem. In fact, it would be safe to say that he would rather

16

chew ground glass than give you the time of day, much less do you a favor. I therefore think it would be safe to assume that if he is taking the time to inform you personally of your new assignment, and is happy about doing it, the assignment is in all probability much less desirable than he is making it out to be.'

'Check.' Phule nodded. 'A bit long-winded, perhaps, but dead on the money with my own assessment.'

'You *did* ask me to elaborate, sir,' Beeker said, a little stung by the 'long-winded' accusation.

'The problem is,' the commander continued as if his butler hadn't spoken, 'how to find out what the trap is *before* we step in it.'

'If I might say so, sir, I believe the general himself has given you the answer to that problem.'

'How's that?'

'You could check the recording again, but as I recall, he specifically instructed you to obtain additional information on the assignment directly from the casino owner.'

'He did, didn't he? Phule smiled, then raised his wrist communicator once more.

'Mother?'

'Yes, O Exalted One?'

'Put a call through for me. I want to speak with Gunther Rafael, *Junior* . . . at the Fat Chance Casino on Lorelei.'

The call took nearly an hour to put through, though most of that time seemed to be spent trying to locate the person who was to receive it. When Gunther Rafael finally did take the call, the image which formed before Phule was less than encouraging.

What the holo-projection showed was an acned youth who didn't look old enough to be admitted to a casino, much less own one.

'Mr. Phule?' the image said, peering at a point slightly to the left of where Phule was standing. 'Hi. Gunther Rafael here. Gee, I'm really glad you called . . . I've been waiting to hear from you for a long time now.'

'You have?' Phule was a little taken aback at this.

17

'Well, yeah. I sent in my request for your services nearly a month ago, and the Space Legion accepted it almost immediately.'

From the corner of his eye, Phule saw Beeker lean back in his chair and stare at the ceiling, and knew the time lapse between the acceptance of the contract and their notification of its existence wasn't lost on the butler.

'I see,' the Legionnaire said. 'Well, I only received the assignment recently, and was hoping you could provide me with a few more details so I could brief my troops before we arrive.'

The youth frowned. 'It's not that hard to understand. I thought I made it clear in my request. I want you to keep those scumbags from taking over my casino, and I don't care if you have to gun every one of them down to do it!'

Beeker was suddenly sitting upright in his chair, staring at the image in disbelief. Of course, the way the cameras were situated, the only image being sent was that of Phule, who held up his hand in a gesture of restraint.

'Mr. Rafael . . .' he began.

'Please, make it "Gunther",' the youth interrupted with a quick smile.

'Very well' – Phule nodded – 'and in return, please call me "Jester".'

'Jester? But aren't you – '

'It's my name within the Legion,' Phule explained with a shrug. 'Anyway . . . Gunther . . . the information channels within the Legion can be slow and often distort the details of the original request, which is why I'm calling you directly. To be sure we're both on the same wavelength, could you briefly explain the assignment to me . . . as if I were hearing it for the first time?'

'Well, since Dad died, I've been liquidating his holdings so I could finally try to make my dream come true: to own and run the biggest and best hotel and casino on Lorelei – '

'Have you ever owned or worked in a casino before?' Phule interrupted.

'No . . . but I know it can be done! I can offer better odds than any other casino on Lorelei and *still* turn a profit.

I worked it all out on paper in college. What's more, I can attract the bulk of the tourists if they know they're getting the best odds *and* that the games are straight.' Gunther's eyes were alight with enthusiasm.

Phule, on the other hand, was unmoved.

'But you've never actually *worked* in a casino before.'

'No, I haven't,' the youth admitted with a grimace. 'That's why I've hired an experienced casino manager, Huey Martin, to run things for me while I learn.'

'I see,' the Legionnaire said, making a mental note of the name. 'Go on.'

'Well, a while back I learned that there was a chance that criminals were going to try to take over my place once it was open, and I didn't know what to do. The police here on Lorelei may be great for keeping the muggers away from the tourists, but they aren't up to handling anything like this! Then I saw the reports on how you managed to stop an alien invasion with just a handful of troops, and figured if you could do that, you should be able to stop common crooks from taking over my casino.'

'So that's the assignment,' Phule said slowly, steadfastly ignoring Beeker, who was now slumped in his chair, his arms folded, one hand over his eyes. 'To guard your casino against a hostile takeover by a gang of criminals.'

'Sure.' Gunther beamed. 'I figure with your uniformed troops standing in full view, the customers will feel safer, and those scumbags will think twice before they try any rough stuff.'

'All right . . . there are several things I'm going to need, Gunther, and I'd appreciate it if you could transmit them to me here on Haskin's Planet as soon as possible. I'm going to want copies of the floor plans and blueprints for the hotel – particularly the casino area – showing electrical and security systems. I also want to see copies of all your personnel files on all employees, starting with Huey Martin's, and . . . did you say you weren't open yet?'

'Well, parts of the casino are open, but I'm doing a lot of remodeling. There's going to be a big grand opening to launch the new operation.'

'We can't leave our current assignment until our replacements arrive,' Phule said, almost to himself, 'then there's time in transit, and . . . Gunther, can you hold your grand opening until at least a week after we arrive?'

'I . . . guess so. Why do you want my personnel records?'

'Let's just say I like to have some idea of who's at our backs while we're standing guard . . . Oh, and speaking of personnel, have you made arrangements for housing my troops?'

'Sure. I was going to have them stay at one of the small hotels down the Strip.'

'Cancel that. I want them to have rooms at the Fat Chance. A hundred rooms and a penthouse.'

'But rooms at the Fat Chance go for –'

'They're supposed to be guarding your hotel and casino,' Phule said pointedly. 'They can't do that if they're at another location when trouble hits, can they?'

'I . . . guess not. All right. I suppose with over a thousand rooms I can spare a hundred. Is that all?'

Phule nodded. 'For the moment. I'll probably be getting back to you soon with some additional requests, but that'll give me a starting point.'

'Okay. I'll tell you, Mr. Jester, I'll sleep a lot easier now knowing you're on the job.'

The youth's image faded as the connection was broken.

For several moments, Phule and Beeker stared silently at the place in the room it had occupied. Finally the commander cleared his throat.

'How in the world did someone that ignorant and naive get to be a multimillionaire?'

'Not to belabor the obvious, sir,' Beeker said softly, 'I believe he inherited it.'

Phule wrinkled his nose in disgust. While he had borrowed seed money from his munitions-baron father, he had long since paid it all back, with interest, and considered his wealth to be self-made. As such, he had little tolerance for those who inherited their wealth, and none at all for those who were foolish with what money they had.

'Oh well,' he said, 'it takes all kinds . . . I guess. At least now we know what we're up against with this assignment.'

'A know-nothing kid trying to run a casino on book theories and hired expertise,' Beeker recited grimly. 'Not exactly the cushy guard duty in paradise that General Blitzkrieg was trying to paint it as, is it, sir? Oh yes . . . and let us not forget the possibility of an attempted criminal takeover.'

'You know, that's the part that bothers me the most.' The commander scowled. 'Check me on this, Beek . . . you stay more abreast of current events than I do. These days, when crime, organized or otherwise, wants to take over a business, do they do it with guns blazing?'

The butler made a soft but rude noise before answering.

'Not to my knowledge, sir. It's my understanding that the usual tactic is to force them into financial difficulty, then buy them out cheap – or, at least, a controlling interest.'

Phule nodded. 'That's what I thought. More like a hostile stock takeover. Well, I've handled those before.'

The butler looked at him sharply.

'If I might point out, sir, the methods the criminal element utilizes to put financial pressure on a business are well outside civilized law. I would suggest it would be prudent not to underestimate your opponents.'

'I appreciate the advice, Beeker,' Phule said, 'but for your information the crowd *I'm* accustomed to playing with has little regard for civilized law. I have not succeeded in the past by underestimating an opponent . . . nor by underestimating myself.'

'Yes, sir. Sorry, sir.'

'Enough of that,' the commander said. 'It's time we got to work. I hope your fingers are rested, Beek 'cause there's a bit of non-Legion business I want you to take care of for me. We're going to be doing some hiring, and I'd like you to do the initial screening and have your recommendations on my desk by noon tomorrow.'

'Very well sir.' The butler was not fazed by the sudden change in mood and topic, nor by the request. The two men had worked together for a long time. 'And our requirements are . . . ?'

'First, I need a solid casino security man – someone with experience and unquestionable references. Top dollar for the right man. Also, I want at least half a dozen instructors who can teach the table games. Check with the dealer's schools – buy one if you have to – but I need them all here. Charter a ship, too, – before our replacements arrive. Offer them all a half year's wages, but we'll only need them from the hiring date until our transport hits the last big port before Lorelei . . . What would that be?'

'Port Lowe, sir.'

'Right. Next . . .' Phule allowed himself a small smile. 'This may be a little out of the ordinary for you, Beek, but I need to set up a cattle call.'

'Sir?'

'An audition. Find out what our first stop is after we leave here, then use the computer to pull up data on available actors and actresses at that location – bit players only. We don't need any recognizable faces.'

'Very well, sir. May I ask what you'll be doing in the meantime . . . in case I need to confer with you on any of this?'

'Me?' The commander smiled. 'I'll be doing my homework . . . seeing what I can learn about organized crime. I think I'll drop into the settlement and pay a visit to our old friend Chief Goetz.'

'That won't be necessary, sir.'

'Excuse me, Beek?'

'I believe you'll find Chief Goetz at poolside here at The Club. He gave me a lift back from the settlement, and he rarely passes on the opportunity to mix with your troops.'

'You got the chief of police to play taxi driver for you?' Phule seemed genuinely impressed.

'Actually, sir, he offered. I was at his home at the time.'

'His home?'

'Yes, sir. I've been tutoring his son in algebra on my days off.'

The commander laughed and shook his head.

'Beeker,' he said, 'what would I do without you?'
The butler smiled. 'I'm sure I don't know, sir.'

Chapter Two

Journal #173

   As I have both noted and chronicled before,
though he is more than effective on an overall
basis, my employer is far from infallible. Not only
do circumstances occasionally catch him off guard,
there are times when his judgment turns out to
be shortsighted or simply incorrect.

   Such was the case in his estimation of how the
Legionnaires under his command would respond
to their new assignment.

   As was our normal procedure, I was excluded
from the actual briefing session, not being a
member of the Legion. Of course, as was my
normal procedure, I elected to keep informed of
my employer's activities by listening in on the
meeting through The Club's two-way paging/in-
tercom system . . .

There was an air of excitement and anticipation as the
company gathered in The Club's combination dining hall
and lounge for their briefing. Speculation as to the exact
nature of their new assignment was, of course, the subject
of much of the scattered discussion, but it was secondary
to the main thrust of their emotions. Almost without exception, the Legionnaires were eager for the chance to put
their new skills, honed by hundreds of hours practice, to
use. While no real protest had been made, they had been
feeling for some time that they were ready for something
more challenging than guarding the planet's swamp miners

once a week, and it looked as if the Legion was finally in agreement with them.

Of course, not everyone was enthusiastic.

'It'll be great to get off this rock and see some *real* fighting, won't it, C.H.?'

Chocolate Harry, the company's massive, pear-shaped supply sergeant, turned his head with regal slowness to survey the Legionnaire who had addressed him through his pop-bottle-thick glasses. One of the few blacks in the company, Harry would be an imposing figure even if he didn't favor a fierce bristly beard to offset his close-cropped hair, or wear his uniform tunic with the sleeves ripped off to display his thick arms, but as it was, the cold stare he leveled was enough to dampen the enthusiasm of his questioner even before he spoke.

'I suppose,' he said slowly at last. 'Personally, though, I'm not lookin' forward to having to move my whole inventory to another location . . . especially since I seriously doubt our new facilities will be as lavish as where we are right now.'

The Legionnaire being addressed suddenly glanced around the room fearfully as if it were about to vanish as they spoke. Until now, he hadn't stopped to think that a new assignment would mean leaving the company's beloved Club behind.

'Then again,' Harry continued, 'there's one big problem with 'real fighting,' as you call it. Unlike the targets you all have been shootin' to shreds, in *real* fightin', the targets shoot back. How many of these folks do you think have ever been shot at before? Let me tell you, troop, it's no fun.'

The Legionnaire who had started the conversation licked his lips and swallowed hard. The truth was *he* had never been shot at before, and, now that he found himself seriously considering the possibility, his earlier enthusiasm for real combat was fading fast.

'Well, *I've* been shot at before,' Brandy said, stepping into the conversation, 'both as a civilian and in the Legion, and as far as I'm concerned it's a lot better when you can shoot back . . . especially if you've got superior firepower and teammates you trust guarding your back.'

The supply sergeant gave a quick bark of laughter in spite of his earlier gloominess.

'You got that right, Top. You sure do.'

He clapped the now-relieved Legionnaire on the shoulder with a friendly hand.

'Don't you worry none, little buddy. Odds are, they'll ignore you completely, what with two big easy targets like the Top and me around. Just stick close to one of us, and they'll never even see you.'

The Legionnaire gave him a nod and weak smile before wandering off to find another, less nerve-racking conversation.

'Quit scaring the troops, C.H.', the top sergeant said softly. 'At least ease up a bit until we find out for sure what we're getting dropped into. Our captain's done a pretty good job of looking out for us so far. Let's give him the benefit of the doubt for a while – at least until we hear something for sure.'

It was a tribute to Phule's personnel management techniques that Brandy, who was once the biggest cynic in the company if not the entire Space Legion, was now a major advocate of optimism, however cautious.

'Oh, you don't have to worry about me backin' him up, Top,' Harry assured her. 'The cap'n's done all right by me so far, and I ain't one to forget someone who's given me a hand up any more'n I'm likely to forget someone who kicked me when I was down. I just get a little intolerant when kids with no scars start tellin' me how great fightin' is.'

Brandy shrugged. 'They'll learn soon enough. Besides,if too many of 'em wise up too quick, then *we* end up out front when the shooting starts.'

'Lord have mercy!' C.H. exclaimed, rolling his eyes in exaggerated horror, then laughed again. 'I never thought of it that way. All right, Brandy, you win. I'll keep my mouth off the troops until they've seen the light all by themselves.'

'Good.' The top sergeant nodded. 'You see, the way I figure it, if the noncoms don't – '

'Atten-Hut!'

The company commander had just entered the room flanked by his two junior officers, and while military courtesy was an option in the Space Legion, the company held him in enough respect and esteem that they rose to their feet as a unit and saluted, holding the pose until he returned the gesture.

'As you were . . . and make yourselves comfortable,' he said, waving them to their seats. 'We've got a lot of stuff to cover tonight.'

The Legionnaires settled back into their original places with a minimum shuffling and murmured cross talk, though more than a few curious glances were cast at the company's junior officers. Like kids asking what a holo-movie was about even as the opening credits were rolling, they looked for some advance clue as to the nature of their new assignment in their leaders' expressions, but those notables kept their faces locked in rigid neutrality.

The more veteran Legionnaires frowned thoughtfully at this. Experience had taught them that noncommittal expressions on officers usually meant bad news. If the news were good, there would be smiles and maybe even a few smug winks being exchanged. As it was . . .

'You all already know that we're being reassigned,' their commander began without preamble. 'While there are still countless details to be worked out, I thought it would be best to at least give you a preliminary briefing in an effort to keep speculation to a minimum.'

'Before I get into the assignment, however, I'd like to address the question of what happens to this facility when we relocate. As you all know, The Club is my personal property. I bought the property and building when I arrived and had it remodeled and am currently renting it to the Legion. Originally I intended to sell the holding when we moved on, and, in fact, have several standing offers from interests who would like to convert it to a country club. I have, however, reconsidered. As I am not in immediate need of additional capital, I have decided to retain ownership of this facility even after our departure. It is my thought that

27

it can serve as a home base for the company and, perhaps, a retreat for those members on leave. If we find that this is a desirable arrangement, then we can discuss the possibility of using the company fund to buy it from me outright ... transferring ownership formally and permanently to the company itself. Should that occur, I think you'll find my asking price more than reasonable.'

The commander allowed a small ghost of a smile to flit across his face as the Legionnaires grinned and nudged each other gleefully at the announcement.

'Now then, as to the assignment itself,' he continued, raising his voice slightly, to which the company responded by falling silent, 'I guess it can best be described as good news/bad news. The bad news is that we've drawn guard duty again, which I know will be a disappointment to those of you who were hoping for some kind of combat assignment.'

Phule paused for a moment, and, as he had expected, the now-traditional voice from the back of the room piped in.

'What's the good news?'

'The good news,' he responded, working to keep his voice and face deadpan, 'is that *what* we are being assigned to guard is the Fat Chance Casino on Lorelei, which I think you'll agree is a step up from standing duty in a swamp. To quote Headquarters directly, it's "easy duty in paradise." '

There were a few heartbeats of silence, then the room exploded. The Legionnaires crowed and cheered, thumping each other enthusiastically on the back.

Phule noticed, however, that not everyone was joining in on the festivities. Several of the company's members, specifically the older, more experienced Legionnaires, seemed unmoved or, in some cases, even wary and thoughtful at the news.

'Excuse me, Cap'n,' Chocolate Harry called, heaving himself to his feet, 'but exactly what is it we're supposed to be guardin' this casino against? I mean, it occurs to me that we're a bit overgunned to be doormen.'

'I wondered about the same thing, C.H.,' the commander

said with a smile, though inwardly he was cursing the shrewdness of a question that prevented him from presenting the situation at his own pace. 'So I gave the owner a call. It seems that his main concern, and the reason for specifically requesting our services, is that he's afraid that a certain criminal element might be trying to take over his casino. It's our job to stop them.'

The celebratory smiles disappeared abruptly at this news, and the Legionnaires began to murmur back and forth.

'A certain criminal element,' Harry repeated dramatically. 'Tell me, Cap'n, is that rich folks' talk for "organized crime"?'

'That's organized crime no matter who's doing the talking, C. H.,' Phule confirmed grimly.

The mutters and conversation in the ranks accelerated noticeably. For some, organized crime was a legendary force they only knew about from carefully phrased media coverage, while others in the company had more firsthand dealings with that subterranean branch of society. Whether their knowledge was from rumor or personal experience, however, it was clear to all that their new 'cushy assignment' had just grown some dangerous thorns.

'Now, it doesn't take a genius to figure out that uniformed security guards won't be much of a deterrent against this kind of opposition,' Phule said, pressing on before the meeting got totally out of hand. 'Any more than uniformed beat cops can keep organized crime out of a city.'

He paused involuntarily to take a deep breath before plunging into the next part.

'That's why I've decided that, for this assignment, some of you will be working under cover, independently and out of uniform, infiltrating the normal hotel and casino staff to gather intelligence for the rest of us. In fact, I'll be calling for volunteers for this duty as soon as the meeting breaks up.'

His eyes sought out the tall Voltron, easily spotted in the assemblage.

'Tusk-anini, you're exempt from this duty . . . as are the Sinthians, Louie and Spartacus. It's my understanding that

29

nonhumans are still a rarity on Lorelei, so you'd be too obvious in any capacity other than as a part of our open presence. Any of the rest of you who are willing to apply for this special assignment, report to me in my office when we're done here.'

'How many are you looking for, Captain?'

Phule didn't even bother to look for the originator of the question.

'I figure that for an effective intelligence network, we'll need about forty or fifty spread through the various hotel areas and shifts.'

The Legionnaires began to glance back and forth among themselves. Forty or fifty Legionnaires meant about one in four of them would not be serving with the rest of the team this assignment.

'That's a fair-sized hunk of our force, sir,' Brandy observed loudly from her front-row seat. 'Aren't you afraid someone will notice if we show up that much understaffed?'

'They would . . . if we showed up in partial strength,' the commander confirmed. 'That's why we're going to have to hire some "ringers" to substitute for the Legionnaires working under cover. I've given Lieutenant Rembrandt the assignment of recruiting – or should I say, auditioning – the necessary number of actors and actresses to bring our uniformed body count up to the required level.'

To Phule, this was a logical choice. Rembrandt, with her artist's eye, would be best at selecting stand-ins, while Armstrong, with his stern Regular Army upbringing, was a natural to help organize and oversee the company's physical relocation to their new assignment.

The Legionnaires, however, heard this news in stricken silence. While they had shown concern over being pitted against the unknown menace of organized crime, the concept of dividing their force seemed to stun them beyond words.

'You will give . . . our uniforms to people . . . not in company? Not in Legion?'

It was Tusk-anini who broke the silence . . . and Phule knew he was in trouble. The big Voltron was one of his most loyal supporters who rarely, if ever, questioned orders. If Tusk was going to get upset over the idea of outsiders standing duty as Legionnaires, then Phule was going to have to talk fast before the rest of the company rose up in open mutiny.

'That's right, Tusk-anini,' he said. 'I'm not wild about it, either, but that's the way it's got to be.'

He quickly turned his attention to the group at large before any more questions could be raised.

'Now, before you all jump all over me about the downsides of this operation, let me cut right to the bottom line of the situation. We've got a hairy assignment that's been dumped in our laps. I didn't ask for it. *We* didn't ask for it, but we've got it. Actually, realizing the dubious opinion Headquarters has of us, we shouldn't be surprised at all.'

That got a few smiles and nudges out of the company. Once considered the losers and rejects of the Legion, the troops under Phule's command now took a perverse pride in their renegade status.

'Basically I'm sure that General Blitzkrieg figures this is an impossible assignment, and that he gave it to us fully expecting us to fall flat on our faces.'

A few growls answered this statement, but Phule pressed on quickly.

'Hey, he may be right. We may *not* be able to stop an organized-crime takeover, but we're going to give it our best shot. Remember what I told you when I first assumed command? About doing the best you can with what you have in any given situation? Well, in *this* situation, to do our best – to have any chance at all of success – we're going to have to send part of our team under cover. They're going to have to give up their pretty uniforms *and* the support they get from them and stand duty all alone. To cover for them, to give them a chance, we're going to have to accept the presence of stand-ins in our ranks. What's more, we're going to have to treat the substitutes as equals . . . *really* let them blend in. Because, if we don't . . .'

He swept the room with his sternest stare.

'If *anyone* gets the idea that not everyone in our uniformed

31

show is genuine, they're going to start looking around for where the *real* Legionnaires are. If they do that, if they catch on to the scam we're running on them, then your teammates, and in some cases your partners, are going to be sitting ducks in a *very* rough shooting gallery.'

'Our partners?' Even his broken accent couldn't hide the horror in Tusk-anini's voice.

Phule cursed his verbal slip. Realizing how upset the company was over the idea of stand-ins, he had decided to hold back this particular piece of bad news until later, but now the cat was out of the bag.

'Affirmative,' he said flatly. 'Between the volunteers for undercover work, and trying to pair the stand-ins with legitimate Legionnaires, I figure a lot of the normal partners in the company will have to be split up.'

Utter silence reigned in the room.

Of all the information he had passed on this evening, Phule knew that this was probably the most unsettling of all. One of the first things he had done upon assuming command of the company was to pair the Legionnaires off with partners or 'wing men.' While there had been some resistance at first, the company was now used to the system, and the partner teams had grown into more than friendships. Telling the Legionnaires that the partners would be split, particularly on top of the other bad news, was roughly like telling them he wanted to cut off their arms.

'Look,' he said, making no effort to keep the regret out of his voice. 'I know it's asking a lot . . . and I can't expect you to like it. To tell you the truth, I don't like it much myself. Still, it's the only way . . . if we're even going to have a *chance* of success on this assignment. I, for one, want to at least give it a shot before we run up the white flag.'

He ran his eyes slowly over the assembled company, then sighed and pulled himself back up into a position of attention.

'Well, that's the bare bones of it . . . the bitter and the sweet. As I said, there are still a lot of details to be worked out. Think it over . . . talk it over. I'll be in my office if any of you want to be considered for the volunteer mission. That's all for now.'

With that, he beat a hasty but dignified retreat from the meeting.

Chapter Three

Journal #174

It seemed that while my employer might have sorely underestimated the reaction of his Legionnaires to his plan, he also underestimated the fierce loyalty they felt toward him . . . a loyalty, I might add, which appeared to be growing steadily.

If, by the way, it seems to you that these accounts always start with an apparently endless parade of meetings, both group and individual, I can only say that this happens to be my employer's particular style of management. Whenever possible, he likes to talk with those in his employment or under his command, both to keep them informed and to learn their reactions to his plans. If anything, I have tried to spare you the tedium of the meetings and discussions he had with the Legionnaires on a weekly and sometimes on a daily basis by omitting them from these journals. Those affecting major events, however, such as the ones in this section, must be included for completeness of my account.

I should also note, as it will become apparent in this section, that while my position still is an individual contractual arrangement with my employer rather than with the Space Legion, I did take a larger role in this assignment than normal.

Beeker raised a speculative eyebrow as Phule stormed into the office.

'Difficult meeting, sir?'

'Difficult?' Phule snarled. 'How does "open revolt" sound?'

'Frankly, sir, it sounds unbelievable,' the butler said, choosing to ignore the redundant nature of his employer's question. 'While your troops may be occasionally unhappy with your orders, I seriously doubt they would ever challenge your position as their leader. Their respect for you borders on reverence.'

Phule took a deep breath, then blew it all out, puffing his cheeks in a near-silent whistle.

'That's true,' he said. 'But they *were* unhappy.'

'Forgive my asking, sir,' Beeker continued mercilessly, 'but wasn't that what you expected? Considering the effort you've put into building camaraderie and a sense of family within the company, it seems to me only natural that they would react with shock and panic when confronted with an assignment which requires their splitting up.'

Despite himself, Phule's face twisted into a wry smile as he cocked his head at his butler.

'Are you trying to tell me I did too good a job, Beek?'

'Not exactly, sir,' the butler returned blandly. 'I am suggesting that you should *keep* doing your job. At the moment your company needs a leader to make firm decisions, however unpleasant . . . not an overly sensitive debutante who worries about popularity polls . . . sir.'

'Ouch.' Phule grimaced. 'Ouch and *touché*. All right, Beek. I'll shut up and soldier. You don't mind if I whine once in a while, though? When the schedule permits?'

'That *is* your prerogative, sir. I shall let you know when and if I find it excessive.'

'I'm sure you will.' The commander laughed. 'And Beeker? Thanks.'

'Just doing *my* job, sir,' the butler said. 'If you have recovered from your ordeal, however, there *is* a matter I wish to discuss with you . . . if you have a moment.'

Reflexively Phule glanced at his watch. 'Well, the volunteers don't seem to be beating down my door . . . not yet, anyway. What do you have, Beek?'

'I believe I have a small amount of vacation time accrued, do I not, sir?'

'As a matter of fact, you have a *lot* of vacation time coming. Why do you ask?'

'I was thinking I might take some of it prior to our arrival on Lorelei . . . if it's convenient, that is.'

Phule frowned.

'I can't say it's really convenient,' he said, 'what with us getting ready for a major relocation. Still . . . what's up, Beek? If you don't mind my asking.'

'I believe your plans call for Lieutenant Rembrandt to depart early? To audition and select a group of actors and actresses to replace those Legionnaires who will be working under cover?'

Phule nodded. 'That's correct.' He had never asked how it was that his butler always seemed to know his plans and decisions without being told . . . mostly because he wasn't sure he wanted to know how this miracle was performed.

'Well, sir, I was thinking I might accompany her on her mission. While I'm sure that she is more than capable of completing her assignment on her own, it occurs to me that there will be a myriad of nonmilitary details and arrangements to be handled in connection with her work, things she may only have minimal experience in dealing with. While I would make arrangements to see to the packing and moving of our own gear before I left, I frankly think my services would be more valuable to her than to you in the upcoming weeks.'

'I see,' Phule said, pursing his lips. 'I don't see where there would be any problem in letting you do that. Let me think about it and get back to you with my decision.'

'Very good, sir. If I might add, however, I assume that Lieutenant Rembrandt will be in civilian garb for her mission?'

The commander nodded. 'I hadn't thought about it, but you're right, Beeker. She'd have to be. Otherwise the media would catch wind of it and tip our hand before we even got started.'

'Well, sir, I, for one, haven't seen the lieutenant in anything except her Legionnaire wardrobe. While I have no reason to doubt the extent of her civilian wardrobe or her ability to supplement it as necessary, I have no basis to be confident of it, either.'

'Point taken, Beeker. Like I say, let me think on it. Just remember . . .'

They were interrupted by a knock on the door.

'Whoops! There's my first victim. Let them in, will you, Beek? On your way out?'

'Yes, sir . . . but first, sir . . .'

'Yes?'

'If I might draw your attention to the time?'

Again Phule glanced at his watch. 'Okay. So?'

'It is my understanding that you're expecting to interview some fifty volunteers tonight?'

'If that many show up, yes.'

'Might I point out, sir, that if each interview only takes ten minutes, it will take more than eight hours to finish them all?'

Phule sighed wearily. 'I know, but it's important that I handle this as soon as possible . . . as you yourself pointed out not too long ago.'

'Of course, sir. I was merely suggesting that you might wish to make an effort to keep each individual interview as brief as possible considering the cumulative time involved . . . resist the temptation to try to settle details tonight that could be handled at leisure over the next few days. While I'm aware that it's my favorite lost cause, you *do* need to sleep occasionally . . . sir.'

The knocking came again, more insistent this time.

'I'll keep it in mind, Beek . . . but no promises. Sometimes I have to go with the flow.'

'I know, sir.' The butler sighed. 'But I felt I had to at least make the effort.'

'Evenin', Cap'n.'

Chocolate Harry, the company's supply sergeant, slouched against the door frame, casually shooting a salute at his commander with one finger.

37

'I'll keep this short, 'cause it looks like you got quite a mob shapin' up out here. Just put me down as one of your scouts.'

'All right, C. H.' Phule nodded, jotting a note on his pad. 'I'll admit I'm a little surprised, though. I didn't think you'd want to be separated from your inventory.'

'I'll admit I'm not wild about it,' Harry said, 'but I figure most of it will be packed and stored anyway for this assignment, and my boys can handle that easy enough. 'Sides, I don't think there's anyone in this outfit who can pass for a civilian as easy as me . . .'specially when it comes to movin' through the less legal portions of polite society.'

He winked broadly at this. While it was normal in the Legion to keep one's pre-Legion life a secret, Harry was very open about the fact that when he joined up he had been on the run from associates who, if not criminal, were at least outlaw.

The commander did not return the smile.

'That brings up an interesting point, C. H. Is it going to be safe for you to operate out of uniform?'

'I've given that some thought myself, Cap'n,' the sergeant admitted. 'There shouldn't be any special trouble for me on Lorelei . . . or if it pops up, it won't be any more dangerous for me out of uniform than in.'

Phule hesitated for a moment, then gave a curt nod.

'All right, then. Check back with me in the next couple days and we'll start working up a cover for you.'

'Oh, don't you worry none about that,' Harry said, uncoiling from the door frame as he got ready to depart. 'Except for maybe a little travelin' cash, I figure I'll do my own job huntin'. That way, if HQ wants to complain about it later, they can't get on your case as an accomplice.'

'Sergeant Escrima . . . reporting for volunteering.'

Phule's smile came easily as he returned the ramrod-stiff salute. He had a genuine fondness for the company's feisty little mess sergeant, though perhaps 'feisty' was a poor description. Escrima was easily the deadliest fighter in the company, especially with sticks or any cut-and-thrust weapon.

'Stand easy, Sergeant,' he said. 'I'll admit I'm glad to see you volunteering. I rather hoped you would.'

'Mmmm . . . Company stay in hotel, nothing for cook to do.' Escrima shrugged, relaxing his pose only slightly.

'My thoughts exactly.' The commander nodded, jotting another note on his pad. 'I assume you're interested in us finding you work in the restaurant kitchen?'

The cook gave a quick nod. 'Things can go wrong in a kitchen – too many things. Need someone there to watch for' – he gestured with his hand slightly as he searched for the right word – 'too many accidents. Bad for food . . . bad for business.'

Phule leaned back in his chair.

'Now, you realize that you probably won't be head cook or chef for the casino hotel . . . that you'll probably have to report to someone else.'

Escrima hesitated for a moment, then bobbed his head again.

'Good,' he said, flashing a quick smile. 'Sometimes it's good not to be in charge. Maybe . . . how you say . . . learn something new for a change.'

The commander shook his head slightly. 'I was thinking more in terms of possible trouble,' he said. 'Say, for example, if someone told you to do something you didn't want to . . . or maybe even criticized your cooking techniques.'

Escrima's dark eyes glittered for a moment. The cook's temper was legendary, and he was particularly sensitive to slights regarding his culinary skills. In fact, his presence in what was once the problem company of the Legion was due to several such spirited discussions . . . which led to hospitalization of his critics.

'I promise, Captain. No trouble . . . I never *start* trouble.'

'Do you mind if we do this together, Captain? I think it will save time.'

Phule could not keep the surprise off his face.

'Brandy . . . Super Gnat. Certainly. Come in together if you wish.'

The two women filed into the office, giving the sketchiest of salutes before seating themselves in front of their commander's desk. Though once standoffish toward each other, they had grown into a close friendship since the company was reorganized and reoriented.

'The reason we're both here,' Brandy said, taking the lead, 'is that we figure you'll have the same objection to either of us volunteering. This way, we only have to go over it once . . . win or lose.'

The commander nodded. 'Very well. Proceed.'

'The way we see it,' the top sergeant continued, 'you'll figure that we can't go under cover because of that pinup spread that we did with Mother – that we'd be recognized as part of the company.'

'It's a factor I'd have to consider,' Phule agreed. 'Also, the fact that Super Gnat represented us in the fencing match with the Red Eagles, which was covered by the media.'

'I was wearing a mask for most of that,' Super Gnat said, waving a hand in vague dismissal.

'True, but you weren't wearing a mask for that photo session . . . or much of anything else, as I recall.'

'That's what we wanted to talk to you about,' Brandy interrupted hastily. 'We wanted to make the point that women can change their appearance dramatically with a change of hairstyle or color, or makeup, or wardrobe.'

'Or just by putting our clothes on,' Super Gnat added with a bawdy wink. 'Tell me the truth, sir. When you look at one of those nudie photo spreads, how much time do you spend looking at the woman's *face*? Would you recognize her if you saw her on the street? Without a staple through her navel?'

'I . . . I'll admit I never gave the subject much thought,' Phule said. Though he tried not to show it, the conversation was making him uncomfortable . . . just as the photo spread in question had when it first appeared. 'If we accept for the moment that you can change your appearance sufficiently

40

to avoid recognition, though, what would you do? Do you have any specific covers in mind?'

The Gnat shrugged. 'No problem there. I used to do a little waitressing from time to time, both dinner and cocktail. I'd probably prefer cocktail waitressing, if given a choice. They circulate through the casino rather than stand duty just in the dining room, and the kind of action you're watching for will probably be going on at the tables, not over a meal. Besides, the tips are better from drinkers.'

'I was thinking more in terms of working with the house-keeping staff,' Brandy supplied. 'That photo spread was fun, but I don't really see myself wearing one of those peekaboo outfits day in and day out. Having a legitimate excuse to be in and out of the guest rooms wouldn't be a bad idea, either.'

The two looked at their commander expectantly.

'Actually,' he said slowly, staring at his notepad, 'the recognition problem wasn't my major concern. Super Gnat should be okay, but . . .' He hesitated, then shrugged and looked at his top sergeant directly. 'I'm not quite as comfort-able with *you* going under cover, Brandy. I had been count-ing on you to help me ride herd on the company while it was standing normal duty. The fact is, Chocolate Harry and Escrima have already volunteered, and the cadre roster is starting to look a little thin even if you stuck around. With you gone . . .' He let his voice trail off, then shook his head.

'I can see where that might be a problem, Captain. But . . .' Brandy hesitated, then leaned forward slightly. 'Can I speak candidly, sir?'

Phule nodded curtly.

'Well, you know how you got on my case when you first took over about being cynical and not trying? This is the first time in . . . hell, I don't know how many years now, that I've *volunteered* for anything. Now that I'm moving, I'd kinda like to see it through. I'm not sure if I'm trying to prove something to you or to myself, but I'd like to give it a shot.'

The commander pursed his lips and stared thoughtfully

41

at his pad again, then realized there was really nothing to decide. If it came to choosing between making things easier for himself or helping Brandy rebuild her self-esteem, there was only one choice that would be acceptable to *him*.

'All right,' he said, raising his eyes to look at them directly. 'We'll tentatively figure you both for undercover volunteers. I'm going to want to see a demonstration of this hair and makeup thing, though. Shall we say, tomorrow afternoon?'

'No problem, sir . . . and thank you, sir.'

The two women rose and saluted, turning toward the door only after their salute was returned.

'Just one more thing . . . Super Gnat?'

The little Legionnaire paused at the doorway at the commander's words.

'Sir?'

'Have you discussed this with Tusk-anini? I don't mean to meddle, but he's very devoted to you.'

At the mention of her partner, the Gnat's usual easy self-confidence wavered.

'I . . . I know, sir . . . And no, I haven't. I wanted to see if you figured I was acceptable first . . . I'll go talk to him now. I think he'll understand. He may be devoted to me, but he practically worships *you*. You were the one who called for volunteers, and I'd be willing to bet he'd put his hand into a fire up to his elbow if you asked him to. He might not like my volunteering, but it'll be mostly because he can't volunteer himself. Give him some time and he'll get over it . . . but even if he doesn't, he won't let it interfere with his performance.'

Rather than being reassured, Phule again felt the pangs of discomfort at this testimonial.

'All right, Gnat. I'll leave it to you. Just let me know if – '

'Say, Captain . . . Excuse me, Gnat.'

Brandy had just poked her head in the door, interrupting the conversation.

'What is it, Top?'

'I was thinking about what you were saying – about being thin on cadre for normal duty. Anyway, it occurred to me

42

that you might want to give Moustache a try as acting sergeant.'

'Moustache?' The commander frowned, searching his memory.

'He got transferred in just before you did,' Brandy supplied. 'I'm not surprised you can't place him. He kind of blends in most of the time. It's my guess, though, that he's had some previous service time in the Regular Army, and probably as more than a line soldier.'

'I'll keep that in mind, Brandy. Thanks!'

'You want me to get him for you? He's outside here in the volunteer line.'

'That's all right. I'll handle him when his turn comes.'

'So, anyway, I was thinking you might want to use me as a washroom attendant or a doorman, sir. I'd probably be a bit less conspicuous than most of the lads – what with my age and all.'

Phule was studying the figure in front of him, noting details more than he was listening to the Legionnaire's words.

The man was above average height and barrel-chested, though his stern posture probably exaggerated both features. His head was as hairless as a billiard ball, except for the bright red handlebar moustache which dominated his face and gave him his Legion name. It occurred to Phule that that facial ornament was doubtlessly dyed, since, judging by the man's age as stated in his file, it should be white. As it was, the only clue to Moustache's advanced years was the wrinkled skin of his neck . . . but even that wasn't noticeable unless one was actually looking for it.

'Hmmm?' The commander blinked, suddenly realizing the Legionnaire had reached the end of his statement and was waiting for a response. 'Excuse me, Moustache. My mind was wandering for a second there. Actually I was thinking . . . are you sure you want to volunteer for under-cover work? You . . . um . . . seem much more at home in a uniform.'

It was a clumsy gambit, but Phule was getting tired and

was hard-pressed to find a tactful way around the Legion rule against inquiring into a Legionnaire's history prior to his or her enlistment. Fortunately Moustache made the job easy.

'Found me out, did you, sir?' he said, breaking into a sudden smile. 'Well, I suppose it was just a matter of time before it came out. Secrets don't last long in an outfit as tight as this one.'

'Is that to say that you've had military experience prior to your signing on with the Space Legion?' the commander urged.

'You might say that, sir. Nearly forty years in the Regular Army before they gave me the boot – forced retirement, that is.'

Startled, Phule glanced at the man's folder again. By the record Moustache was well on in his years, but if he had been in the Regular Army for nearly forty years, then he must be at least . . .

'Before you say anything, sir, I *did* shave a few years off my birthday when I filled out my enlistment papers. While the Legion is reputed to accept all applicants, I didn't want to take the risk of being turned down.'

'You were really that eager to join up?'

'Frankly, sir, it was my last hope. You see, sir, when they retired me from the Regular Army, it didn't take long to find out there wasn't much of a place for me in civilian life. I was way too old to go into police work, and bein' a night watchman always struck me as a race to see which gathered dust and cobwebs faster: the guard or the stuff he was supposed to be guarding.'

'I suppose just taking it easy and enjoying your retirement wasn't included on your list of options?'

'Not bloody likely,' the Legionnaire snorted. 'The Army always kept me busy – until one of their computers started counting up my birthdays, that is. After years of keeping the lads busy, even with "make-work" assignments, the idea of just doing nothing sounded uncomfortably like being dead. I mean, sir, inactive is inactive, whether you're sittin' in a rocker or six feet under.'

'It sounds like you had some rank before you retired,' Phule observed cautiously.

'Let's just say I was a noncom and leave it at that, sir. I've been trying not to make a big thing of my experience. Seen too many new blokes to an outfit come in ringing the mission bell and preaching to the heathens how they should be doing things. The noncoms you have seem to be doing a right good job, especially since you got them back on track. Truth is, it's been a bit of a treat for me to be back in the ranks – letting others do the thinking and just following orders.'

'I see,' Phule said, then reached for his notepad. 'Well, Moustache, I'm afraid your vacation is over, as of now. I'm refusing your offer as a volunteer, and instead am assigning you duty as an acting sergeant for this assignment. We'll see about making it permanent when it's all over.'

'Yes, sir. Very good, sir.'

The Legionnaire snapped into a rigid, parade-ground salute, but Phule did not return it immediately.

'Just one more thing, Moustache. Excuse me for asking, but exactly what is that accent you have, anyway?'

'Holo-movie, sir,' the Legionnaire said, flashing another quick smile. 'I never could master the Southern American drawl that's so popular with noncoms, so I settled for the next best thing. Studied every war holo I could find with a proper British sergeant major in it. It may not be authentic, but after forty years, it's habitual . . . sir!'

And so it went, hour after hour, volunteer after volunteer.

True to Beeker's prediction, even with making an extra effort to keep the interviews brief, it was late even by Phule's standards when the last Legionnaire had been dealt with. Finally alone, he tried to review his notes, but set them aside with a sigh when his eyes refused to focus.

He didn't really need to read the list to confirm what he already knew. While he had more than enough volunteers for a full complement, there was one name missing from the roster, one he had been counting on since receiving the assignment.

Glancing at his watch, he debated briefly over whether he should call it a night and deal with this problem in the morning. At this hour, the Legionnaire in question would probably already be asleep, and . . .

With a conscious effort, the commander accepted a mental compromise. He'd just make a casual walk-by of the Legionnaire's room and then, if the lights were out, he'd get some sleep himself.

'Come in, Captain. I've been expecting you.'

Sushi set aside the book he had been reading and beckoned his commander through the open door and into a chair.

'Sorry to be calling so late,' Phule managed, sinking into the offered seat, 'but there were a lot of volunteers for the new duty – more than I expected, really.'

'More than you need?'

'Well . . . yes and no,' the commander hedged, glancing around the room. 'Where's your partner?'

'Do-Wop? He headed into town to do a little celebrating. Late as it is, I expect he won't be back until morning.'

'Good, good,' Phule said absently. Now that he had found Sushi, he wasn't quite sure what to say to him. 'I, um . . . wanted to talk to you.'

'Let me make this easy for you, Captain,' the Legionnaire said, holding up a hand. 'You want to know why I didn't volunteer. Right?'

'Well . . . yes. If it isn't prying, that is. I would have thought the assignment would be a natural for you. Considering . . .'

He let his voice trail off, leaving unsaid what was already common knowledge between the two of them.

Phule knew Sushi – or, at least, had a passing acquaintance with him – from before their respective enlistments in the Space Legion. They had traveled in the same, or similar, circles, both coming from exceptionally wealthy families. Phule also knew, as did a few in the company, that Sushi was an embezzler and that most of the money he had stolen had gone to finance a passion for casino gambling.

'I should think the answer is obvious.' Sushi shrugged. I'm a compulsive gambler. I love high-stakes risks the way an alcoholic loves a bottle. That was bad enough when the only thing to lose was my own money and reputation – or that of my family's company, as it turned out – but to have *our* company's reputation riding on my control . . .' He shook his head. 'I just think it would be safer all around if I stood normal duty and avoided the tables completely. The only sure way I've found to stop gambling is not to start.'

Phule leaned back in his chair and stared at the ceiling for a moment, frowning thoughtfully.

'This *is* a volunteer mission,' he said finally, 'and I wouldn't want to frog-march you into it, Sushi, particularly not if it means asking you to go against a decision you've made for your own good. The problem is . . . let's face it, you're probably the only one in the company who *really* knows casinos as a gambler. I had been hoping you'd take the role of one of those high rollers – the big-stakes players that the casinos give red-carpet treatment to. You could move around openly with more freedom than the team members who we infiltrate into the staff, since they will be pretty much limited to those areas defined by their jobs, plus you'd have a better feel for normal operations and when there was anything going on at the tables that warranted closer inspection.'

'Sounds like you were counting on me as one of your main spotters,' Sushi said, chewing his lip slightly.

'I was,' Phule admitted. 'But, still, I can understand your reluctance. I'll just have to figure out some other way to – '

'Don't bother, Captain,' Sushi interrupted. 'I'll do it on one condition. If I feel like I'm losing control, or if in *your* personal opinion I'm plunging too hard, you'll pull me out of there, even if it means locking me in my room with a guard to keep me away from the tables. Agreed?'

'Agreed.' Phule nodded with a smile. 'Okay. That's a load off my mind. Let's see . . . you'll need a bankroll to play with . . . shall we say, a hundred thousand for starters?'

'Excuse me, Captain, but if – and I stress *if* – I happen to come out ahead, who gets the profits?'

'Well . . . I hadn't given it much thought, but I suppose if you're gambling out of the company fund, then any winnings should go back into that fund.'

'In that case,' Sushi said, flashing a schoolboy's grin, 'I think I'll provide my own bankroll, if you don't mind. I *did* squirrel away a few dollars before I enlisted, in case of just such a rainy day.'

Chapter Four

Journal #197

I will not attempt to chronicle the endless details involved in packing up the company for relocation. For one thing, they are boring and tedious; for another, they contribute little to the account of this particular assignment. Perhaps most important, however, is the simple factor that I was not present for those proceedings. Let it suffice to say that knowing my employer's habit of wanting to put his personal stamp on everything, and Lieutenant Armstrong's tendency to be overly formal and by the book when carrying out orders, however minor, I'm rather glad I was elsewhere at the time, at least until I observed the condition of my employer's wardrobe after having left it to someone else's care.

I, of course, was occupied elsewhere, specifically on the planet Jewell, assisting Lieutenant Rembrandt in her efforts to find and recruit the actors necessary to replace those Legionnaires who would be working under cover for this assignment.

As I find is often the case with higher executives, my employer had grossly underestimated, or simply chosen to ignore, the difficulties involved with performing a specific task delegated to a subordinate, choosing instead to lump all his assistance and advice into the brief phrase 'Just do it. Okay? Make it happen!' While this may be a successful method for said executive to shift the bulk of the responsibility for a task off his own shoulders, it effectively leaves the designated subordinate to, as they say, 'twist in wind,' bear-

*ing the brunt of the blame for the methodology,
as well as the results, of their efforts.*

*With my own humble assistance, however,
Lieutenant Rembrandt had completed her assignment prior to the company's arrival on Jewell,
or, should I say, completed* most *of it.*

Phule barely recognized his senior lieutenant as he disem-
barked from the shuttle at the Jewell spaceport. In fact, he
might have missed her completely had she not been standing
next to Beeker in the waiting area.

Rembrandt had forsaken her usual long-braided ponytail,
and her dark brown hair now hung loosely almost halfway
down her back. There was no sign of her customary black
Legionnaires uniform, either, as she was dressed in a decep-
tively simple white blouse and dark skirt combination,
topped off with a camel-colored sweater worn over her
shoulders like a cape, with the arms tied loosely around her
neck. Her wardrobe, combined with the stack of folders she
was hugging with both arms and the pencil stuck behind
her ear, gave her the appearance of the young assistant of
someone in some branch of the entertainment field – which
was, of course, what she was striving for.

'Lieutenant . . . Beeker,' Phule said, coming to a halt in
front of them. 'That's a new look for you, isn't it,
Rembrandt?'

Rembrandt's normally pale complexion suddenly
exploded with a bright pink blush.

'Sorry, sir. Beeker said . . . I mean, I felt . . . Well, you
said we shouldn't let anyone know I was with the Space
Legion, so I thought . . .'

'Whoa! Stop the music!' the commander said, holding
up a restraining hand. 'There's no need to apologize,
Lieutenant. I was just teasing you a little. You look fine . . .
really. In fact, you look exceptionally good in that outfit.
You should wear skirts more often.'

Rather than looking relieved, Rembrandt's blush deepened to the approximate red of a tomato in a seed catalog.

'Thank you, sir,' she mumbled, averting her eyes. 'Beeker helped pick it out.'

Painfully aware that his efforts to lighten the mood were only making matters worse, Phule cast around desperately for a change in subject.

'So . . . what have you got for me there?' he said, looking pointedly at the folders Rembrandt was clutching.

'These are the résumés of the actors and my notes on them for your review, sir,' the lieutenant said, gratefully slipping into the more familiar military mode as she thrust her load at her commander.

'Excellent,' Phule said, accepting the stack and idly opening the top folder to glance at the contents. As he did, the three-dimensional holo-photo which was the inevitable inside cover of an actor's portfolio sprang to life, projecting a miniature person who seemed to be standing on the folder. He ignored it, scanning the printed pages instead. 'I assume they'll be ready to load and board this evening?'

Rembrandt licked her lips nervously.

'I . . . those are only my final recommendations, sir. I've been holding off finalizing them pending your approval.'

The commander's head came up with a snap.

'You mean they haven't been notified to be ready for departure?'

'Well, I have them on standby, but I explained that *you* had to approve the final selection, so they're –'

Phule slapped the cover shut on the top folder, squashing the actor's image in the process, and handed the entire stack back, interrupting her in midsentence.

'Get them on the horn and tell them they're hired,' he said firmly.

'But sir! Don't you want to –'

'Lieutenant,' the commander cut her short, 'I gave you this assignment because I trust your judgment. If you say these are the best candidates, then that's what we'll go with.'

'But I'm not sure of a couple of these, sir. I was hoping you could –'

'Being sure is a luxury you rarely get as an officer, Lieutenant. You make the best guess you can in the time allowed, then *make* it the right choice.'

'But . . .'

'Our main criterion is that they fit into uniform sizes that we have in stock. Outside of that, they're mostly window dressing. As to personalities . . . well . . . if you'll recall, we took potluck with this company to start with. I doubt there is anyone in there that will be more of a problem case than the Legionnaires we're already dealing with. Agreed?'

'I . . . I guess so sir.'

'Fine. Like I've said before, Rembrandt, you need to be more decisive. I don't have time to duplicate your work – and neither do you if we're going to give the new bodies time to pack and get on board before lift-off. I suggest you start moving.'

'Yes, sir!'

Momentarily forgetting her civilian garb, Rembrandt drew herself to attention and fired off a salute before fleeing her commander's presence.

'Well, Beek,' Phule said, turning to his butler at last, 'except for that, how are things going?'

'Rather better than they are for you, it would seem . . . sir.' Beeker's voice was utterly devoid of warmth.

'How's that again?' Phule frowned. 'Is something wrong, Beek?'

'Not at all, sir. It's always a treat to watch the finesse and compassion with which you handle your subordinates. Of course, I *have* noticed that your skill level seems to drop in direct proportion to the amount of sleep you've been getting . . . sir.'

The commander shot a glance in the direction which Rembrandt had disappeared.

'What you're trying to say, in your traditionally subtle way, of course, is that you think I was a little hard on Rembrandt just now. Right?'

'I suppose from your point of view, sir, you were being quite tolerant,' the butler observed blandly. 'I mean, you *could* have had her stood up against a wall and shot.'

'I'll take that as a "yes."' Phule sighed heavily. 'I guess . . .'

'Or then again, flogging is always effective, if a bit outdated,' Beeker continued as if his employer hadn't spoken.

'All right, all right! I get the point! I guess I've been a bit tense lately. Relocating the company has been more of a hassle than I anticipated.'

'I wouldn't know, sir,' Beeker said, shrugging slightly. 'What I *do* know, however, is how hard Lieutenant Rembrandt has been working on the assignment you so casually dumped on her, *and* how concerned she's been about whether or not you'd approve of her efforts, much less her results.'

'Which is why she wanted me to review her choices before finalizing them,' Phule said, finishing the thought. 'Of course, my barking at her is only going to hurt, not help, her confidence, which is the exact opposite of what I wanted to have happen.'

'It's hard to see where anything positive will come from your current stance . . . in my own, humble opinion, sir,' the butler confirmed mercilessly.

Phule gave another sigh, running a hand over his face like he was trying to wipe water from it, and seemed to deflate back into himself.

'Sorry, Beek,' he said. 'I seem to be running tired these days. You know, when I was giving the crew going under cover their final briefing, Armstrong had to point out to me that I was getting redundant – that I had reviewed the procedures on their new communicators three times even though there hadn't been any questions. Can you believe that? Armstrong? Keeping *me* from making an idiot of myself in front of the troops?'

'Lieutenant Armstrong has come a long way,' Beeker observed, 'but I see your point. I think, however, that your troops, like myself, will be inclined to worry rather than be critical over minor flaws in your performance.'

'Yeah. Well, that still doesn't change the fact that I'm not functioning at peak efficiency, especially in the manners department. What can I say other than I'm sorry?'

'You could try saying the exact same thing – only to Lieutenant Rembrandt,' the butler said. 'After all, it is she and not I who is the offended party in this situation.'

'Right.' Phule nodded, glancing down the corridor again, as if expecting to see his senior lieutenant appear at the mention of her name. 'Maybe I can catch her before – '

'As for myself,' Beeker continued, 'what I would probably most like to hear is that you plan to take some time to catch up on your sleep . . . sir.'

'Excuse me, what was that, Beek?' the commander said, pulling his attention back to the conversation.

'You asked a rhetorical question, sir,' the butler explained. 'I was merely taking advantage of it to state my own opinions.'

'Oh.'

'And in *my* opinion, sir, what is most important at the moment is not that you apologize for past errors in judgment, but rather that you get some sleep to lessen the probability of compounding the situation with future errors.'

Phule frowned.

'You think I should get some sleep?' he said finally, reducing things to their simplest form.

'It would seem in order, sir. By your own admission, you're "running tired." '

'Can't do it – not now, anyway,' Phule insisted, shaking his head. 'I have too much to do before the actors' briefing tonight. I can't afford the time.'

'If I might suggest, sir, I don't believe you can afford *not* to get some sleep, *particularly* if you're getting ready for an important presentation. Perhaps you could delegate some of your planned preparations?'

Phule thought for a moment, then nodded slowly.

'I guess you're right, Beek. It's bad enough if I'm snapping at the troops that already know me, but if I start leaning on the newcomers . . .' He shook his head again, more emphatically this time. 'Okay, I'll try to get some sleep. But only if you promise to wake me up a couple hours before the briefing.'

'Consider it promised, sir.'

'And Beeker? It's good to have you back. Sarcasm and all.'

'It's good to *be* back, sir.'

The actors' briefing went smoothly . . . much more so than I had ever hoped, considering the circumstances.

Because of the secretive nature of their work, Lieutenant Rembrandt had specifically not informed them of any details regarding the 'parts' they were auditioning for, other than the necessary warnings that there might be some danger involved, and (apparently more important to the actors) there would be no 'billing' or other credits for their individual performances. In short, the only reward the actors could expect from their roles would be financial. As might be expected, having come to know my employer's style of problem solving, as mysterious and sketchy as the information was, the offered pay scale was generous enough that there was no shortage of applicants to choose from.

Still, it must have come as no small shock to at least some of them to learn that the 'troupe' they had been auditioning for was none other than the Space Legion, or that in accepting, they had effectively 'enlisted.' The ease with which they absorbed and adapted to this news is a tribute to their professionalism . . . or their greed.

'That pretty much concludes the basic information I wanted to cover at this first meeting,' Phule said, giving his notes one final scan. 'Now, I'm sure that you all have questions. Let me remind you, however, that we have a lot of time before we reach Lorelei, and that specific information on standing duty will be covered in later briefings which will include the entire company. Also, some of your questions might be better asked, and answered, in private. Lieutenants Rembrandt, who you've already met, and Armstrong will be available throughout the trip to discuss individual problems, or, if it will make you more comfortable, you can speak with either Sergeant Moustache or myself.'

He paused to gesture toward the individuals mentioned, who were currently standing at parade rest on either side of him, reinforcing the introductions which had been made at the beginning of the meeting.

'Now then,' he continued, 'are there any questions you would like to raise in front of the group at large? Things that would affect all of the temporary Legionnaires?'

The actors, seated in auditorium formation at one end of the transport's ballroom, exchanged looks for a few moments. Since the company leaders appeared before them in the unexpected black uniforms to start the briefing, silence had reigned, and even now everyone seemed reluctant to speak.

'Mr. Phule?'

'That's "Captain Jester" or just "Captain" for the duration.' The commander smiled gently. 'Yes? You have a question?'

'You said that we were free to withdraw if we wanted to, now that we've heard the whole story. How would that work, exactly? I mean, now that we've lifted off and are en route, wouldn't it be kind of hard for us to get back to Jewell?'

'You would be provided with a return ticket to Jewell – at our expense, of course – *after* we had completed our assignment,' Phule explained. 'In the meantime, you would be held incommunicado on Lorelei. While you were our guests, all expenses would be paid as well as a small stipend, but it should be noted that your earnings would be substantially less than what will be paid if you honor your contracts and stand duty with us.'

There was some mumbling in the assemblage at this announcement, but Phule held up his hand for silence.

'Believe me, I regret having to take this position, but we can't run the risk of having too many people wandering around who know about the substitution we're attempting. It would be dangerous to our undercover members, as well as to those of you who *do* stand duty, if information is leaked that not all the Legionnaires guarding the casino are combat-trained. I cannot stress enough the need for secrecy on this assignment. Now, obviously, we'd rather you all agreed to stick around, but it will be understood if you choose to withdraw at this time. I can only apologize that the situation required that we kept you in the dark as long as we have. Take your time and think it over, but I'd appreciate it if you'd let me know as soon as you've made up your minds so we can try to arrange for replacements if necessary.'

'Just how dangerous will standing duty be, Captain?'

'Minimal,' the commander said firmly. 'We haven't worked together before, so you have no way of knowing my personal style. Let me assure you, however, that if I thought there was even an average chance of physical danger, I wouldn't be putting you in this spot. All we have so far is a rumor, unconfirmed, that there may be an attempt to take over the casino by organized crime. Even if it's true, I'm expecting more of a financial attack than any kind of physical harassment. That chance does exist, however, so it would be less than honest of me to withhold the information while you were making up your minds, though I'll admit the pay scale you were offered to lure you into this position was inflated, in part, to compensate for the potential hazard. Also, rest assured that we are not entirely without plans if things *do* get a little rough. I say specifically a *little* rough since it is my understanding that organized crime has long since abandoned armed confrontation due to the legalities and publicity involved. Each of you is being teamed with an experienced Legionnaire, and I suggest that in event of trouble, you step back and let them handle it as they have been trained to do. Also, if any of you are still nervous, hand-to-hand combat training will be available during the trip, and while it might not make you experts, it should provide you with the basic skills necessary to get you out of any awkward situations which may arise. Frankly we're hiring you as decoys, not as combat troops. If things *do* take a turn for the worse, you have my personal guarantee that your contracts will be "terminated with cause" from our end, and you will be free to leave.'

He swept the assemblage with his eyes.

'Any other questions?'

The actors looked around as well, but there were no takers.

'Very well.' Phule nodded. 'I'll be trying to spend some time with each of you, individually and informally, during the trip in an effort to get to know you better. In the meantime, if you'll follow Sergeant Moustache now, you'll be issued uniforms and given your teammate assignments. If you would, please change into your new uniforms and report back here in an hour.'

He allowed a faint smile to flit across his face.

'I'm giving a cocktail party to introduce you to the rest of the company and welcome you to our ranks. It will be a good time for you all to start getting to know each other.'

Despite my employer's good intentions, his cocktail party was something less than a roaring success.

While the regular Legionnaires had long since resigned themselves to the inevitability of their new assignment, and had even accepted the necessity of breaking up their established two-person teams, the idea of 'outsiders' standing duty with them as equals was still unpopular. Though they were careful to keep their feelings hidden from their commander, it was readily apparent to a careful observer that little warmth was spared on their new 'colleagues.'

This was particularly noticeable at the cocktail party . . . though almost as interesting, if you are a confirmed people watcher like myself, were the opening gambits as the actors themselves began to jostle to establish a pecking order within their own numbers. Without blatant eavesdropping, the exact details of the various conversations remained a mystery, but the general content could often be distinguished simply by observing the body language of the individuals involved . . .

Tiffany was not used to being ignored. Not that she was beautiful in the classic sense – surviving as an actress required a brutal honesty which forbade her that particular delusion – but her mane of auburn hair, slightly slanted cat eyes, and ample curves exuded an earthy sensuality that usually guaranteed that men would make room for her in any conversation. As such, she found herself growing increasingly vexed at feeling all but invisible in a room filled by a crowd which was predominantly male.

Fighting a frown (frowns cause wrinkles, darling), she surveyed the gathering again. The chairs from the earlier briefing had been pushed back against the walls, creating an open area in which the Legionnaires stood clustered about in small groups – small *closed* groups which seemed oblivious to all else in the room except those people they were talking to immediately.

After having eased up to a few of these groups, only to finally wander away again when no one acknowledged her presence, Tiffany was ready to try a new tactic. Moving in a controlled drift, she took up a station near the mini-bar which had been set up at one end of the room . . . like any good predator, waiting for her prey near the water hole.

True to her observations, she didn't have long to wait. If nothing else, the actors had *that* in common with the Legionnaires. Neither group was likely to squander the opportunity of free drinks at an open bar.

One Legionnaire detached himself from his group and strode over to the bar.

'Scotch, double, rocks,' he told the bartender in the universal shorthand of a confirmed lounge lizard.

Tiffany gulped the remainder of her existing drink in one swallow and stepped into line behind him.

'Hi there,' she said brightly, flashing her best smile. 'I'm Tiffany.'

The Legionnaire glanced at her. 'Hello.'

Realizing the man was not about to supply *his* name, she switched quickly to another conversational ploy.

'So . . . have you been in the Space Legion long?'

'Yes.'

Again the abruptness of the response left her without anything to say.

'Well – '

'Your drink, sir,' the bartender interrupted, pushing his offering across the bar.

To Tiffany's surprise, the Legionnaire reached into his pocket.

'You're paying?' she blurted. 'I thought this was a free bar.'

The man fixed her with a brief, level stare.

'It is,' he said. '*We* still tip the bartender, though. Just because the captain's paying for the drinks is no reason to short the help for their work. Like the captain says: "You don't break someone else's rice bowl." '

With that, he tossed a bill on the bar, gathered up his drink, and left to rejoin his group.

'Something for you, miss?' the bartender said pointedly.

'Hemlock, neat,' she muttered, staring after her departed victim.

'Excuse me?'

'Nothing. Give me a rum and Coke. Heavy on the rum, no lime.'

It was clear that 'bright and friendly' wasn't working. Maybe she should change gears and see if the crowd was up for 'sultry and a little horny.'

'Chilly out tonight, isn't it?'

Tiffany glanced around.

'Lex! I thought that was you at the briefing. Let me tell you, darling, it's good to see a friendly face. I was starting to think I had grown another head – and an ugly one at that.'

'It isn't just you,' her savior assured her. 'They seem to be unreceptive to any of us – even me!'

The 'even me' tag line was, of course, typical of Lex. A male model turned actor, his success had heightened his already substantial opinion of himself. It had been noted more than once that the only thing bigger than his ego was, unfortunately, his talent. When he was 'on,' he had the gift of appearing to totally focus his attention, making whoever he was dealing with at the time feel that they were the most important, interesting person in the universe. This impression was conveyed even when the other 'person' was a camera lens or the 'third wall' of a stage, giving him the ability to affect an audience as few actors can. It was only when he was relaxed that his true disdain for others showed, encouraging most to maintain him as an acquaintance rather than as a friend.

Tiffany knew him only in passing from one production they had worked together, and normally would avoid his company. Even now, as desperate as she was for someone to talk to, she couldn't resist 'zinging' him a little.

'Well, *some* of us seem to be doing okay,' she said, pointing with her chin to a far corner where a petite young girl was engrossed in a conversation with a towering Legionnaire with a huge, warthog head.

Lex followed her gaze.

'Who? *Her?*' He managed to convey both disgust and dismissal by intonation alone. 'She isn't really one of us. She's only done a few things, all amateur. In fact, this was her big try at breaking into professional acting.'

Tiffany cocked an eyebrow at him.

'How do you know all that?'

'I talked to her earlier, after the briefing.'

'And she wouldn't give you a tumble, eh?' she finished for him with a grin.

'Don't be a bitch, Tiffany,' Lex said, unruffled. 'Just because I didn't come after you first is no reason to be catty.'

'Say ... what are you doing here, anyway?' she said, indulging in a small frown. 'I thought they were looking for relative unknowns. Didn't I hear you landed a part in a holo-soap?'

'I didn't list that on my audition sheet,' Lex said, glancing around nervously. 'And I'd appreciate it if you'd keep it quiet. My part was canceled after a half dozen episodes, and it was only in planetary syndication, anyway. I guess our recruiter-in-disguise there doesn't watch the soaps ... which is just as well for me. Frankly, Tiff, I need the money. I went a little wild with my spending when I landed the part. Got so excited I didn't read the contract close enough. Missed the "character cancellation" clause completely.'

'Gee, that's tough,' Tiffany said sympathetically, and meant it. Though she might not like Lex as a person, he was still a fellow professional, and she could understand how crushing it would be to think one had finally gotten their big break, only to have it jerked away from them. 'Don't worry, I won't say anything.'

Lex gave a quick smile of thanks, then turned his attention to the party again.

'So . . . what do you think so far?' he said, scanning the crowd. 'Are you going to stick around or sit this one out?'

'Oh, I'm *definitely* going to work this one,' Tiffany said. 'As to the job itself . . . unless these clowns loosen up a little, it could be a long tour, if you know what I mean.'

'Hey. They're no different from us,' chimed in a lanky individual who had just stepped up to the bar and overheard Tiffany's comment. 'Think of them as a road troupe that have been working together for a long time. We're the new replacements, and they aren't going to cut us any slack until we've shown them what we can do.'

'Hey, Doc!' Lex said, waving for him to join their conversation. 'Didn't get a chance to say hi earlier. Was that your son with you?'

'Sure was.' He raised his voice to call across the room. 'Yo! Junior! Come over here a minute.'

The gangly teenager Tiffany had noted before rose from the chair he had been holding down and began ambling toward them.

'He sure has grown,' Lex said, making the obligatory observation.

'Sure has,' the newcomer confirmed. 'I'm thinking of maybe using him for a stand-in for *me* in some of the rougher gags.'

Even though she didn't find the man particularly attractive, Tiffany found her curiosity piqued. Lex usually held himself aloof from his colleagues, and generally had no use for men at all, unless they were producers, directors, or someone else important enough to further his career. The latter possibility was enough to capture her undivided attention.

'I don't think we've met,' she said, holding out her hand. 'I'm Tiffany.'

'I'm sorry,' Lex said, slapping his forehead melodramatically with his palm. 'I thought everybody knew Doc . . . well, everybody who counts. Tiffany, this is Doc. Short for "Scene Doctor." He's made me look *real* good the times we've worked together.'

'How so?' Tiffany asked, then realized she was talking to the back of Doc's head.

That individual was craning his neck, trying to get a better look at the scene that was unfolding a few steps away where his son had been stopped by one of the Legionnaires waiting in line for a drink.

'You look pretty young to be a Legionnaire, sonny.'

Unruffled, the youth shrugged.

'The casting director – I mean, the lieutenant – didn't seem to think so,' he said easily.

'Oh yeah?' the Legionnaire sneered. 'Tell me . . . have you ever killed a man?'

'No,' the youth admitted. 'But I almost did once.'

'Really?' his challenger said, clearly taken aback by the unexpected answer. 'What happened?'

'I almost ran over him with a forklift.'

There was a few seconds' pause, then the Legionnaire flushed a bright red.

'Are you trying to get cute with me, kid?'

'Take it easy there, hoss,' Doc said, stepping forward to drape an arm around his son's shoulders. 'He was just trying to answer your question truthfully. You don't have to worry about him pulling his own weight, either. He does his job as well as the next man, and better than most. Here, I'll show you.'

With that, he made a fist with his free hand and suddenly launched an overhand punch into his son's face. There was a painful smack of flesh hitting flesh, and the youth went sprawling.

All conversation in the room ceased as abruptly as if it had been recorded background noise and someone pulled the plug.

'*Jeez!*' the wide-eyed Legionnaire gasped, staring at the

63

figure on the floor. 'What'd ya go and do that for? I was just – '

'*Stand easy!*'

At the barked command, the others in the room relaxed slightly and returned to their conversations, though many a curious and suspicious glance was directed at their group.

'Oh no,' the Legionnaire said softly, almost in a groan.

The company commander was bearing down on them, his face set in a grim mask, while his junior officers and a few of his sergeants materialized out of the crowd to trail along casually in his wake.

The entourage halted before the offending group, and the commander swept them all, standing and prone, with a steely gaze before fixing his eyes on the distraught Legionnaire.

'Well? Should I ask?' he said in a tone as icy as the void outside the ship's hull.

'I didn't do *anything!* Really, Captain!' the Legionnaire protested desperately. 'We were just standing here talking and – '

'It's no big deal, sir,' Doc said, stepping forward. 'My son and I were just giving the others here a little demonstration. Didn't think it would get everyone riled up.'

'Demonstration?'

'That's right.'

Doc extended a hand down to his son, who seized his wrist and bounced lightly to his feet, apparently unharmed.

'Guess you haven't had a chance to go over our files, Captain,' Doc continued easily. 'Junior and me are stuntmen.'

'I see,' the commander said, thawing slightly. 'Well, I'd appreciate it if you'd refrain from any further "demonstrations." Or at least give us a bit of warning. We try to discourage fighting, or even the appearance of fighting, at social gatherings.'

'No problem . . . sir.' Doc shrugged. 'Sorry, but we're still learning the ins and outs of this crew.'

'You'll catch on,' the commander said, relaxing into a smile. 'In fact, if you're willing, I'd appreciate it if you'd give a demonstration for the whole company sometime, and maybe even a few lessons if you're . . .' He broke off suddenly, his eyes narrowing with a passing thought. 'By the way,' he said with forced casualness, 'before we get *too* far off the subject, may I ask what prompted this little demonstration just now?'

'I – I was saying that the k – the *gentleman* here seemed a bit young to be a Legionnaire, sir.'

The commander ran a quick, appraising eye over the youth.

'Nonsense,' he said firmly. 'He may *look* young, soldier, but he's the same age you are. Isn't that right?'

'He is?'

'*Isn't that right?*'

'Oh . . . yes, sir!'

'Because if he wasn't, he wouldn't be able to stand duty with us in a casino. Understood?'

'Yes, sir. Understood, sir.'

'Very good.' The commander nodded. 'Be sure to spread the word to the others.'

'Right away, sir.' The Legionnaire saluted and fled to the cover of his original group.

'Sorry if that's a problem,' Doc said, 'but Junior here's been travelling with me ever since his mom died. We hire out as a team, sort of a package deal. The lieutenant there said she wasn't sure she could take us, but I thought she had cleared it with you before she gave us the final call.'

Something flitted across the commander's face, but was gone before it really registered.

'Nothing we can't work out.' He smiled. 'Besides, he seems as solid as any of our regular troops, though that may not seem like a compliment to some. Anyway, glad to have him aboard . . . and the same goes for all of you, for that matter. Now, if you'll excuse me, I've got to circulate a bit.'

'Good luck, Captain,' Tiffany chirped as he turned to leave.

'Thank you . . . umm . . .'

65

'Tiffany,' she supplied with a smile, arching her back slightly.

The commander's eyes flickered over her, a bit more slowly than when he had been assessing Doc's son.

'Right,' he said. 'Well . . . later.'

'Wipe your chin, Tiffany,' Lex said softly, nudging her as she watched the commander walk away. 'Really. I thought you liked them a bit broader in the shoulder than that.'

'He has other attractions,' the actress purred, following the captain with predator's eyes.

'Oh? Like what?'

She glanced at him in genuine surprise.

'You mean you really don't know?' she said. 'My God, I spotted him as soon as he came in for the briefing. He even *told* us who he was.'

Lex shrugged. 'So he's rich. So what?'

'Rich doesn't *start* to cover it,' Tiffany insisted. '*That*, gentlemen, is Willard Phule, the fourth richest man in the universe under forty-five who isn't gay or married and monogamous.'

Doc frowned. 'How do you know that?'

'How does a bug know when it's going to rain?' Lex said dryly. 'Yes, I start to see the attraction he has for you, Tiff.'

'Hey, a girl's got to look out for her future,' the actress said. 'Our business trades on looks, and makeup can only cover so much so long. Catch you later, guys. I have more questions to ask our captain – just to make sure he doesn't forget who I am.'

Chapter Five

Journal #203

Despite the dubious beginning, relations between the Legionnaires and the actor/auxiliaries improved steadily during our voyage to Lorelei. While not quite accepting their new comrades into the fold, the company seemed at least willing not to condemn them as a group, judging them instead on their performance and character traits as individuals.

In part, this was doubtless due to the shared experience of the in-flight lessons on casino gambling and scams taught by Tullie Bascom and the instructors from the school he ran for casino dealers.

I will not attempt to detail the techniques for cheating and detecting cheats which were imparted in these lessons, as it is my intention to chronicle the career of my employer, not to provide a training manual for larceny at the gaming tables. Suffice it to say that the instruction was sufficiently challenging and intense that it drew the force together, in part to practice on each other, and in part to swap tales of embarrassing slips and failures.

Watching the eagerness with which the company attacked its lessons, however, I could not help but wonder if they were preparing for the upcoming assignment, or if, perhaps, they were rabidly squirreling away information for their personal use.

Apparently I was not the only one this occurred to . . .

Tullie Bascom's report had run long, much longer than anyone had expected after he appeared for the meeting without notes. Twenty-five years of working casinos, mostly as a pit boss, however, had sharpened his eye and memory to a point where he rarely wrote anything down – names or numbers. Instead, he appeared to speak off the top of his head, rattling on for hours as he reviewed each of his student's strengths and weaknesses, while the commander and the two junior officers flanking him filled page after page on their notepads with his insightful comments.

This was a closed meeting, convened in the commander's cabin, and was, in all probability, the final session before Tullie and his team left the ship at its last stop prior to the final leg of the journey to Lorelei.

After the last Legionnaire was reviewed, Phule tossed his pencil onto his notepad and leaned back, stretching cramped muscles he hadn't noticed until just now.

'Thank you, Tullie,' he said. 'I'm sure I speak for all of us when I say the job you've done has been most impressive – both with the lessons and with keeping us informed of the company's progress.'

He paused to glance at his two lieutenants, who nodded and mumbled their agreement, still a little dazed at the volume of data which had just been dumped on them.

'You paid top dollar. You get my best shot,' Tullie responded with a shrug of dismissal.

'I can't think of any questions on individuals that you haven't already covered in depth,' the commander continued, 'but if it's not asking too much, can you give us your impressions of the force as a whole?'

'They're some of the best I've ever trained,' though I'd appreciate it if you didn't tell them I said that until after I've left,' the instructor admitted easily. 'Of course, it's not often that I get students who can attend multiple sessions, one right after the other, day after day, like we've been doing on this trip. Usually I'm training folks who have to work their lessons in around their paying jobs, at least until they get certified.'

'Do you think they're ready to hold down a casino on their own?' Phule pressed.

Tullie scratched his right ear and frowned for a moment before answering.

'They'll catch the casual cheats easy enough,' he said. 'As to the pros, I don't know. Your boys are good, but the grifters who can do you *real* damage have been polishing their routines for years. Some of 'em you can't spot even if you know what you're watching for.'

'Like a good sleight-of-hand magician,' Armstrong observed.

'Exactly,' Tullie said. 'Some of these mechanics even show you what they're going to do – that they're going to "second-deal" a card and when they're going to do it – and you *still* can't see it when they work it at normal speed. I can't, and I've been training my eye for years.'

The commander frowned. 'So how do you catch them?'

'Sometimes you don't,' the instructor admitted. 'If they don't get greedy – just hit once or twice and keep moving – they can get away with it clean. About the only way to spot bad action is to watch the patterns. If one player starts beating the odds on a regular basis, or if one table starts losing more often than can be explained by a bad run, you'll know you've got problems. Just remember not to get hung up on trying to figure out how they're doing it. You can lose a lot of money waiting for proof. If something doesn't ring true, shut the table down or run your big winner out of the casino. Of course, if you've got an experienced staff of dealers and pit bosses, they should be able to handle that without coaching from you.'

'If you say so,' Phule said, grimacing a little. 'I just wish we didn't have to rely so heavily on people outside our own crew.'

'Well, I can say for sure that your boys are head and shoulders above any casino security force I've ever seen,' Tullie pointed out. 'Most guards are just for show – to discourage folks from trying to get their money back by stickin' up the joint. I'd say that any team of pros that tries to work their scam assuming your team is window dressing

69

will be in for a nasty surprise. They may not be able to spot *every* scam, but if the opposition gets even a little sloppy, they'll know it in a minute.'

'I guess that's the best we can do.' Phule sighed. 'I only wish we had some kind of extra edge.'

'You do,' the instructor insisted. 'I told you before, that little girl you got, Mother, is gonna make it real hard for anyone to get cute. She's *superb*. And I don't say that about many people. Easily the best "eye-in-the-sky" person I've ever seen. Even my own people had trouble pulling stuff while she was watching. In fact, I'd like to talk to her before I leave about maybe hiring her myself when her enlistment's up . . . if it's all right with you.'

'You can certainly *try* talking to her,' Phule said, smiling, 'but I don't think you'll get far. She's deathly shy when it comes to face-to-face conversation. That's why we had the whole camera and microphone setup in the first place. If you really want to talk to her, I suggest you borrow one of our communicators and talk to her over that.'

'That reminds me,' Tullie said, clicking his fingers. 'I wanted to be sure to thank you for setting up that crazy camera and mike rig. It's the weirdest thing I've seen in a long time, but it worked like a charm. In fact, I'm thinking of trying the same thing back at my school and adding "eye-in-the-sky" to my curriculum. I owe you one for that. I don't think there's another school going that offers that kind of training.'

What Tullie was referring to was the special training Phule had arranged for the company's communications specialist, Mother. Knowing that her shyness would negate her effectiveness on public duty, he had suggested to her, and she agreed, that she stand duty in the casino's eye-in-the-sky center. This was the room in any casino which monitored the closed-circuit cameras hidden in the ceilings over the various gaming tables. These cameras were equipped with zoom lenses to allow close scrutiny of any dealer, player, or card, and were one of the casino's main defenses against cheats on either side of the table.

In an effort to train her for this duty, Phule had rented

a half dozen closed-circuit cameras and microphones and set them up over the tables where the Legionnaires were receiving their instruction so Mother could hear and see what was going on in her accustomed anonymity. Tullie had been skeptical about the arrangement at first, until Phule gave him a headset so that he could carry on a two-way conversation with Mother as the lessons were in progress. Even the cynical instructor was impressed with the speed with which Mother picked up the table routines, and her ability to spot any deviation from them, though it wasn't clear if he was more taken with the innovative training system or with Mother herself.

'Is that to say I can expect a discounted rate for your services?' Phule asked innocently.

Tullie favored him with a smile.

'I can see why your troops like you, Mr. Phule,' he said. 'A sense of humor like yours doesn't come along just every day.'

'That's what people tell me,' the commander said, smiling back to show he hadn't really expected the instructor to cut his profits. 'Well, unless there are any further questions, I think we've pretty much covered everything.'

He glanced at his lieutenants for confirmation, but it was Tullie who spoke.

'If you don't mind, Mr. Phule, I've got a question myself.'

'What's that, Tullie?'

'Well, like I said, your boys have picked up a lot of information about gambling scams during this flight, and part of our deal was that none of my school's records would show them as students, right?'

'That's right.' Phule nodded. 'What's the point?'

'So how can you be sure you haven't just footed the bill for my training up a new pack of grifters? What's to keep them from taking what they've learned and going into business for themselves once they get out of the Legion? And I don't mean by opening a training school, either.'

'Mr. Bascom,' Phule said carefully, 'we also train our troops to use firearms despite the fact they could use that same training to be maniacal killers in civilian life. We give

71

them the training in the skills they need to stand duty in the Space Legion, and beyond that we have to trust them not to misuse that training once their enlistment's over.'

'Trust them? That bunch of crooks?'

Armstrong dropped his notepad and glanced fearfully at his commander, who was staring fixedly at the gambling instructor.

'Excuse me,' Phule said in a dangerously soft voice. 'I didn't quite hear that.'

Tullie shrugged. 'I just meant that I've never seen so many blatant or potential criminals assembled in one – '

'I think what the captain means, Mr. Bascom,' Rembrandt interrupted hastily, 'is . . . if you could, perhaps, *rephrase* your statement?'

The instructor finally caught the warning in her voice. The Space Legion commander doubtlessly already knew the caliber of the troops under his command, but they were still *his* troops, and derogatory comments about them, however true, were ill advised.

'I . . . umm . . . just meant that your boys seem to show a real . . . *flair* for larceny,' Bascom said, backpedaling hastily. 'I was just a little worried . . . Well, there's always a *chance* that they might be tempted to *misuse* what I've been teaching them. That's all.'

'*I* trust them,' Phule intoned in a voice that would have sounded more in place coming from a burning bush. 'End of subject. Do you have any other questions?'

'No. I . . . no,' Tullie said. 'That covers everything.'

'Very well,' the commander said. 'Then, if you'll excuse us, there are a few things I have to go over with the lieutenants. Again, thank you for your work with the company. Be sure to relay my thanks and appreciation to your instructors.'

'I'll do that,' Bascom said, and fled gratefully from the meeting.

'Do you believe that?' Phule huffed after Tullie's departure. 'The man suspects our troops may be less than upstanding citizens!'

The three officers looked at each other for a moment, then exploded into laughter.

There was an edge of hysteria to their gaiety, not surprisingly like people who had been too long without sleep and under pressure who finally found an outlet for their tension.

'Guess he's never worked with the Space Legion before,' Armstrong gasped, trying to catch his breath.

'Well, certainly not with *our* crew, that's for sure,' Rembrandt agreed, wiping a laugh tear from one eye.

'Seriously, though,' the commander said, bringing himself under control at last, 'Tullie does have a point. Be sure to brace the company about keeping their hands in their pockets, at least until this assignment's over. No showing off, and no grifting for pocket-change pots. We're supposed to be the guards on this caper, and it wouldn't do to have anyone get busted for the exact same thing we're policing the casino for. That kind of media coverage we don't need. Besides, I think it would be tactically sound not to let on how much we do or don't know just yet.'

'Gotcha, boss,' Rembrandt said, flipping an index-finger salute at him. 'You want us to tell them as a group or as individuals?'

'Both,' Phule said firmly. 'A general announcement should do for most of them, but I think some of them would benefit from a *personal* reminder that we're watching them and won't tolerate any nonsense this time around.'

'So what else have you got for us, Captain?' Armstrong said, picking up his notepad.

'Nothing, really,' Phule said, stretching his arms. 'I just thought I'd give you two a chance to ask any questions that Tullie shouldn't be hearing. I figure I'll give you some time to review your notes before we get down to the final shift assignments – that and get some sleep. You two have been pushing yourselves awfully hard on this trip so far.'

Rembrandt gave out a snort.

'Look at who's talking,' she said. 'You'd better get some sleep yourself, Captain, or Beeker's going to sneak something into your food.'

'Beeker *never* thinks I get enough sleep.' Phule shrugged, dismissing the subject. 'You get used to his grumbling after a while. So anything either of you want to go over just now. Anything at all, not just Tullie's report.'

'Not that I can think of, sir,' Armstrong said, giving his notes one last glance. 'As near as I can tell, we've got everything covered.'

The commander nodded. 'I know. And to be honest with you, that worries me a little.'

'How so?'

'Well, there's an old saying in business,' Phule said with a rueful smile. 'If you think you've got everything covered, it means there's something you're overlooking.'

'Cheerful thought,' Rembrandt observed wryly, then glanced at the commander with a mischievous twinkle in her eye. 'As a matter of fact, I have one question for you, sir – if you're *really* throwing the floor open.'

'Shoot.'

Rembrandt sneaked a wink at her partner. 'I was just wondering, how are you doing at staving off the Red Menace?'

The Red Menace was the nickname the Legionnaires had assigned to Tiffany, mostly due to her blatant and obvious efforts to herd Phule into her bed. Of course, to her face, the moniker was shortened to just 'Red.'

'Isn't that question a bit personal, Lieutenant?' the commander growled in mock severity.

'Yes and no, sir,' Armstrong chimed in with a grin. 'You see, the crew is giving odds as to your holding out, so you might say it affects the morale of the whole company, which, as you keep telling us, *is* our business.'

'Really?' Phule said. 'What odds?'

Armstrong blinked and glanced at Rembrandt, who admitted her own ignorance with a shrug.

'I . . . I don't actually know, sir,' he sputtered. 'It's just something I've heard. Why? Is it important?'

'Well, if the payback's big enough, I just might put some money down myself, then rake in the whole pot – if you know what I mean,' Phule said through a yawn.

There was no response, and he glanced at his lieutenants, only to find them staring at him.

'Hey! It's a joke. Okay?' he clarified. 'You know I don't fool around with women under my command – or you *should* know it by now.'

His junior officers rallied gamely, though their late laughter was a little forced.

'Of course' – Rembrandt grinned – 'as one of the subcontractees, it could be argued that Big Red isn't *really* under your command.'

'For the duration of this assignment she is,' Phule said grimly, 'and if she wants to do any chasing after that – '

A knock at the door interrupted them, and they looked up to find Tusk-anini framed in the doorway.

'Excuse, Captain,' the giant Voltron rumbled. 'Must talk to you . . . soon.'

Phule waved. 'Come on in, Tusk. We were just finishing up here. Say, how's your new partner – what's her name – Melissa working out?'

'Nice girl. Very smart,' the Legionnaire said. 'But not fighter like Super Gnat. Not worry, Captain. I watch out for her.'

'I'm sure you will,' the commander said. 'So what brings you calling? Is it all right if the lieutenants hear it, or is it personal?'

'Not personal . . . company business.'

'Okay. What have you got?'

The Voltron raised the small stack of paper he was holding into view.

'You ask me . . . look at records for casino employees? See where they hired from?'

'That's right.'

Tusk-anini was a closet insomniac and a rabid reader, and Phule had utilized this by making him into a company clerk, reviewing the massive paperwork necessary to run a company and interface with Headquarters. More recently, as part of the plan to infiltrate the casino with undercover Legionnaires, the commander had asked the Voltron to go through the employment records of the existing casino employees, making a list of the various employment agencies they had been hired through. With that information, it would be a relatively easy matter to engineer a computerized break-in, sneaking carefully prepared résumés and references into the appropriate files.

'You look at this, Captain,' the Voltron said, passing the stack to Phule. 'All these hired from same service. Golden Employment Agency.'

'All right,' the commander said, idly leafing through the sheets. He had every confidence in Tusk-anini, and if the Voltron said they were all from the same source, he was sure they would be. 'So what's the problem?'

'It not exist. No such agency.'

Phule sat bolt upright as if someone had just plugged in his chair.

'Are you sure?' he said, staring at the pages as if they would talk to him themselves.

'Yes, Captain. Otherwise not bother you. Check many times. No such agency . . . ever.'

'I don't get it, sir.' Rembrandt frowned. 'How could so many employees use the same fake reference?'

'It means we aren't the only one sneaking people onto the staff,' the commander growled. 'That's the trouble with being impressed with your own cleverness. You tend to forget that there are other people out there just as clever.'

'All have same person approve reference check. Huey Mar-tin,' Tusk-anini supplied, stumbling a little over the name.

'The new casino manager,' Phule said grimly. 'If *he's* bent, we could have an uphill fight on our hands. Great work, Tusk-anini! If you hadn't caught this, we could have walked into a swinging door.'

'Thank you, Captain,' the giant said, drawing himself up proudly to an even greater height.

'We'll take it from here . . . and Tusk? Don't say anything to anyone else about this. Okay?'

Can keep secret, Captain. Not worry.'

The officers sat in silence for a few minutes after Tusk-anini had left.

Finally Phule heaved a sigh.

'Remember what I was saying about thinking everything was in hand?' he said.

'This assignment just keeps getting better and better,' Armstrong spat bitterly. 'If you don't mind my saying so, sir, Headquarters' idea of an easy job in paradise leaves a lot to be desired!'

'What are we going to do, Captain?' Rembrandt asked, ignoring her partner's irritation. 'Should we alert the owner that he's got a rat in the woodpile?'

'Not just yet,' Phule said thoughtfully. 'First of all, we don't know for sure what Br'er Huey is up to. He might just be indulging in a little featherbedding.'

'Featherbedding, sir?'

'Filling the roster with friends and family members,' Armstrong explained.

'We're going to hold off sounding the alarm until we've had a chance to check things out firsthand,' the commander continued, almost to himself. 'Fortunately Tusk-anini's alertness has provided us with a list of exactly who we have to be watching.' He tapped the stack of records with a smile. 'Lieutenant Rembrandt, be sure this entire list *and* the complete files of everyone on the list get passed to Mother. In the meantime, I'll get busy and do a detailed check on one Huey Martin.'

'What if it turns out that he *is* crooked, sir?' Armstrong said. 'Him and the people he's been hiring?'

'Then we lower the boom on him,' Phule said grimly. 'But not until just before the grand opening. If he *is* a part of a bigger scheme, we'll let him think it's working, then pull the rug out when it's too late to switch to an alternate plan.'

'But we can't wait that long to dump *everybody* on the list,' Rembrandt protested. 'The casino couldn't find that many replacements on such short notice.'

'They can't, but we can,' the commander responded with a grimace. 'It's going to hurt a little, though. I'll have to reopen negotiations with Tullie for him and his instructors to stay on as a stopgap reserve – and I just gave him a rough time for the sake of a cheap laugh.' He shook his head ruefully. 'I just *love* negotiating contracts with someone who's already annoyed at me.'

'Maybe you could wait to talk to him, sir,' Armstrong suggested. 'Maybe it would be easier after he's had a chance to forget about the last round . . . and you've had a chance to get some sleep.'

'It's a tempting thought,' Phule said, rising to his feet, 'but I'd better try to catch up with him now. I don't think I could sleep, anyway, with this hanging over our heads.'

A casual stroll through the ship's more popular gathering spots failed to locate Tullie Bascom, so Phule began a more careful search through the less frequented areas.

'Excuse me . . . Gabriel, isn't it?' he said to a Legionnaire he found sitting alone in one of the smaller lounges.

'Sir?' the man responded, rising to his feet.

'As you were,' Phule said, waving him back to his chair. 'I was just wondering if you had seen Tullie Bascom recently.'

'I think I heard him come by a while ago,' the Legionnaire reported. 'I didn't look around, but he was telling someone that he was going to his cabin to get some sleep.'

'Okay. Thanks.' The commander sighed and headed off down the corridor toward his own quarters.

So much for that idea. Maybe it was just as well. He should probably do a little more checking as to the actual necessity for contracting Tullie's crew for backups before beginning negotiations. Besides, his lieutenants were right – he *could* use a bit of sleep to clear his mind. Maybe he could get Beeker to . . .

Phule suddenly halted in his tracks as realization struck him.

The Legionnaire, Gabriel, had been sitting alone in the lounge.

While Phule and Tusk-anini weren't the only night owls in the company, the Legionnaires by and large were social animals, tending to gather together in their off hours, and to his knowledge Gabriel was no exception. Rather than being at one of the normal ship hangouts, however, the

Legionnaire had been sitting alone, without a book or work in sight – not even a deck of cards.

Abandoning his plan for sleep, the commander retraced his steps back to the lounge.

Gabriel was still sitting there, sprawled in an easy chair with his head tipped back, staring at the ceiling.

'Are you feeling all right, Gabriel?' the commander said, speaking gently.

While some of the Legionnaires were borderline hypochondriacs, others were more like children, hiding it when they felt ill rather than reporting to the ship's doctor.

'What? Oh. No, I feel fine, sir,' Gabriel said, suddenly aware that he was no longer alone with his thoughts.

'Is there something bothering you?' Phule pressed. 'Anything you'd like to talk about?'

The Legionnaire hesitated. 'It's . . . well . . . I'm afraid, sir. Of this.'

He made a vague gesture, encompassing the air in front of him.

'I . . . I'm not sure I understand.' Phule frowned. 'What is it you're afraid of? The new assignment?'

'No . . . *this*,' the man said, repeating his gesture. 'You know . . . space travel.'

'I see,' the commander said. He had encountered nervous travelers in the past, but not recently, and he tended to assume that everyone was as accustomed to space travel as he was. 'Haven't you ever been on a ship before?'

'Sure,' the Legionnaire said. 'A couple of times. But it always affects me the same way. I keep thinking about what will happen if anything goes wrong. Life pods may be effective for interplanetary travel, but for interstellar, we wouldn't stand a chance. The only choice would be between dying fast or slow.'

Phule thought for a moment, then heaved a sigh.

'Sorry, Gabriel,' he said. 'I can't help you with that one.'

'That's okay, sir,' the Legionnaire said, hanging his head slightly. 'I guess it's a silly fear, anyway, in this day and age.'

'I didn't say that!' the commander snapped, then ran a

hand across his eyes. 'Don't put words in my mouth, Gabriel, please. I soak up enough grief over what I *do* say.'

'Sorry, sir.'

'There *are* no silly fears,' the captain continued. 'If you're afraid of something, it's *real*, and it affects your thinking and performance no matter how invalid or valid someone else thinks it is. It's like there's no *minor* pain when it's yours. If it hurts, it hurts. What you got to do is figure out how to deal with it, not use up your energies trying to decide if it's real or not.'

Phule leaned against the wall, crossing his arms over his chest until he was almost hugging himself.

'All I meant to say was, I can't do or say anything to set your mind at ease. Telling you not to be afraid doesn't change anything. I can tell you there's no danger, but we both know that things *can* go wrong, and there's nothing I can do to lessen the danger that hasn't already been done. I could cite the low accident stats on space travel, but you're already aware of those yourself, and it hasn't made any difference. Realizing that, about the only thing I *can* do is beat a hasty retreat – for my own protection.'

'Your own protection, sir?'

'Fear is contagious,' the commander explained with a shrug. 'If I tried to compare notes with you on the dangers of space travel, there's a chance that all I'd do is start worrying myself, and I can't afford that. You see, Gabriel, there are lots of dangers in our lives that we can't do a thing about – traffic accidents, bad food – dangers that have a low probability rating, but that if they hit will be devastating. All I can do – all anyone can do – is to do my best to put them out of my mind. It may seem like a head-in-the-sand approach to fear, but the only option I see is letting the worries eat you alive – paralyze you to a point where you cease to function. To my thinking, that means you're dead, whether you're still breathing or not. I'd rather try to focus on things I *can* do something about. I can't danger-proof the universe, or even guarantee my own personal safety. I have no way of telling for sure exactly how long my life is going to be, but I'm determined that while I'm alive, I'm going to be a doer, a worker – not a do-nothing worrier.'

He broke off, realizing that his fatigue was making him prattle.

'Anyway,' he said, forcing a conclusion, 'I'm sorry I can't help you with your problem, Gabriel, but frankly it's out of my league.'

'Actually you have, Captain.' The Legionnaire smiled.

'I have?'

'Well, at the very least you've given me something to think about. Thank you, sir.'

Strangely enough, of all the problems that had beleaguered him that day, it was the final conversation with Gabriel that haunted Phule's thoughts and kept him from dozing off when he finally tried to sleep. Despite the Legionnaire's claims that the commander's talk had helped him, Phule felt that his help and advice had been inadequate.

Group dynamics, personal image, military strategy, and, of course, finances – all these things the commander felt qualified in helping and training the people under his command. But deeper problems? Matters of the soul?

With a flash of insight, Phule decided to do what he had always done when confronted with a problem beyond his personal abilities: find an expert. Sliding out of his bunk, he marched over to his desk, fired up his Port-A-Brain computer, and blearily composed a personnel request to Legion Headquarters. If his Legionnaires needed spiritual guidance, then, by God, he'd get them a spiritual expert. A chaplain!

There was an almost tangible load lifted from his mind as he hit the Send key, but close on its heels came the crushing weight of exhaustion. Staggering back across his cabin, Phule toppled into his bunk and fell into a deep, dreamless slumber.

Chapter Six

Journal #209

The in-flight classes and lectures arranged by my employer had given the company every confidence that they were ready for their new assignment. This belief was, of course, encouraged by their commander and his officers, who made a point of keeping their own fears and suspicions from their troops. Thus it was that upon their arrival, the Legionnaires were eager to begin their duties, while the company's leadership was already suffering from a lack of sleep due to their anxieties.

Nothing in the briefings, tapes, or brochures, however, succeeded in preparing them for the total impact of Lorelei itself.

The space station known throughout the galaxy as 'Lorelei' was officially an antique. One of the first privately owned stations, it was originally named 'the Oasis,' constructed on the old spoked-wheel design, and had been built as an outpost to supply the far-flung colonies and outbound explorer ships – an expensive outpost to be sure, as there was no competition to keep their prices down.

As civilization pushed outward, however, the so-called frontier moved on, leaving the station to compete with an ever-increasing number of spaceports and supply depots – places with newer designs and, therefore, lower maintenance expenses. Only one thing saved the station from extinction during that period: its reputation and tradition of being a 'safe haven' or a 'liberty port.' That is, even though people lived and worked at other colonies and spaceports, when they wanted to play or vacation, they headed for the Oasis.

The owner, not government, made the rules at the Oasis, and little was forbidden or outlawed that might generate revenue for the station's coffers. Not surprising, one of the main pastimes that was not only allowed but encouraged was gambling.

Eventually a combine of investors recognized the station's potential and bought it away from the original owner's estate. Hundreds of millions were put into renovating and remodeling the station, not to mention an extensive advertising campaign to change the station's image to that of the ultimate resort and family vacation spot, and the station was renamed 'Lorelei.'

The new name was due, in part, to the station's beacon, which was said to be strong enough to cause interference in neighboring solar systems. If the ever-present advertising was not enough, the beacon made sure no one passed through that sector of space without hearing of Lorelei's lures and charms. 'Once you visit Lorelei,' the catchy slogan ran, 'you'll never want to leave!'

The reality was a little grimmer: Once you visit Lorelei, you might not be *able* to leave. Not that there was physical danger, mind you . . . it would be bad publicity to hurt a tourist. The real danger was on Lorelei was its famous, vampiric casinos.

The inside of the space station's wheel design had been filled in and painted to look like a massive roulette wheel, which, while it was eye-catching to those in ships with view points, had a practical function as well. The surface of the wheel was actually a massive solar energy cell, endlessly gathering power from the stars and feeding it to the casinos . . . and they needed it!

The casinos were dazzling to the point of being awe-inspiring, each trying to outshine, outglitz its neighbors. Though there was no 'sunlight' on the station, the massive, circular main corridor needed no streetlights, nor did the electric shuttle vehicles moving tourists from destination to destination require headlights. The same artificial gravity which kept the buildings to four stories or less, forcing the casinos to spread out rather than up, was actually a boon to designing their exterior light displays. Freed of the physics of engineering by the abruptly lessening gravity above the buildings, the casinos' light displays were spectacular, as they almost floated in the 'air,' fighting for the attention of passing tourists. These displays around 'the Strip' kept the stations interior lit to near-daylight brightness – near daylight as the wattage was carefully controlled to create an illusion of darkness above the casinos, thus enhancing the effectiveness of the light shows. There was no day or night on Lorelei, only a perpetual twilight through which the tourists, vacationers, and, of course, gamblers walked, rode, or, eventually, staggered in their pursuit of pleasure. The only concession to normality was that the rooms in the casino hotels all had blackout curtains, so that one could shut out the light when, and if, one wanted to sleep.

Of course, the carefully maintained illusion on Lorelei was that no one slept. The casinos never closed, and neither did the restaurants or shops. Entertainment booked to lure people into one casino or another was simply advertised as 'every three hours' rather than specific showtimes.

In short, there was a studied sense of timelessness which permeated Lorelei – for a specific reason. The longer people gambled, the better it was for the casinos. While there might be the occasional 'lucky hit' or 'hot run,' if the players kept betting long enough, the house odds would catch up with them, and all their winnings, plus whatever they were willing to lose of what they brought with them, ended up in the casino vaults.

This was the real trap of the Lorelei's song, and many who arrived by private ship left by public transport. Others, who could no longer afford even public transport, were absorbed into the station's work force until they could raise enough money to leave, which rarely happened, as they would usually succumb to the temptation of the tables once more, trying desperately to 'build a stake' while the house yawned and raked in their savings. Those that did manage to escape, vowing never to return again, were quickly replaced by the next shipload of eager faces and fat wallets, each planning to have a good time and maybe win an instant fortune on the lucky roll of a card.

There was a seemingly endless supply of these replacements, as the publicity machine of Lorelei was mercilessly effective, and unceasing in its quest to find yet one more way to keep the lure of Lorelei in front of the public. Thus, it was no surprise to insiders that the media had been alerted and was waiting when the Omega Mob arrived on Lorelei.

'Excuse me, Mr. Phule?'

The Legionnaire commander halted, not ten paces from stepping off the gangplank, and blinked in surprise at the figure blocking his way. The pudgy man was wearing a fluorescent-green jumpsuit with a large blue bow tie, leaving one with the quick impression of being confronted by a prizewinning frog.

'Actually it's "Captain Jester" when I'm on duty,' he corrected gently.

'But you *are* Willard Phule? The megamillionaire turned soldier?'

Phule flinched a bit, as he always did when publicly confronted with his wealth-generated fame, and shot a quick glance at the company. The Legionnaires were ambling off the ship, some gawking at the casino light displays while others started to crowd close to see what was happening with their commander.

'That's correct,' he said levelly.

'Great!' the man exclaimed, seizing Phule's hand and giving it a hurried pump. 'Jake Herkamer, here. I was wondering if we could have a few minutes of your time for a quick interview on your new assignment?'

As he spoke, he made a magician's pass, and a microphone appeared in his hand. Simultaneously the portable floodlights came on, alerting Phule to the presence of holo cameras, which, until then, had been undetected.

85

'Umm . . . could this wait until I get my troops settled in the hotel?' Phule hedged.

'Good point! Hey, guys! Get some shots of the soldiers before we lose them in the hotel!'

Phule felt his muscles tighten as the camera crew obediently began to pan over the gathering Legionnaires, who mugged or glowered for the cameras depending upon their individual inclination. While he had known all along that this assignment would put his force in the public eye more than ever before, he also knew that there were several Legionnaires who had joined up specifically to escape from their earlier lives, and were therefore quite nervous about having their pictures and current location broadcast by the media.

'Rembrandt . . . Armstrong!'

'Sir!'

'Here, sir!'

The two lieutenants materialized at his side.

'Form the company up, over there, while I take care of this. If it runs more than a couple of minutes, move them out to the hotel. Get them away from these cameras.'

Turning back to the reporter as the junior officers started off, he forced a smile.

'I suppose I could spare a few minutes,' he said.

'Great!' the reporter beamed. 'Hey, guys! Over here! Start shooting. Now!'

He leaned into the microphone, showing an impressive number of teeth.

'We're here today with Willard Phule, or, as he's known in the secretive Space Legion, Captain Jester. He and his famous elite force of Legionnaires have just arrived on Lorelei. Tell me, Captain, are you and your force here for business or pleasure?'

Of course, I have no way of telling how the interview upon our arrival was received by the viewers, as it went out on stellarwide broadcast and, as I've mentioned before, I am not omnipresent.

From subsequent events, however, I feel I am able to project with some accuracy how it was viewed in at least two locations: back on Haskin's Planet and here on Lorelei.

'Hey, Jennie! Come here a sec! I think you'll want to see this!'

Annoyed at the interruption, Jennie Higgens glanced up from the notes she was reviewing for that night's broadcast.

'What is it? I'm kinda busy here.'

'Your boyfriend's being interviewed on interstellar, and Jake the Jerk's got him.'

'Really?'

Jennie decided the notes could wait a little longer and joined the small cluster of newsroom staff crowding around the monitor bank. Due to the multiscreen nature of their business, they had the monitors set to display the broadcasts on flat screens to avoid the chaos of multiple projections.

'It's a bit of an experiment,' Phule was saying, *'a test to see if the Space Legion can be effective in more commonplace, civilian security roles. Of course, being stationed here on Lorelei is a real treat for my force. It really is a spectacular place. Can your cameras pick up some of the light displays behind us?'*

Unnoticed by her fellow reporters, Jennie narrowed her eyes a bit at this. She had barely seen Phule in the weeks before his force's departure from Haskin's, and then only hurriedly – supposedly due to the pressures of preparing for their new assignment. So this was the tough duty he had been so engrossed in, eh?

'But don't you feel that the rather massive firepower of a Space Legion company is unnecessary for normal security duty?' the interviewer pressed, ignoring Phule's attempts to divert the interview from his force to the casino light displays.

'Oh, we won't be carrying our normal weapons on duty in the casino, Jake.' Phule laughed easily. *'But I've always found it's easier not to use equipment you have than to use equipment you don't have, if you know what I mean.'* For the briefest second, his eyes flickered from the interviewer to look directly into the camera, as if he were speaking personally to one of the viewers.

'I've got to admit, your boy gives good interviews,' one of the reporters commented to Jennie. 'He's giving the

87

impression of being just plain folks, but still managing to come across as someone you wouldn't want to tangle with. Nothing to scare the tourists off there.'

'Yeah, but look at some of the plug-uglies in his crew, though. They scare *me* just looking at them.'

'Those aren't the really mean ones,' Jennie put in. 'Wait until you see . . .'

Her voice trailed off to silence as she stared at the monitor, focusing now on the figures in the formation behind Phule rather than on the commander himself. As if reading her thoughts, the camera did a slow pan of the force, showing the formation from one end to the other.

A small frown appeared on the reporter's forehead as she studied each face in turn. Something was wrong here. While she was interviewing them, not to mention while she was dating their company commander, she had gotten to recognize many of the Legionnaires on sight – and there were faces missing in the formation!

Where was Chocolate Harry? He would stand out in any crowd. And the woman standing next to Tusk-anini was small, but she wasn't Super Gnat. For that matter, where was Brandy? The company's top sergeant should be standing prominently in front of the formation, yet she was nowhere to be seen.

'Are you taping this?' Jennie asked, not taking her eyes from the screen.

'Yeah, I figure it might have some local interest if we want to replay it here. Why?'

'Oh, nothing.' Jennie was suddenly all smiles and innocence. 'I just forgot to ask Willard for a picture before he left, and this might make a nice remembrance until we see each other again. Can you make me a copy when it's over?'

'You got it.'

As the technician turned his attention to the screen once more, however, Jennie's smile vanished and she edged backward out of the group.

'Sidney?' she murmured, drawing one of the photographers aside with her. 'Have you still got those shots you took when we were doing the big spread on this crew while they were stationed here? All of them, not just the ones we used.'

'Sure. Why?'

'Get them and see if you can find the tapes from their competition with the Red Eagles. Then meet me in viewing room two – pronto.'

'What's up?'

'I'm not sure' – she smiled darkly – 'but unless my intuition is failing me completely, I think there's a story brewing on Lorelei.'

In a large penthouse, discreetly screened from the light shows in one of Lorelei's lesser casinos, the holo-images of the Omega Mob were arrayed across the sunken living room like so many ghostly specters.

Watching them with her characteristically frozen stare, Laverna sat on one end of the sofa, so rigidly immobile she might have been taken for a part of the room's furnishings. Specifically she almost reminded one of a floor lamp, as her skin was very nearly the color of the black baked enamel so often found on those appliances, and her long body was thin almost to the point of being skeletal. Still, there was an easy, elegant grace to her movement as she rose and walked to the closed bedroom door and rapped on it sharply with her knuckle.

'Maxie?' she said, raising her voice slightly to be heard through the door. 'You'd better come out here.'

'What?' came the muffled response from within.

'It's important,' Laverna said shortly.

Her message delivered, she returned to her seat without waiting for additional discussion or comment. She had voiced her opinion, and her opinions were rarely challenged.

Scant seconds later, the bedroom door opened and Maxine Pruet emerged into view wrapped in a housecoat. She was a small woman in her early fifties, with high, angular cheekbones that might have been called 'striking' when she was young, but now, combined with her piercing eyes and silver-streaked hair, could only be referred to as 'severe.' Because of the timelessness of life on Lorelei, she, like many of those who dwelt here, had no regular sleep patterns, sleeping only occasionally and briefly as fatigue demanded. Despite her years, however, Maxine was still very energetic and active, setting a demanding pace for those who worked for her.

'What is it, Laverna?' she said without rancor.

'The new security force has just arrived,' Laverna said flatly. 'I thought you should take a look at them.'

'I see.'

Maxine stepped down into the sunken living room, walking through several of the images as she did so as if they weren't there, which, of course, they weren't, and joined her assistant on the sofa, studying the figures in silence like a prim aunt watching children at a piano recital as the interview rattled on.

'So. Our Mr. Rafael's called in the Army,' she said at last. 'I'm not sure I understand why you feel this is important. The security force has a minor impact, at best, on my plans. Uniformed guards are little more than a decorative deterrent.'

'Take another look at their commander,' Laverna instructed. 'The one being interviewed.'

Maxine obediently turned and peered at the lean figure in black.

'What about him? He's not much older than Mr. Rafael himself.'

'That's Willard Phule,' Laverna said. 'Probably the youngest megamillionaire in the galaxy. You may not know it, but he's a bit of a legend in financial circles – a real tiger when it comes to corporate infighting and takeovers.'

'How very interesting,' Maxine said, studying the figure with a new respect. 'Forgive me, Laverna, but I'm still tired and sleepy, and my mind is a little slow right now. What is it *exactly* that you're trying to tell me here?'

Now it was Laverna's turn to shrug.

'To me, this changes the game,' she said. 'Whether he knows it or not, Rafael has just hired himself some real heavyweight help. I thought you might want to reconsider your whole idea of taking over the casino.'

While Maxine might give the appearance of being some-one's grandmother or, perhaps, a maiden aunt, this impression couldn't be further from the truth. Locally she was known simply as 'Max' or 'the Max.' She had married into organized crime while still young, and surprised every-one by successfully stepping into her late husband's shoes after his untimely demise during a shoot-out with unsympa-thetic authorities. She had sold off most of the 'business interests' her husband had maintained, focusing her entire energies and resources on one speciality – casinos.

Max liked casinos, officially because of their money-laun-dering capacity, which earned her a steady income providing that service for other crime families, but, in actuality, because she liked the glittery life-style that prevailed at those establishments. She was a common fixture at the tables around Lorelei, though she rarely placed a bet for more than the table minimum. The tourists who gambled beside her never realized that she held controlling interest in nearly ever casino on the space station, but the permanent residents knew who she was and treated her with the appro-priate deference.

Despite her years of experience in behind-the-scenes casino work, however, Maxine had a lot of respect for Laverna, which was why the black woman was in her cur-rent, favored position of being Max's main advisor and confidante. Not only did Laverna have advanced degrees in both business and law, she was by far the coldest analyst of risks and odds Max had ever met. Maxine, though she prided herself on her levelheadedness, still might be swayed by feelings of anger, vengeance, or ego, but Laverna was as emotionless as a computer, weighing all pluses and minuses of any endeavor before bluntly stating her opinion, however unpopular. The others in the organization called her 'the Ice Bitch,' or just 'Ice,' but there was always an undercurrent of respect in the title. If Laverna said this uniformed gentle-man could affect their plans, Maxine would be foolish not to give her words serious consideration. Still, Max was a gambler.

'No,' she said finally, shaking her head. 'I want this

91

casino. This Mr. Phule may know numbers and corporations, but I know casinos. If anything, it adds a bit of spice to the challenge. We're going to take this enterprise right out from under his nose, and if he gets in our way, we'll just have to persuade him to stand aside.'

Laverna glanced at her employer sharply, then looked away again. Max's casual mention of 'persuasion' was, of course, a reference to violence – the one point the two women disagreed on. What was more, it was far from an empty threat.

Maxine had proven herself to be a more than competent general for her troops on the occasions when other crime factions had thought her territory easy pickings and tried to move in. Nor was she averse to getting personally involved in the bloodshed.

The sleeves of Max's housecoat were loose, as were the sleeves of all her clothes. This was to accommodate the custom pistol and spring holster that she always wore. It was a very small caliber, .177 to be exact, the same size as a BB, and the sound it made when firing was no louder than a man snapping his fingers. The small size of the hollow-point bullets meant that she could fit twenty-five of them into a magazine no larger than a matchbox, yet they were deadly if they hit a vital organ, and Max was a crack shot who could hit anything she could see.

Laverna knew this, and while she acknowledged the constant potential for violence in their profession, she didn't approve of it.

'Suit yourself,' she said shrugging again. 'You pay me for my opinions, and you've heard my thoughts on this one. By the way, if you're seriously thinking of leaning on that child, remember he has a couple hundred troops of his own backing him. What's more, that isn't the Regular Army, that's the Space Legion, and it's my understanding they aren't big on playing by the rules.'

'Oh?' Maxine said, raising one eyebrow. 'Well, neither are we. See if you can locate Mr. Stilman, and tell him I want to see him in about an hour. I'm still a little tired. Not getting any younger, you know.'

Her decision made, Max retreated into the bedroom, leaving Laverna to stare at the holo-images alone again.

Chapter Seven

*Even as the company was settling into their
new quarters and beginning to stand duty, their
undercover colleagues were filtering into the space
station.*

*I have endeavored to keep these events as
sequential as possible to avoid confusion. This
effort has been hampered, however, by the sketchy
nature by which the facts have been reported to
me — directly or indirectly — as well as by the
previously noted timelessness of life in the casinos.
Much of the difficulty in chronicling the company's arrival on Lorelei is due to the fact that
its undercover members were traveling as individuals by a wide variety of transports independent of the 'official' group, and were establishing
their presence both before and after the company's
formal, publicized entrance.*

*Often, my only clue as to 'what happened
when' is by the chance passing reference to an
event known to me, or which, by simple logic,
would have had to take place prior to an event
which I was aware of.*

*Such was the case regarding Chocolate Harry's
arrival . . .*

Although Lorelei was known mostly for its famous Strip,
which ran down the center of the station for its entire
circumference, there were back streets as well. These
housed the businesses necessary to keep the casinos operat-

ing such as laundries and warehouses, as well as the hole-in-the-wall hotels where the minimum-wage employees made their home. Also found here were the mini-hospitals and pawnshops, carefully hidden away to avoid reminding the space station's visitors of the less frivolous side of life on Lorelei. This off-Strip area, though lighted adequately by normal standards, always seemed dark in comparison to the gaudy light displays along the Strip proper, and tourists needed no warnings to give it wide berth, clinging instead to the better-traveled areas which clamored for their attention and money.

It was along one of these back streets that Harry tooled his hover cycle, enjoying anew the freedom from his normal Legion duties. Though he genuinely liked the uniforms Phule had provided for the company, it felt good to be back in his denims, threadbare but velvet soft from years of hard wear.

His arrival on Lorelei had been surprisingly easy, especially considering his current, disreputable appearance. The only difficulty he had encountered was in off-loading his beloved hover cycle. The spaceport officials were noticeably reluctant to allow it in the space station, and he had had to spend several hours filling out forms, initialing tersely phrased lists of rules and regulations, and, finally, paying several rounds of fees, duty charges, and deposits before they grudgingly cleared it for admission.

It didn't take a genius to realize that much of the ordeal was specifically designed to frustrate the applicant to a point where he would be willing to simply store the vehicle until his departure, but Harry had used every trick in the book, as well as a few new ones, to keep his hover cycle while he was in the Legion, and he wasn't about to pass using it now that he was back in civilian garb.

The reason for this 'screening' was quickly apparent. All the air on Lorelei was recycled, and while the support systems were efficient enough to handle the monoxide generated by the people on the station, excessive engine use would have taxed it severely. Consequently there were few vehicles on Lorelei aside from the electric carts that shuttled gamblers back and forth along the Strip. The formula was simple: The limited air supply could support people or vehicles – and vehicles didn't lose money at the tables.

Despite his apparent nonchalance, Harry knew exactly where he was going. In fact, he had known since before he left the ship. His information had come in the form of a warning from one of the ship's porters.

'Goin' to Lorelei, huh?' the man said as they were talking one night. 'Let me tell you, brother, you keep yourself out of a place there called the Oasis. Hear? Bad enough to lose your money at those places where they smile and call you "sir" while they rake in your chips. There's bad folks hang out at the Oasis. More trouble than the likes of us can afford.'

Casual pressure had yielded no more details, as the man was apparently passing along hearsay rather than firsthand experience. Still, it told Harry what he needed to know.

The Oasis itself looked harmless enough as Harry parked his cycle in front and pushed through the door. If anything, it seemed to be several cuts above the average neighborhood bar. Rather than being disappointed, he was heartened by the place's appearance. It was only in the holo-movies that criminal hangouts looked like an opium den in a bad cartoon strip. In real life, those who successfully worked the non-legal side of the street had money and preferred to do their drinking and eating in fairly upscale surroundings.

'Gimme a draft,' he said, sliding onto a stool at the bar.

The bartender hesitated, running an appraising eye over Harry's clothes until the Legionnaire-in-disguise produced a thick wad of bills from his pocket, peeled one off, and tossed it casually on the bar. The bill was of sufficiently high denomination that it would have been noticeable most places in the galaxy, but this was Lorelei, where gamblers often preferred to make their wagers in cash, and the barman barely gave it a glance before going off to fetch his drink.

The drink appeared and the bill vanished in the same motion, only to be replaced a few moments later by a stack of bills and change. Harry carefully separated a bill from the stack before pocketing the rest, pushing it forward on the bar as a tip. The bait worked, and the barman materialized again to claim the perk.

'Excuse me, my man,' Harry drawled before the man could retreat again. 'I was wonderin' if maybe you could help me out?'

'Depends on what you need,' the bartender said, his eyes wary, but he didn't leave.

Moving slowly, Harry withdrew a wristwatch from his pocket and laid it gently on the bar.

'What can you give me on this?'

Shooting a quick glance around the bar, the man picked up the watch and examined it, front and back.

'This came from off-station, right?' he said.

'Does it make a difference?'

The bartender looked at him hard.

'Yeah, it does,' he said, and tapped a finger on an inscription on the watch's back. 'I figure you aren't Captain Anderson *or* his grateful crew. If you picked it up here on Lorelei, I'm holding trouble in my hand. They come down hard on pickpockets and muggers up here – bad for the tourists.'

Harry held up both hands with the fingers spread like a magician accused of cheating at cards.

'The captain misplaced that beauty *before* our last stop,' he explained, 'and stopped askin' around about it two days out. By now, he and his ship should be well on their way. If there was a chance he was still lookin', I wouldn't be showin' it around like this.'

The bartender studied the watch again.

'Tell you what,' he said at last. 'I'll give you twenty for it.'

Harry rocked back on his stool like the man had taken a swing at him.

'Twenty?' he echoed. 'Excuse me, but that's a pretty steep cut. I knew I wasn't gonna get a one-for-ten deal, bein' new here and all, but that's barely one for a hundred!'

'Suit yourself.' The bartender shrugged, setting the watch down. 'Take it back if you think you can get a better offer. Let me show you something, though.'

He ducked out of sight under the bar, then emerged again and plopped a cardboard box next to Harry's beer.

'Take a look,' he said.

The box was two-thirds full of wristwatches and jewelry.

The bartender smirked. 'This is Lorelei, my friend. Gamblers will hawk or pawn anything to raise money for a ticket off-station – or, more often, another pass at the tables. When the box gets full, I run it over to one of the pawnshops, and I'll be lucky to get back what I paid for most of it. I just do this as a public service for our customers.'

Harry didn't bother to express his disbelief at this, but he found it hard to believe the Oasis had a Boy Scout working its bar. More likely, the man shipped his booty off-station and split the take with whoever did his selling at the other end.

Instead, he picked up his beer, took a sip, then smiled.

'All of a sudden, twenty sounds real good,' he said.

The man picked up the watch again and tossed it into the box, replacing it under the counter before turning to the cash register and ringing up a 'no sale' as he extracted a twenty.

'Tell me,' Harry said as he accepted the offering. 'Any chance of finding some work around here? I got a feeling that, between the casinos and the prices up here, my roll isn't gonna last all that long without some help.'

'You'll have to talk to the manager about that,' the bartender said. 'There's a lot of turnover up here, but he does the hiring and firing. He should be in in an hour or so, if you can hang around.'

'I gots nowhere to go,' Harry said, flashing his teeth. 'Is my hawg okay out front there?'

For the first time the bartender showed surprise, raising his eyebrows.

'You got a hover cycle up here?' he said. 'I thought I heard one right about the time you came in, but I figured it was my imagination. That or wistful thinking.'

'You sound like you used to ride yourself.'

'Sure did.' The man grinned. 'Didn't you notice the bugs in my teeth?'

Harry threw back his head and gave an appreciative guffaw, slapping his thigh with one hand. It was a *very* old joke, probably predating hover cycles themselves: How do you tell a happy cyclist? By the bugs in his teeth!

It was still around, though, and served almost as a recognition signal between hover cycle enthusiasts, since no one else remembered it, much less laughed at it.

'That was a long time ago, though,' the bartender said, his eyes looking into the distance as he smiled at the memory. 'I rode for a while with the Hell Hawks.'

'That's a good club.' Harry nodded approvingly. 'I rode with the Renegades myself.'

'No foolin'?' the man said, recognizing the name of one of the oldest, largest hover cycle clubs in the galaxy. 'By the way, my name's William. Used to be 'Wild Bill' when I was riding.'

'Just call me C.H.,' Harry supplied.

The two men shook hands solemnly, though the Legionnaire-in-disguise was mentally groaning at his slip. He was supposed to be working under a different name for this caper, but in the enthusiasm of talking hover cycles, his Legion name, which happened to also be his old club name, just popped out before he thought. He would have to pass the word to Mother that he wasn't using his planned alias and hope that the word of his whereabouts didn't reach the Renegades.

'Tell you what,' the bartender said, leaning close. 'When the manager comes in, let me talk to him first . . . maybe put in a good word for you.'

'Hey. I appreciate that.'

'And let me get you another brew while you're waiting . . . on me.'

As the bartender headed off, Harry turned on his stool and rested his elbows on the bar, surveying his new home.

There was a small dining area attached to the bar, not more than a dozen tables, though those tables were widely spaced, leading Harry to believe it was more of a gathering point than a profit generator. Only a few of the tables were occupied, and those customers, by their dress and manner, seemed to be locals rather than tourists.

One group in particular drew his attention. The only man at the table had the broad-shouldered no-neck look of an astroball player, and he was listening intently to a woman old enough to be his mother – if not his grandmother. What really caught his eye, however, was the third member of the party. Sitting beside the old lady was a tall lean Negress whose severe, angular features failed to hide the fact that she was bored with or disinterested in the discussion of the other two.

As if she felt his eyes, she glanced over to where Harry was sitting and their eyes met. He raised his beer in a silent toast to her, showing all his teeth in a friendly smile. Rather than responding, however, she let her eyes go out of focus, her face impassive, looking right through him as if he wasn't there. A near-physical chill swept over Harry like a wind off a glacier, and he turned back to the bar where the bartender was just delivering his fresh beer.

'Say, Willie,' he said. 'What's the story on the group against the far wall? They look like regulars.'

'I don't know who you're talking about,' the bartender replied without looking.

'The monster and the two women,' Harry clarified. 'The ones sitting right over . . .'

He started to point, but William snaked out a hand and caught his wrist.

'I said "I don't see anything",' his new friend intoned, staring hard into Harry's eyes as he emphasized each word. 'And if you're going to work here, you don't, either. And you *sure* don't point at them. You catch what I'm sayin'?'

'Got it.' Harry nodded slowly. 'They aren't here tonight. Never have been, never will be. Casual conversation or under oath.'

'Good,' William said, releasing his wrist. 'I thought you'd understand. Sorry to grab you like that, but you almost bought into some *big* trouble before I could give you a full briefing.'

Harry picked up his beer and propped his elbows on the bar.

'No problem' he said easily. 'I appreciate your watching my back for me. Speakin' of briefings, though, just between the two of us, my vision is a lot more selective when I know just what it is I'm not seein'.'

William moved a few steps away and leaned casually against the bar.

'Well,' he said, talking prison-style, without looking directly at Harry, 'what you *aren't* seeing is the Main Man on this whole station.'

The Legionnaire-in-disguise frowned slightly.

'That's funny. I always thought that kinda dude usually kept a low profile, but I could *swear* I've seen him somewhere before. Has the media been shootin' him or somethin'?'

The bartender let out a snort. 'If you're an astroball fan, you've seen him, all right. Remember Ward Stilman?'

'Sure do!' Harry said, sneaking another look at the group in question, but using the bar mirror this time. 'So that's him, huh? Damn! I used to love to watch him bust up people before he got tossed out of the pros.'

'That's him,' William confirmed. 'But he's not the one I was talking about. The old biddy's the *real* mover and shaker on Lorelei. Stilman's just her chief muscle.'

Harry's eyes flickered over to the older woman he had been ignoring so far.

'Her? *She's* "the Man" up here?'

'*Be*-lieve or *be* dead,' the bartender said, flashing a tight smile. 'You may have heard that someone called Max is running things. Well, that's short for "Maxine," and that's her. She's got a piece of every casino on this station and is *real* good at keeping the tourists in and the competition out. I'll tell you, C.H., if you start thinking about picking up some extra change with a bit of part-time larceny here on Lorelei, you don't worry about the cops – you look over your shoulder for Max. She *does* hire free-lancers from time to time, by the way, but ain't real tolerant of independents, if you know what I mean.'

'How 'bout the stone mama sitting next to her?' Harry said, shifting the conversation to the original object of his attention.

'That's the Ice Bitch.' William grinned. 'Some say she's the actual brains of the operation, others say she's just a walking calculator for Max. *Everybody* says that if you want to make a pass at her, you'd best have your frostbite insurance paid up.'

'I can believe *that*,' Harry said, shaking his head. 'I damn near caught cold from across the room a minute ago when she looked at me.'

The bartender's smile evaporated.

'Steer clear of that one, C.H.,' he said earnestly. 'In fact, you're wisest not to mess with any of them. I'll tell you, when those three get together – like they aren't right now – it means someone is about to get put through the grinder. Whatever it takes, just be sure it's never you.'

It has been accurately observed in military history that no battle plan ever survived contact with the enemy. Such was the case in the opposition's first attempt to 'feel out' my employer's troops.

Accounts of the incident vary, which is not surprising, as it was a brief skirmish that was over almost before it began . . .

Huey Martin, manager of the casino portion of the Fat Chance complex, did not bother trying to hide his disdain as he surveyed the Legionnaires wandering through what used to be his unchallenged domain. His feelings went unnoticed, however, as they were next to impossible to distinguish from his normal, dour expression.

At first he had been more fearful than resentful when his wet-behind-the-ears employer informed him that he was bringing in a Space Legion company to serve as security guards. What had looked like a pushover job was suddenly jeopardized by an unknown factor.

Watching the Legionnaires since their arrival, however, the concern he felt gave way to amusement and, eventually, contempt. Far from being experienced casino guards, they seemed to be no more knowledgeable about the table games than the average tourist. One by one, Huey let his planted dealers shift back to their normal grifting routines, and so far not a one of them had been detected by these uniformed clowns, even when they were seated at the table with the hustle going on literally under their noses. Instead, they cheered and clapped like children as they raked in their winnings, apparently oblivious to the fact that their winning streak was being boosted by dealers who were working to empty the casino's coffers.

A faint smile drifted across the manager's face.

It would be deliciously ironic to use the Legionnaires to break the casino, but the Max had her own timetable for that, and Huey would never have the nerve to try to deviate from her express orders. Besides, it was easier to pass big winnings to big bettors, and the Legionnaires all seemed content to cling to minimum bets at the low-stakes tables – at least, so far.

A small flurry of noisy activity drew his attention, and his smile tightened again.

Some of the Legionnaires, among them the two sluglike Sinthians, were posing for pictures, pointing their guns at a slot machine as the cameras gobbled up film recording the scene: guards holding up a one-armed bandit. The tourists loved it.

With only a small portion of the casino open, the Legionnaires had far less to do than they would after the grand opening. In the meantime, they had lots of time on their hands to explore the space station or, as they were more inclined to do, hang around the Fat Chance and pose for the tourists who came nosing around looking to meet this highly publicized force.

As far as Huey was concerned, that was all they were good for, and even there he firmly believed the job could be done better by models in hula skirts. Models would be more fun to look at, and cheaper.

A familiar figure entering the casino caught his eye, and Huey realized it was time for him to slip out of the complex for a walk. It would be best if he wasn't on the premises for what he had been warned was about to transpire.

Contrary to popular belief, planned violence is usually much more effective than the spontaneous, berserker variety. The main difficulty, of course, was finding personnel capable of the former. Ward Stilman, Maxine's field general when it came to physical action, had thought long and hard before selecting just who he wanted to carry out this mission. Lobo was far and away the best choice.

Though not particularly imposing physically, Lobo's work as a baggage handler at the spaceport had given his long, simian arms deceptive strength. Even more important for this assignment, however, was his eerie ability to soak up punishment without apparently feeling it or losing his head. In fact, he was something of a minor legend on Lorelei after he successfully took on three soldiers on leave in a fight. The brawl had lasted nearly fifteen minutes – long for a no-holds-barred dispute – but at the end of it Lobo had emerged victorious, though more than a little battered, while his opponents had to be carried to the Lorelei hospital.

The job as given to him by Stilman was simple enough, though slightly puzzling. He was supposed to try to goad one of the Legionnaire guards into a fight, both to test their effectiveness as fighters and to see how much provocation was necessary for them to take action. Above all, Lobo had been cautioned numerous times *not* to strike the first blow – not to fight back at all, for that matter. Supposedly this was to minimize the chance that the Legionnaires would simply resort to using the tranquilizer dart sidearms they were carrying, and instead be forced to try to subdue him physically.

Though he hadn't said anything at the time, Lobo wasn't wild about being assigned to play punching bag for some uniformed jerk. Not that he minded the possibility of pain or injury; it was the idea of not fighting back that bothered him. Still, it wasn't often that Stilman came to him with work, and he was eager to prove himself.

Lobo was impressed by Ward Stilman as he had rarely been impressed with anyone in his life, and wanted to move up in that notable's esteem. If the man wanted him to take a dive, he'd do it, but he wanted to be sure it was as spectacular as possible.

He pondered this as he ensconced himself at a table in the cocktail lounge that opened into the casino, the only lounge still open during the remodeling. This, too, was covered by his instructions: to establish his presence before starting trouble, so it wouldn't look like he walked in with that end specifically in mind.

Lobo had followed Stilman's career in astroball, as had most who loved that rough-and-tumble sport, until the league tossed him out for consistently exceeding the level of viciousness allowed by the rules, though the clamor from the media, not to mention several threatened lawsuits by hospitalized individuals who were unfortunate enough to have faced him on the field, doubtless played a factor in their decision. In person, however, Ward Stilman was even more intimidating than when viewed in the holos. The man had a disquieting habit, on the field or off, of standing absolutely motionless – not stiff or tense, but poised, as if he were waiting for just the right cue to spring for your throat. The media, of course, had picked up on this trait, calling him 'the Statue' or, playing on his name 'the Still Man,' but watching him in a stadium or even in holo was not the same as trying to remain relaxed when he was looking specifically at *you*. Whenever they talked, Lobo found himself moving very slow and deliberately, hoping subconsciously that by making his own actions clear he would not trigger an attack accidentally. Not being used to feeling fear, Lobo at once admired and resented the effect Stilman had on him, and aspired toward the day that Stilman would view him as an equal. The trouble was, how could he demonstrate his own courage and effectiveness while keeping his hands in his pockets, soaking up damage from some Army amateur?

The answer came to Lobo in the form of two Legionnaires who ambled into the bar while he was waiting for his drink. In an instant, Lobo knew he had his target.

The woman was nothing much – short, with the soft

curves of lingering baby fat. But her companion! Lobo mentally licked his lips in anticipation.

Even Stilman would have to be impressed that Lobo had chosen this monster to pick a fight with, especially a fight he was destined to lose. What was more, 'monster' was an accurate description of the Legionnaire he was targeting. The guy was some kind of alien, huge with a big warthog head and all-black animal eyes. At a glance it was easy to see that he would have to be one of the 'heavyweights' for the security force.

'That will be five dollars, sir,' the cocktail waitress said, interrupting Lobo's thoughts as she delivered his drink.

The opportunity was too good to let pass.

'What do you mean, *five dollars*?' he snarled, raising his voice. 'I thought drinks were *free* in these casinos.'

Though she was small, easily as small as the uniformed Legionnaire accompanying the monster, the cocktail waitress held her ground, apparently used to dealing with loud drunks.

'That's at the tables, sir,' she explained patiently. 'Drinks are complimentary while you're playing, but here in the bar we have to charge you. If you'd like, I can take it back.'

'Oh hell . . . *here!*' Lobo spat, fishing a bill from his pocket and throwing it at her. 'Just don't expect a tip, too.'

The waitress smoothed the bill, quickly checking its denomination, then retreated without another word.

Glancing around the bar in mock anger, Lobo caught the Legionnaires watching him, as he had expected.

'What are *you* looking at, *freak?*' he challenged, ignoring the woman to deal directly with the monster.

The massive Legionnaire shrugged and turned back to his companion.

'*Hey!* Don't look away when I'm talkin' to you, *freak!*' Lobo pressed, rising from his seat and approaching the other table. 'What are you doin' in here, anyway? Doesn't this place have a leash law for *pets?*'

The woman opened her mouth to respond, but the monster laid a restraining hand on her arm.

'Sorry . . . not mean to stare,' the monster said haltingly. 'My eyes not like yours. Sometimes look like I stare.'

'Hey! He even *talks* funny!' Lobo said, turning to make his appeal to the bar's other customers only to find the few occupied tables had been deserted, their occupants seeking quieter surroundings for their drinking.

'Tell you what, babe,' he said, focusing on the smaller Legionnaire. 'Why don't you send this freak back to his kennel and let *me* buy your next round?'

'I'm happy where I am, thank you,' the woman shot back coldly.

'With *him?*' Lobo laughed. 'You military chicks can't be *that* hard up! What you need is a *real* man.'

'Not talk like that,' the monster rumbled. 'Dangerous.'

'Oh yeah?' his tormentor sneered. 'You want to try to do somethin' about it . . . *freak?*'

Of course, what the Voltron was referring to was something that Lobo was missing completely, focused as he was on his target. The small waitress who had served him his drink was now marching toward him from behind, still holding her now-empty metal drink tray.

'Come on, freak!' Lobo taunted. 'Let's see what you've got.'

With that, he leaned forward and slapped the monster playfully on the side of its snout just as the waitress stepped in close behind him, raising her tray.

Chapter Eight

Journal #214

As I have noted, it took a while for my employer to determine that the casino his force was guarding was, indeed, under attack, much less who his adversaries were.

The opposition, on the other hand, as instigators of the attack, had no such difficulty, though they, in turn, were lacking hard information as to the exact nature and temperament of the force arrayed against them.

I find it particularly interesting, however, that some of the main problems encountered by both commanders throughout this campaign came from within, not without.

There was a muffled knock along with a muffled call of 'Housekeeping,' and Phule opened the door to admit his top sergeant, barely recognizable in her maid's uniform.

'I can only be here a few minutes, Captain,' she declared hurriedly. 'The story is I'm supposed to be checking to be sure the beds were made today, and if I take too long, the rest of the staff will start to wonder.'

'All right, Brandy, I'll try to keep this brief,' Phule said tersely. 'I assume you've heard about Super Gnat's little brawl?'

'It's all over the hotel,' Brandy said, 'though from what I hear, it wasn't much of a fight.'

'Well, have you talked to her about it?'

'Just for a few minutes in passing,' the top sergeant said. 'She seems to be all right. Why do you ask?'

'Didn't you say anything to her about breaking cover?' Phule pressed, ignoring the question.

Brandy shrugged. 'Not that I recall.'

Phule started to snap something angrily, then caught himself.

'All right,' he said stiffly. 'I want you to get her aside . . . pin her ears back for me. Understand?'

'No, I don't, sir,' the top sergeant said, perching on the edge of the room's dresser in a pose much more in keeping with her old Legion manner. 'Just what is it she's done that's supposed to be wrong?'

'Are you kidding?' the commander snarled. 'She stepped in on a fight and jeopardized her whole cover as a cocktail waitress.'

'I don't think so, Captain,' Brandy countered. 'The way I heard it, she just bopped a tray – didn't use any of the nasty stuff she's been trained in.'

'The man's in the clinic with a concussion,' Phule said pointedly.

'So? He got drunk and tried to pick a fight in a bar – and a casino bar at that. I don't think it's out of line that he got roughed up a little. You think that *real* waitresses can't get mean if you start acting up?'

'Usually they call for security,' the commander argued. 'They don't wade into it themselves when there are two security guards sitting right there.'

'– who couldn't do anything without it looking like they were overreacting to a minor incident,' Brandy added. 'Seriously, Captain, would you really expect the Gnat to stand there looking helpless while someone slapped Tusk-anini around? You know how close they are . . . *and* about the Gnat's temper.'

'I guess it would be too much to hope for.' Phule sighed, deflating slightly. 'It just caught me by surprise is all. I hadn't stopped to think that anything like this might happen.'

'Planned or not, I think it all turned out for the best,' the sergeant said with a smile. 'The incident got handled without our uniformed troops raising a hand. Instead of a possible lawsuit, the guy's going to want to forget about it as soon as possible. There's no glory in getting taken out by a female half your size, and he's *sure* not going to want to publicize it.'

'You're probably right, Brandy,' the commander said, 'but it still worries me. When I sent part of the team under cover, I figured they would be acting as eyes and ears for the company, not as fists. Gathering information is one thing, but if anything goes wrong, if anyone catches on to who they really are, they're going to be out there alone, without support.'

'Speaking as one of them, Captain,' Brandy drawled, 'we figured that danger was a part of the assignment. That's why you called for volunteers. Besides, nobody joins the Space Legion to be safe.'

'Okay, okay! You've made your point,' Phule said, holding up his hands in surrender. 'Just' – he glanced away as he searched for the right words – 'keep an ear open, will you, Brandy?' The words were so soft they were barely audible. 'If you hear of anyone targeting her, don't wait to check with me or anyone else. Pull her out – quick!'

'Will do, Captain,' the sergeant said, uncoiling from the dresser. 'Well, I've got to get back to work now.'

She started for the door, then turned back with one hand on the knob.

'And Captain? You might want to try to get a bit more sleep. You look terrible.'

As if in response to her words, Phule's wrist communicator chimed to life.

'Yes, Mother?' he said, triggering the two-way system.

'Hate to bother you, Fearless Leader,' came Mother's familiar, jaunty voice, 'but we've got a situation developing downstairs that I think requires your personal attention.'

'Just a second.'

The commander put his hand over the speaker and shrugged helplessly at Brandy.

'So much for getting some sleep,' he said with a grimace. 'Like you said, I've got to get back to work. Thanks for the concern, anyway.'

Brandy had concerns of her own as she left Phule's room. Though the troops were doing their best to screen their commander from minor problems, going to the junior officers or simply dealing with the hassles themselves, the captain was still driving himself far too hard on this assignment. She was just going to have to pass the word for everyone to tighten up a little more – to try to operate as independently as possible without playing 'Mother May I?' with their commander.

A small smile crept onto her face.

She wondered what the captain would say if he knew that she and the others on housekeeping were using their passkeys and their training with lockpicks to search the guests' luggage for any clues of larcenous intent. He said he wanted information, and their standing orders had always been to use whatever was necessary to get the job done!

In the same lounge where the 'incident' had taken place, another meeting was going on, though to the casual observer it would appear to be nothing more than a few friends relaxing over drinks. The mood of the gathering, however, was anything but relaxed.

'He's still a bit groggy,' Stilman was saying, 'but he swears he never even saw the guy start to swing. Now, Lobo may not be too quick upstairs, but he's been in enough fights to know what he's talking about, and he says this big guard is the fastest guy he's ever tangled with!'

He glanced fearfully out the open side of the lounge into the casino as if expecting to see the Legionnaire under discussion appear at any moment.

'I don't know,' he concluded. 'Maybe Lobo just picked the wrong guy to lean on. Maybe this alien type has faster reflexes than normal. Maybe . . . I don't know.'

'Maybe you just sent the wrong guy on the assignment,' Laverna said. 'Maybe you should have used somebody who could think as well as fight.'

'Hey, stay out of this, Ice,' Stilman snapped, turning his head slightly to glare at her. 'You may know numbers, but *I'm* the expert when it comes to rough stuff. Remember?'

111

'Are you aware, Mr. Stilman, that though they are very intelligent, Voltrons have slower reflexes than humans?' Maxine said carefully, ignoring the byplay.

'Really?' The big man scowled. 'Well, maybe Lobo tied onto one of their athletes or something.'

Maxine sighed heavily. 'Tell him, Laverna,' she said.

'Listen up, Stilman,' her companion said with a smirk. 'The word *we've* got is that your man didn't get taken out by the guard. Word is, he got hit from behind by one of the cocktail waitresses.'

'What?' Stilman didn't even try to hide his astonishment.

Maxine nodded. 'That's right, Mr. Stilman. The account was quite detailed. Apparently she hit him with her tray.' Her eyes took on a hard glitter, as did her voice. 'The account also states that Lobo was engaged in hitting the guard at the time. Slapping him, actually.'

Stilman shifted in his seat – a rare movement which betrayed the degree of his discomfort.

'Lobo didn't say anything about that when I talked to him,' he declared. 'I specifically told him *not* to throw the first punch.'

'Well, I'll leave that to you,' Maxine said, 'though I rather think he's already paid a high enough price for the fiasco. Speaking of that, did you take care of his bill at the clinic?'

'Yes, I did,' Stilman said hastily, glad to have something positive to report. 'I told them to put it on your account.'

'Good.' Maxine nodded. 'Incompetent or not, we have to take care of our own. In the meantime . . .' She let her gaze wander out into the casino. 'Let's move on to the other reason we're here . . . why I chose this place for our meeting. I want to get a look at the cocktail waitress who was so effective at dealing with your man.'

'With your *handpicked* man,' Laverna added pointedly.

Stilman ignored her.

'What does she look like?' he said, sweeping the casino with his own eyes. 'Do we have a description?'

'She shouldn't be too hard to spot,' Laverna said. 'She's supposed to be the smallest person on the staff. Guess she makes up for it by having such fast reflexes.'

112

'Look, Ice,' Stilman began, but Maxine cut him short with a gesture.

'I'm afraid we're going to have to postpone our search,' she said, staring at something out in the casino. 'I'm afraid we have a bigger problem to deal with.'

'What is it, Maxie?' Laverna said, craning her neck to see.

'The oriental gentleman at the *pai-gow* table,' Maxine clarified, not shifting her gaze.

Stilman frowned. 'Which one?'

Pai-gow was a form of poker utilizing dominos and dice which originated in Old Earth Japan. While nearly every casino offered it in some form or other, most gamblers descended from Western cultures still found the play too intricate for comfort, so the tables were invariably filled by those who were raised gambling on the game.

'The one on the far end . . . in the white shirt.'

Stilman followed her eyes. 'So?'

'Look at his arms,' Maxine instructed.

The man's shirt was of very fine cotton, and his arms were clearly visible, though it took a moment to realize that it was his arms one was seeing. Adorning the arms, from shoulder to wrist were colorful swirls of tattoos, so vivid that, to a casual glance, they almost seemed to be a paisley pattern on an undergarment.

Maxine knew that the significance of the decorations was not lost on her companions as they both reacted, Laverna with a low whistle and Stilman with a narrowing of the eyes.

'I think I'd like to speak with that gentleman,' she said. 'Could you invite him to join us, Mr. Stilman?'

'What . . . now? Here?'

'Yes, now. But not here,' Maxine said with a tight little smile. 'We've taken a suite of rooms here at the Fat Chance. It's occurred to me that I should be a bit more closely involved in monitoring this project.'

'Please . . . have a seat,' Maxine said to the slender, youthful Oriental as Stilman ushered him into the suite. 'So nice of you to accept my invitation.'

The man's face was impassive, but there was anger in his voice and movements.

'I wasn't aware I had a choice,' he said, sinking into the offered chair.

Maxine raised her eyebrows in mock surprise.

'Mr. Stilman,' she said, 'didn't you make it clear that I was extending an *invitation* to our guest?'

'I asked him nice,' the big man growled. 'I didn't lay a hand on him.'

'Well, no matter,' Maxine said. 'As long as you're here. We were just admiring the tattoos on your arms.'

The man glanced down quickly as if to assure himself that the decorations were still in place.

'I see,' he said.

'They're very beautiful.' Maxine smiled. 'Might I ask the circumstances under which you got them?'

The Oriental rose abruptly to his feet.

'They are a personal matter,' he hissed. 'Not to be discussed with strangers.'

'*Sit down, sir!*'

Maxine's voice cracked like a whip, and the man responded to the authority in her tone by quickly resuming his seat.

'Let's cut the crap, shall we?' Maxine purred, leaning forward to cradle her chin in one hand. 'Unless I'm mistaken, those tattoos mark you as a member of the Yakusa . . . sometimes crudely referred to as the Japanese Mafia. If that is correct, I would be most curious as to what you're doing on Lorelei and why you haven't been to pay your respects.'

For a moment, the man's eyes widened with surprise, then they narrowed warily.

'Forgive me,' he said with careful formality. 'But these are things one does not speak of with strangers.'

'I'm sorry,' Maxine said with a smile. 'You don't seem to know who I am. I had assumed Mr. Stilman had informed you before you arrived. Allow me to introduce myself. I'm Maxine Pruet, though you may have heard me referred to simply as "Max".'

The man stared at her for a moment, then seemed to remember himself and sprang to his feet.

'I didn't know. My superior did indeed instruct me to convey his compliments,' he intoned with a stiff bow from the waist. 'Forgive me, but I only received my orders recently, and they were very brief and sketchy. I thought . . . that is, I wasn't told . . .'

' – that I was a woman?' Maxine smiled. 'I'm not surprised, really. Your organization is even more rooted in old chauvinisms than my own. It stands to reason that if my name came up in conversation, my gender would be tactfully omitted.'

She returned his bow with a slow nod of her head. 'And who might you be?'

'I . . . my name with our organization is Jonesy.'

'Jonesy?' Laverna blurted in surprise from her place in the corner.

The man glanced at her and gave a brief, rueful smile.

'I travel extensively for our organization,' he explained, 'and it was thought that the name "Jonesy" would be easier for outsiders to pronounce and remember than the one which was more ethnically correct.'

'An interesting theory,' Maxine observed. 'It does, however, bring us back to my original question. What brings you to Lorelei, Mr. Jonesy? Business or pleasure?'

'Please, just "Jonesy," ' the man corrected gently. 'A little of both, actually. I was originally here for a vacation, but, as I mentioned, I recently received a call from my superior instructing me to investigate certain business opportunities for our organization.'

'And just what might those business opportunities be?' Maxie pressed. 'I don't mean to pry, Mr . . . Jonesy, but I would like some reassurance that they aren't in conflict with our own interests.'

'I . . . ' Jonesy glanced at Stilman, who was standing between him and the door. 'I was instructed to investigate the possibility of our organization acquiring full or partial ownership of this casino hotel.'

His words hung in the air like a death sentence.

'I don't understand,' Maxine said carefully. 'There has always been a sort of gentleman's agreement between our organizations regarding territory. Why are you attempting to move into an area which has always been acknowledged as mine?'

'My superior told me to specifically assure you that we are not moving against *you*,' the man explained hastily. 'We will continue to respect your current holdings, and we will not compete with you for *this* property.'

'Then what . . .'

'Please, allow me to explain,' Jonesy said, holding up a hand. 'We are, of course, expecting you to attempt to gain control of this casino as you have the others on Lorelei. There has, however, been media coverage of a new security force hired to protect this facility. My superiors are impressed with the reputation of this force and the individual who leads it, and are unsure if your organization is capable of opposing it. I have simply been instructed to observe your efforts. It you are unsuccessful in adding the Fat Chance to your holdings, then my superiors feel they will be free to make an attempt of their own. In such a case, they feel they would not be opposing you in any way, but simply moving on an unclaimed opportunity. I hasten to repeat, however, that this will only be done if, and only if, your own efforts prove fruitless.'

'I didn't know vultures were Japanese,' Laverna observed dryly.

'That will do, Laverna,' Maxine said primly. 'If you would, Jonesy, the next time you speak with your superior, please convey to him my appreciation for his concern *and* his alertness in spotting an apparent business opportunity, but assure him that I have every confidence in our ability to maintain our unblemished record in this area, Space Legion or no.'

'I will be pleased to do that,' the man said with a shrug, 'but words of confidence lose their strength in the face of actual performance.'

'And what's *that* supposed to mean?' Maxine said. 'Please, Jonesy. If you have something to say, just say it plainly.

116

We're trying to have a meeting here, not write fortune cookies.'

'I believe there was an incident in the bar involving one of your men,' Jonesy said calmly. 'At least, we assume he was one of your men, since his medical expenses are being charged to your account. If that is true, then the results of that encounter do little toward justifying the confidence you have in your plan.'

Maxine gave a short bark of laughter.

'Is that what this is all about?' she said, then leaned forward, showing all her teeth. 'That was, at best, a diversion, Jonesy. A little something to show young Mr. Rafael that the force he has hired is more than adequate for handling any trouble that might arise. The truth is, we *instructed* our man to lose – to build the guards' confidence while providing us with information on their operating methods.'

The man frowned. 'I see.'

'Perhaps if I outlined for you what our *real* plan is, you'd be better able to convince your superiors that their interest is not only premature, it's pointless.'

Jonesy was humming to himself when he finally returned to his own room, though the tune was none other than the catchy advertising ditty from the Lorelei beacon.

Unlocking the door, he was just reaching for the light switch when a voice greeted him from the darkness.

'What the hell do you think you're doing, Sushi?'

Startled, Sushi managed to click on the lights, and discovered his company commander sprawled in one of the room's chairs, squinting against the sudden brightness.

'Good evening, Captain. You gave me a bit of a turn just now. I didn't expect to see you.'

'*I* gave *you* a bit of a turn?' Phule snarled. 'You've had the whole force in an uproar since you showed up with those tattoos. I had to move fast to keep them from charging to the rescue when that goon picked you up.'

'Really?' Sushi said, raising his eyebrows. 'I'll have to apologize. I didn't mean to panic everyone.'

'Well, you panicked *me!*' the commander snapped. 'Now, what's with the tattoos? Why are you posing as a member of the Japanese Mafia?'

'What makes you think it's a pose, Captain?' the Legionnaire countered blandly. 'Our regular uniforms are long-sleeved. Have you ever seen my arms before?'

Phule gaped at him.

'Relax, Willard.' Sushi laughed, resorting to Phule's civilian name. 'You were right the first time. It's a disguise. I just wanted to pull your leg a little to try to get you to loosen up. You seem awfully tense.'

'Do you blame me?' the commander said, settling back in his chair with a glower. 'All right, I'll bite. Where did you get the tattoos?'

'As a matter of fact, Lieutenant Rembrandt put them on for me,' Sushi said, holding up his arms to display the decorations. 'Aren't they great? I told her what I wanted in general, but the actual design is hers.'

'Are you saying you cleared this masquerade with Rembrandt?' Phule said, ignoring the display.

'To be honest with you, Captain, I don't think she realized the significance of what I was asking.' Sushi smiled. 'I'll admit, I wanted it to be a surprise.'

'Oh, it was a surprise, all right,' the commander snorted. 'But I'm still waiting for you to tell me why you're doing this.'

'Isn't it obvious? You said you wanted to know what was going on here, didn't you? I simply figured that the best way to get reliable information was to go to the source – to try to infiltrate the opposition. Once I settled on that objective, it became clear to me that the best way to achieve it was to pose as a visiting dignitary from another criminal faction, of which the Yakusa was a natural choice.'

'Did it occur to you that it might be dangerous?' Phule said, his original anger giving way to the concern that spawned it.

'Of course.' Sushi smiled. 'Remember what I said when you asked me to go under cover? About being addicted to high-risk games and not being sure I could control myself at the tables? Well, I've found the answer. The tables are pretty tame compared to the game I'm playing now. To be honest with you, I'm having more fun than I've had in years.'

'Games? Fun?' the commander said, his temper starting to rise again. 'Aside from the danger of the locals figuring out your charade, what are you going to do if you run into a member of the *real* Yakusa? I don't think they'd take kindly to your trying to pass yourself off as one of their representatives.'

'I think you're underestimating me, Captain,' the Legionnaire said. 'I may refer to it as a game, but as a habitual gambler, I've studied the odds very carefully. It's doubtful it will ever occur to the locals that I might be an imposter for the very reason you've just mentioned: Who would ever think of posing as a member of the Yakusa? What's more, it's extremely doubtful that I'll run into anyone from that organization, since they've been carefully staying away from Lorelei for years.'

'How do you know that?'

'I made a few calls,' Sushi said with a smile. 'While my family is quite scrupulous about avoiding criminal enterprise, myself being a notable exception, it nonetheless is aware of the underworld network and maintains several contacts for the sole purpose of information and communication. That raises another point, Captain.'

The Legionnaire dropped his smile.

'I'm not sure how familiar you are with the Yakusa, but it's not really a single organization. Like its Western counterparts, it's actually made up of several families who operate under a mutual truce. If I *did* run into a member, I'd simply claim to be from another family. I'm familiar with the general recognition codes.'

Sushi's smile started to grow again.

'The interesting thing that occurred to me as I was planning this, Captain, is that it's almost legitimate. What you're doing with the company is not that dissimilar from the forming of a Yakusa clan, and on this assignment I *am* your representative. In fact, if you'll look closely at my tattoos,

119

you'll see that Rembrandt has worked our unit's logo into the pattern several times.'

'Speaking of your tattoos,' Phule said, barely sparing them a glance, 'am I correct in assuming that they aren't permanent? What happens if they start to come off at the wrong time?'

'No chance of that happening.' Sushi grinned. 'They don't come off with water, just alcohol, and Rembrandt says they should last for months. She even gave me a touch-up kit to use just in case.'

'And if someone spills a drink on your arm?' the commander pressed.

The Legionnaire looked startled.

'I . . . I hadn't thought of that, Captain. Thanks for the warning. I'll be extra careful in the future – or maybe just wear regular long-sleeved shirts so they won't show at all.'

Phule shook his head with a sigh.

'It sounds like you're set on this plan,' he said. 'In any case, it's too late now for me to try to talk you out of it.'

'Don't worry, Captain. It's working like a charm. In fact, I've already gotten quite a bit of information for you, like an outline of the opposition's whole game plan.'

'Really?' Phule was suddenly interested. 'Then there *is* an attempt to take over the casino?'

'There certainly is,' Sushi confirmed. 'And the mastermind is a woman named Maxine Pruet.'

If the Legionnaire was hoping for a reaction of surprise, he was to be disappointed.

'. . . who runs most of the crime here on Lorelei,' the commander said, finishing for him. 'Yes, we already know the name. We just weren't sure she was actually trying to move on us. So she's the moving force behind Huey Martin, eh? That's good to know. We weren't sure if he was part of a whole or just operating independently.'

'You already know about the casino manager?' Sushi said, a trifle crestfallen.

'The man's crooked as a snake, and so are the dealers he's hired,' Phule said easily. 'We spotted that they were grifting early on, and have just been waiting for the right

120

time to lower the boom. If that's their big plan, we've got it covered.'

'Oh, there's a lot more to it than that, Captain,' Sushi informed him. 'For openers, Max says they've gotten into the casino's computer.'

'*What?*'

Phule was suddenly bolt upright in his chair.

'And that's not the worst of it,' the Legionnaire continued. 'You know how you were saying that we're supposed to be keeping organized crime from getting a toehold in the casino ownership? Well, it's too late. They've already got it.'

Chapter Nine

Journal #215

In earlier entries, I have made passing reference to my employer's temper. While he is as prone as the next person to occasional flares of irritation or annoyance, these pale to insignificance when compared to his real anger.

Anyone who has been the focus of his attention when he is in such a mood usually goes to great lengths to avoid repeating the experience in the future, myself included. Fortunately he is not normally quick to anger, and peaceful coexistence is not only possible but probable as long as certain topics and situations are avoided.

One situation which is guaranteed to trigger an explosion, however, is if you'll pardon the pun, when he feels he's been made to play the fool.

Gunther Rafael looked up from his work as the door to his office slammed with sufficient force to blow papers off his desk. It didn't take a genius to tell that the black-clad figure that had just entered was upset.

'Is something wrong, Mr. Phule?'

'Why didn't you tell me Maxine Pruet was part owner of the Fat Chance?' the Legion commander demanded without preamble, storm clouds billowing on his face.

The youth blinked. 'I . . . I didn't think it was important. Is it?'

'Not *important?*' Phule raged. 'For God's sake, *she's* the head of the gang that's trying to take over your operation! The organized crime we're *supposed* to be *saving* you from!'

'She can't be,' Rafael said, frowning. 'She's one of the most respected business people on Lorelei. In fact, I think she owns some of the casinos here.'

'She has controlling interest in *all* of them except yours, and she's working on that right now!'

'But she was the one who – oh my God!'

The stricken look on the youth's face as full realization dawned on him was sufficient to cool Phule's anger somewhat.

'Look, Gunther,' he said levelly, 'why don't you tell me exactly what happened?'

'There's not much to tell,' Rafael stammered, still shaken. 'She gave me a loan for my remodelling – even suggested it, in fact. She paid me a social call to welcome me as the new owner and seemed quite open in her admiration of the facility, though she did suggest it could use some renovation.'

'And when you said you didn't think you could afford it, she offered to lend you the money,' the Legionnaire supplied.

'That's right,' Rafael said. 'She said she was looking for a short-term investment to hide some money from the tax men. It seemed like a good deal at the time. She even offered an interest rate below what the bank would charge me.'

'She did, did she?' Phule scowled. 'What were the other terms of the loan? *All* the terms?'

'Well, I can't remember them all, but I have my copy of the contract right here,' the youth said, quickly rummaging through one of the desk's file drawers. 'Basically she gave me the money against twenty-five percent of the Fat Chance. When I pay it off, her share drops to five percent, as a permanent interest.'

'Twenty-five percent?' Phule echoed. 'That doesn't sound right. From what I hear she usually goes for controlling interest. Let me see that contract.'

'I still don't see how it can . . .' Rafael began, but Phule cut him short.

'Here it is!' he declared, pointing to a spot in the document's depths. 'The "Late Payment" section. According to this, if you fail to pay the loan off on time, you not only forfeit the right to buy back her shares, but she gets additional points of the enterprise up to –'

'Forty-nine percent,' the youth supplied. 'I know. But even then it's not controlling interest. I don't know what you're worried about, though. The loan isn't due until a week after our grand opening, and that alone should generate enough money to pay her off.'

'Assuming there are no problems with the opening,' Phule growled, continuing to scan the document. 'The trouble there is your casino manager's on Maxine's payroll, and he's been staffing your tables with crooked dealers. I'm willing to bet that when you open your doors, they won't be working to rake money in for the house – they'll be passing it out!'

Gunther blinked. 'Huey's part of this?'

'That's right. Where did you find him, anyway?'

'Well, Maxine recommended . . . Oh!'

'I see,' the Legionnaire said, shaking his head. 'It all starts to fit together. And what kind of a deal do you have with *him*?'

'He actually is working fairly cheap,' the youth protested. 'Barely minimum wage and – oh my God!'

'Don't tell me, let me guess.' Phule sighed. 'A salary *and* two percent of the Fat Chance. Right?'

Gunther nodded dumbly. 'Maxine negotiated the deal for me.'

'I figured as much,' the commander said, tossing the contract back onto Rafael's desk. '*That's* where she'll get the missing two percent to give her controlling interest. Huey will side with her on every vote . . . if she hasn't had him sign it over completely.'

The youth leaned back in his chair, shaking his head.

'I still can't believe it,' he said. 'Maxine. She's been like a mother to me.'

'Believe it,' Phule said grimly. 'Your "mother" has tied an anchor around your neck and is about to push you off the end of the pier. I suggest you start learning how to swim.'

'But how?' Gunther said, almost as a plea. 'If you're right, and she's sabotaged the tables, there's no way I can make enough to pay off the loan.'

'Don't worry about the tables,' the commander said. 'We happen to have an honest set of dealers standing by ... *and* a new casino manager. It'll cost, but we can probably clean house in time to save the casino. I think you'll agree that the time to strike is just *before* your grand opening. That way, we minimize the chance of Maxine switching to an alternate plan.'

'You mean we can beat her? You've solved the problem?'

'Not so fast,' Phule said, holding up a hand. 'We have other worries besides the tables. When was the last time you had your computer programs checked and audited?'

'The computer?' Rafael frowned. 'It was checked just before you arrived. Why?'

'We've gotten word that part of Maxine's plan is to fiddle with your computer,' the Legionnaire said. 'Who cleared the computer?'

'There's an outfit here on Lorelei that specifically checks the casino computers,' Gunther said. 'They're completely reliable and bonded. In fact, Huey said – '

'Huey?' Phule interrupted.

'That's right!' the youth gasped. 'Huey was the one who recommended them. If he's working against us ...'

'Then odds are your computer is now a time bomb,' the commander finished grimly. 'All right, let's take it from there. What else does your computer control?'

'The whole complex is hooked into it. The hotel ... even the theater's lights for our entertainment specials.'

'Does the casino hook into it for anything?'

'No, I don't – *yes!* The computer controls the video slot machines!'

'All of them?' Phule scowled. 'Including the ones with the progressive multimillion jackpots?'

The casino owner could only nod.

'That could be disastrous,' the Legionnaire said. 'What

happens if we pull the plug on them? Just shut down the slots until this whole thing is over?'

Gunther shook his head. 'We can't do that. The slots are one of the biggest draws we have – any casino has – not to mention the most profitable. If we shut off the slots, we can kiss the whole opening goodbye.'

Phule sighed. 'Then we'll just have to get the programs fixed. And that means . . . Damn, I hate to do that!'

'Do what?' the casino owner said.

'What? Oh . . . sorry. It means doing something I *really* don't like to do: ask a favor of my father!'

One of the Old Earth authors, Hemingway, I believe, is attributed with the observation 'Rich people are just like anyone else . . . only richer.'

During my association with my employer, I have grown to appreciate the truth of these words more and more. The truly rich are different, in that in times of crisis, they reflexively use money and power on a scale so alien to the average person that they almost seem to be of another species. (It should be noted here that I still consider myself to be an "average person." Though it has been mentioned that I'm comfortably well off financially, that condition is relatively recent, and I therefore lack the abovementioned reflexes of the truly rich. That mental state requires a lifetime, if not generations, of conditioning.)

Where they are like everyone else is in the problems they encounter . . . for example, in dealing with their parents . . .

'Hello . . . Dad? It's me. Willard . . . your son.'

The Legionnaire commander had retreated to the relative privacy of his own room for this call, choosing not to communicate with his father from Gunther's office. This, in itself, was an indication of his uncertainty of how the conversation would go.

'I know,' the holo projection in the room said gruffly. 'Nobody else has the clout to pull me out of a negotiation meeting.'

Seated in a corner, safely out of the camera's view, Beeker

took advantage of the rare chance to compare the two men side by side.

If anything, Paul Phule looked more like a military commander than his son did – or the majority of active military officers, for that matter. His manner and bearing displayed what his heir potential might achieve in maturity. Where his son was slender, the elder Phule had the lean, fit look of a timber wolf. His features had the sharp, angular planes of a granite cliff, whereas his son's face still showed the softness of youth. In fact, the only visible clue to his age was the white hair at his temples, but even that seemed a testimony of his strength rather than a hint of senility. All in all, anyone seeing Paul Phule would arrive at the conclusion, not incorrectly, that this was not a man to be trifled with, particularly if he was annoyed, as he seemed to be now.

'Well, you've got me,' the image growled. 'What's the problem *this* time?'

'Problem?' the commander said. 'What makes you think there's a problem, sir?'

'Maybe because the only time you call me is when you're in some kind of a scrape,' his father pointed out. 'It wouldn't kill you to write once in a while, you know.'

'As I recall,' the commander said testily, 'the last time I called you was on that weapons deal with the Zenobians. That didn't turn out too bad for you, did it? An exclusive on a new weapons design in exchange for some worthless swampland?'

'A deal you closed *before* you had the swampland under contract, as I recall,' the elder Phule defended. 'I'll concede the point, though. Sorry if I'm a bit touchy. This meeting is a lot rougher than I thought it would be, and it's getting under my skin. The irritating part is that what I'm offering is better than what they're asking for, but they won't budge. It's tempting to just let them have their way, but you know what will happen down the road if I do.'

'They'll claim you set them up,' the younger Phule supplied. 'Gee, that's tough, Dad.'

'Whatever,' Paul Phule said. 'That's my problem, and I shouldn't let it interfere with us. So why *did* you call?'

From Beeker's vantage point, he could see his employer wince just a bit before answering as he realized he had inadvertently painted himself into a corner.

'I'll keep this short, realizing you're in the middle of a meeting,' the commander said. 'Basically, Dad, I need to borrow your Bug Squad. Rent them, actually.'

It is to the elder Phule's credit that he did not indulge in any 'I told you so's at his son's expense, but instead simply addressed the problem at hand.

'My what?' he said, scowling.

'The Bug Squad,' the Legionnaire persisted. 'At least, that's what you used to call them. You know, Albert's crew – the computer auditors.'

'Oh. Them.' Paul Phule nodded. 'Sorry, son. I can't help you there.'

'Come on, Dad,' the commander said. 'You know I wouldn't ask if I didn't *really* need them. Neither of us has time to play games on the price. I'll go two points on our next deal, but beyond that . . .'

'Whoa! Hold it, Willie,' the elder Phule said, holding up a restraining hand. 'I didn't say I *wouldn't* help you. I said I *couldn't*! Albert and his team don't work for me anymore. They split off and formed their own company. Now I have to contract them myself for any work I need.'

'I see,' the Legionnaire said thoughtfully. 'Tell me, was the parting amicable?'

'What do you mean?'

'Are you and Albert still on good terms, or is he going to dig in his heels if anyone mentions the name Phule to him?' the commander clarified. 'It sounds like I'm going to have to approach him on my own, and I'm trying to figure out if I'll have to go through an intermediary or not.'

'Oh, there were no hard feelings involved – at least, not from his side,' Paul Phule said. 'He's not an easy man to deal with, though. He doesn't even give *me* a discount for his services, even after I footed the bill while he recruited and trained the team he's running.'

'Well, you didn't hire him for his personality,' the Legionnaire responded with a chuckle. 'And weren't you the one who always told me that loyalty had to be earned, not hired?'

'Don't start using quotes on me unless you want to soak up a few in return,' the elder Phule warned darkly. 'Now, are there any other *nonproblems* I can help you with? Like I said, I'm in the middle of a meeting.'

'No, that covers it. If you can just tell me how to get through to Albert, and I'll get out of your hair.'

'Stay on the line and my secretary will give you that info,' the elder Phule instructed. 'I've got to run, myself. You know how your grandmother is if you keep her waiting too long.'

'Grams?' The Legionnaire blinked. 'Is that who you're meeting with?'

Paul Phule grimaced. 'That's right. And she's in one of her "holy crusade" moods, and you know what that means.'

The commander gave an exaggerated shudder in response.

'Well, good luck, Dad,' he said. 'No offense, but it sounds like you're going to need it. Say hello for me, if you think it will help.'

'And listen to her run on about you and your Boy Scout troop again?' the elder Phule said. 'Thanks, but no thanks. Got to go now . . . My best to Beeker.'

'So that's it in a nutshell, Albert,' Phule concluded. 'Can you help me?'

The holo-image of the computer specialist nodded slowly. It had the pale, unripened complexion of someone who habitually uses a cathode-ray tube for a sunlamp.

'I'll have to pull a couple people off other things, but yes, I think we can handle it.'

'Good,' the commander said. 'How soon can we look for you?'

'I'll have to check the flight schedules, but I imagine we can be there in a couple weeks. It's not that far from where we are now.'

'Not fast enough,' Phule said, shaking his head. 'We've

got to have things fixed before the grand opening, and that's in a week. Charter a ship if you have to, but – '

'Impossible,' Albert interrupted, shaking his head. 'We might be able to *get* there in a week, but to diagnose any program problems, much less fix them, simply can't be done in that time frame.'

'Double your fee,' the commander said flatly.

'But then again,' the analyst said, without blinking an eye, 'if you can download the programs to us so we can be going over them in flight, all we'll have to do on-site is load the revisions. It'll be tight, but I guess we can manage.'

'Right.' Phule nodded. 'A pleasure doing business with you, Albert.'

He broke the connection with a sigh.

'Well, at least *that's* taken care of.'

'If you say so, sir.'

The commander cocked an eyebrow at his butler.

'I know that tone of voice, Beek,' he said. 'What's the problem?'

'If I might ask a question, sir?'

'You mean why don't I just loan Rafael the money to pay off Maxine?' The commander shook his head. 'Aside from the ethical question involved with buying our way out of a problem this big, there's the matter of sheer logistics. The kind of money we'd need I don't have handy in ready cash. It would mean having to liquidate some of my long-term assets, which I don't want to do, and even if I did, it would take more time than we have. Max wants the casino, and she's not about to let Rafael off the hook for anything less than cash on the barrelhead.'

'I understand, sir,' Beeker said. 'However, if I may, that wasn't my question.'

'Oh?'

'If I heard correctly, you were instructing Albert and his ... Bug Squad ... to focus their attention primarily on detecting and correcting any computer programming inconsistencies applying to the video slots in the casino. Is that correct?'

'That's our biggest vulnerability. Yes.'

'Well, I can't help but wonder, sir, if it's wise to completely ignore the other areas which might be affected by
computer tampering. It's been my experience that the
people who program computers are very much like the
machines themselves when it comes to dealing with users.
They do specifically what they're instructed to – usually –
but seldom anything else. That is, I doubt they will address
any of the other problem areas under their current instructions.'

'C'mon, Beek,' Phule protested. 'You heard him. They're
going to be hard-pressed to fix the slots in the time frame
we've got. Any other assignments will only slow things up.'

'Then you may have to consider alternative solutions to
the other problem areas . . . sir,' the butler said blandly.

'But they're only . . .' The commander caught himself
and stopped, rubbing one hand across his eyes. 'Okay,
Beeker. Out with it. Which areas other than the slots are
you worried about?'

'Well, sir, if I understand the situation, the computer also
controls the lights and sound system for the showroom
stage.'

'That's right. So?'

'I believe, sir, that the showroom and its featured entertainers are one of the primary draws the casino uses to
attract its clientele. In short, if there's no show, there may
not be many people attending the opening to play the slots,
making the question of the slots program relatively irrel-
evant.'

'I see,' Phule said. 'Then we – '

'What's more,' the butler said as if he hadn't been interrupted, 'I believe that Mr. Gunther has booked Dee Dee
Watkins for the opening, and – '

'Who?'

Beeker rolled his eyes in not so mock exasperation.

'Really, sir,' he said. 'You really *should* read more than
the financial pages once in a while. Dee Dee Watkins has
been a rising holo star for several years now, and she's just
put together a nightclub act to tour, which is supposed to
premiere at the grand opening.'

131

'Oh.'

'Not quite yet, sir,' the butler corrected. 'You see, while I have not had the privilege of reviewing Ms. Watkins's contract personally, my recent experience with Lieutenant Rembrandt while hiring our own actors leads me to believe that a performer of her standing will have a clause in her bookings requiring that she be paid in full even if she does not perform, providing the reason for her performance is a failure on the part of the booking party to supply stage equipment of at least minimal professional standards – which I would assume includes lights and a *functioning* sound system. I would further assume that her fees for performing, while, perhaps, not of the same magnitude as the potential losses from multiple jackpots at the video slots, are, nonetheless, substantial – and I *know* how you dislike paying people *not* to perform their contracted services.'

He paused, then nodded at his employer.

'*Now*, sir.'

'Oh,' Phule responded dutifully.

Silence hung in the air as Beeker waited respectfully for his employer to digest this information.

'Okay,' he said. 'I can see where that will have to be addressed. Any other jewels of insight?'

The question was meant facetiously, but that was always a danger in the company Phule kept.

'As a matter of fact, sir,' Beeker said, 'it occurs to me that you might also want to arrange for some sort of audit or backup system for the front desk of the hotel.'

'The front desk?'

'I believe the computer is utilized rather heavily for both the reservations and the billings for the hotel, and aside from the annoyance of double bookings, there is a long-standing law that in such an event, the hotel is responsible for finding the extra guests equivalent lodging *and* absorbing the cost.'

'And there are a lot of tour groups who are supposed to have reservations for the opening,' Phule finished grimly.

The commander produced his Port-A-Brain minicomputer from his pocket and pulled up a chair next to the room's holophone.

'Get on the horn and order us some coffee,' he said. 'We've got a lot of work to do. And Beek?'

'Yes, sir?'

'I don't want to hear any grumbling about my not getting enough sleep. Not for a while, at least.'

That Lawrence Bombest was surprised to receive a holocall from Willard Phule was an understatement. While he had formed a grudging respect for the job Phule had done upgrading the attitudes of his down-at-the-heels Space Legion company while they were temporarily housed at the Plaza, Bombest would not in his wildest dreams fantasize that the two of them were at all close.

In his position of manager at the Plaza Hotel, one of the oldest, most respected hotels on Haskin's Planet, it had been his duty to act as guardian of those stately facilities, and while the Legionnaires had turned out to be much better behaved than he had originally feared, more often than not it had placed himself and their commander in adversarial roles. As surprised as he was at the mere existence of the call, however, he was dumbfounded at its content.

'I know we're both busy, Bombest,' the ghostly holo-image said, 'so I'll cut right to the chase. Would you be willing to take a brief sabbatical from the Plaza to manage a hotel here on Lorelei? Say, for about a month?'

'I . . . I'd have to think about it, Mr. Phule,' the manager stammered, caught totally unprepared by the question.

'Unfortunately we don't have a lot of time,' the image said, shaking its head. 'Yes or no?'

'In that case, I'm afraid the answer would have to be no,' Bombest said. 'If nothing else, my commitment here would forbid it. I'd have to apply for the necessary leave time, and arrange for a replacement . . .'

'I'm afraid you're underestimating me again, Bombest,' Phule broke in. 'That's already been handled. I cleared it with Reggie Page . . . you remember the name? The CEO of the Webber Combine that owns the chain? Anyway, I've explained the situation to him, and he's agreed to give you the time off, with pay, of course, and to arrange for a replacement until you return. By the way, I hope it goes without saying that you'll be generously compensated for your work here, as well as having an expense account, so that your combined income for the period will be substantial.'

'So this was all done in advance?' Bombest said.

'There was no point in asking you if you weren't going to be available,' the image said, 'and, no offense, Bombest, I figured I had a better chance of getting through to Reggie *and* getting a timely answer than you did. Anyway, the question isn't whether or not you *can* do it, it's whether you *will* do it. You're the only one who can answer that.'

'I see. If you don't mind my asking, Mr. Phule, why me? Forgive me, but I was under the impression that we didn't particularly get along while you were staying here.'

'Oh, I don't pretend that I *like* you, Bombest,' Phule said with a tight smile, 'and I don't expect that you particularly care for me as a person. Our styles are far too different for us to ever be "good buddies." You are, however, the best I've seen at what you do, which is handling problems at a hotel, and I happen to be in a jam right now where I need that talent. The question isn't if we are or will be friends, but if you're willing to work with me.'

Bombest pursed his lips. 'I don't suppose you've checked the availability of flights from Haskin's to Lorelei, along with your other inquiries?'

'Actually I've gone a bit further than that,' the image responded. 'When – excuse me, *if* – you're ready to go, you'll find the governor's military ship standing by at the spaceport to bring you directly here. As I said, we're on a tight timetable.'

This bit of information spoke volumes to Bombest. While there had been no love lost between himself and Phule, their relationship was positively rosy if compared to the Legionnaire commander's interaction with the military governor of the planet. While details of those encounters were never made public, it was no secret that they fought like cats and dogs whenever their paths crossed. The fact that Phule would approach the governor for the use of the official space launch, not to mention what he must have had to commit to obtain it, was a tribute to how badly the commander wanted Bombest's services. Much more so than a casual call to Reggie Page.

'Very well, Mr. Phule,' the manager said, making up his mind. 'I'll do it. There are a few matters I have to clear up before I go, but they shouldn't take more than an hour or two. Then I'll be on my way.'

The image smiled. 'Excellent. Welcome aboard, Bombest. I'll be looking forward to seeing you.'

After the connection was broken, Bombest had a few moments to reflect on the call which had just turned his immediate future topsy-turvy.

To his surprise, he realized that the money being offered had not been the major factor in his decision, though it had paved the way. The *real* deciding point was that he had been flattered at the lengths to which the Legionnaire commander had gone to obtain his services. For someone of Willard Phule's stature and experience to say you were the best he knew at what you did *and* that he needed you was enough to make you move heaven and earth to prove his opinion of you justified.

For the first time, Bombest began to understand exactly how it was that Phule was able to get zealous loyalty where others were hard-pressed to get obedience.

Chapter Ten

Journal #227

To say the final days before the casino's grand opening were a study in freneticism would be like saying Genghis Khan dabbled in real estate.

There were a myriad details to be handled, and my employer, with his customary tendency to position himself in the heart of things, managed to involve himself with most of them.

Of course, they all had to be dealt with immediately.

'I was told I could find Captain Jester here?'

'He here . . . but in meeting. Not to be disturbed.'

'We'll see about that!'

The verbal exchange was conducted at sufficient volume that it penetrated the room's door, and the Legionnaires assembled had ample forewarning of the interruption even before the door opened.

Tusk-anini had specifically been chosen to stand guard on the meeting, as his sheer presence was enough to intimidate most would-be intruders. Unfortunately intimidation alone was not enough to deter the petite bundle of energy which now burst through the door. Though dressed casually in jeans and a sweater, she carried herself as regally as a queen – or, to be more accurate, a spoiled princess throwing a snit fit. The sight of a dozen black-clad Legionnaires sprawled about the room, staring at her like a pack of panthers, was, however, sufficiently unnerving to at least bring the young lady to a halt.

'Captain Jester?' she said hesitantly.

'Yes?'

The commander rose lazily to his feet from his seat on the sofa.

'I need to talk to you right now. I was told – '

'Excuse me,' Phule said, holding up a restraining hand with a smile. 'Now that you know who I am, may I ask who *you* are?'

Though they eventually grow to dislike the intrusions on their privacy by droves of nameless admirers, big-name entertainers nonetheless depend on public recognition for their livelihood. It is therefore more than a little jarring to them to be confronted by someone who is not only unimpressed by but unaware of their identity.

'Tough house,' the intruder muttered, almost to herself. 'All right, Captain. We'll play it your way. I'm Dee Dee Watkins, the featured attraction for the casino's grand-opening show.'

'Got it,' Phule said with a curt nod. 'Forgive me for not recognizing you Ms. Watkins. Though I'm familiar with the name, I rarely have time to watch the holos, and am woefully ignorant when it comes to the various entertainers, much less their current positions in the pecking order. Now then, what can I do to help you?'

'I was just checking on the showroom's availability for rehearsals and was told that I was going to be working with a live stage crew instead of a computerized setup – by *your* orders.'

'That's correct,' the commander said. 'Is there a problem with that?'

'Aside from the fact that a live crew never handles their cues the same way twice, not at all,' the singer said sarcastically. 'Look, Captain, it's been a long time since I worked in front of an audience. I'm going to have my hands full remembering my *own* cues without wondering whether or not the follow spot is going to be on me or on the piano when it comes up.'

'I guess my information was incorrect,' Phule said. 'I was told that you would *prefer* to work with a live crew, provided they were competent, of course.'

'Oh?' Dee Dee frowned. 'Who told you that?'

'I'm afraid I did, love.'

She turned toward the speaker, then did a visible double take.

'Lex? My God, is that you? I didn't recognize you in that getup. Did you enlist or something?'

The actor shot a quick glance at Phule before answering.

'Just a temporary arrangement, I assure you,' he said with a smile too easy to be genuine. 'As far as the stage crew goes, would it help at all if I gave you my *personal* reassurance that things will be handled properly?'

'*You're* working crew?' Dee Dee said incredulously.

Lex's smile tightened slightly.

'I'm *managing* the crew,' he corrected, 'but I've worked with them long enough that I feel confident they can handle it.'

'I didn't know you knew anything about the techie side of theater.'

'I've worked a few summer-stock tours,' the actor said with a shrug. 'In that situation, you do a bit of everything. One week you're playing the lead, the next week you're working lights – '

'Sorry to interrupt this reunion,' the commander broke in, 'but there are still a lot of things we have to cover in our meeting. If there are no further questions, Ms. Watkins?'

'Can I be excused from the rest of the meeting, Captain?' Lex said. 'We've already covered the stuff that concerns me, and there are a few things I'd like to go over with Dee Dee while she's free . . .'

'Go on ahead,' Phule said, sinking onto the sofa once more. 'But report back to me when you're finished. I want to be sure to be kept apprised of any modifications in your original plan.'

The actor nodded his agreement and left, relishing the envious looks he gathered from the other men in the room.

'Sorry for the interruption,' Phule said, as if he were responsible for the disruption caused by the singer. 'Now then . . . back to business. I want you to pass the word through the company that I'm going to need the services of a forger. I repeat, a *forger*, not a counterfeiter . . .'

'Excuse me . . . Mr. Beeker . . . sir?'

Reluctant to let anything intrude on his rare off-duty time, the butler nonetheless paused at the hail, to find Bombest hastily emerging from behind the front desk.

'It's simply "Beeker," sir,' he said.

'Yes, of course,' the manager replied absently. 'I was wondering if I might speak with you for a moment?'

'In regards to what, sir?'

'Well' – Bombest glanced around as if he were afraid of eavesdroppers – 'I've been going over the reservations – manually, as Mr. Phule suggested – and I'm afraid we're going to need an extra hundred rooms for the opening.'

'Why?'

The manager shrugged. 'I can only assume computer error. Most of the reservations were entered correctly, but they don't seem to appear on any – '

'I meant why are you bringing this to *my* attention . . . sir?' Beeker said. 'I have no authority in these matters. Surely you were provided with a procedure by which you could report any irregularities through normal channels.'

'I was,' the manager admitted, 'but . . . well, frankly I've been reluctant to speak with Mr. Phule directly. He seems quite preoccupied with the arrangements for the opening, and I hate to interrupt him unless it's important.'

'I'm sure he would feel it was important enough to warrant interruption,' the butler said. 'After all, he felt it was important enough to import you specifically for the task, didn't he?'

'I . . . I guess so,' Bombest said hesitantly. 'I've barely spoken with him since my arrival, though. I didn't expect a brass band, mind you, but my lack of contact has left me feeling that there are higher priorities than my work occupying his mind.'

'More likely it's a tribute to his confidence in you, Mr. Bombest,' Beeker said easily, long accustomed to soothing the ruffled feathers and bruised feelings which invariably followed in his employer's wake. 'He doubtless feels that you are able to carry out your duties with minimal guidance or input from him.'

The manager's posture, never sloppy, improved noticeably at these words.

'I never thought of it that way,' he said.

'If, however, you still feel uncomfortable dealing directly with my employer,' the butler continued smoothly, 'might I suggest you speak with one of his officers? Lieutenant Armstrong or Lieutenant Rembrandt? I notice you're wearing one of the company's wrist communicators. I'm sure Mother will be able to put you in touch with them or relay your message if they're unavailable.'

Bombest glanced at the communicator on his wrist as if seeing it for the first time, then grimaced slightly.

'I suppose that's the only way to handle it,' he said. 'You know, Beeker, this is part of the problem.' He tapped the communicator with his forefinger. 'When Mr. Phule contacted me for this job, I was prepared to work as a hotel manager, but at times I feel more like a secret agent. Between the wrist radios and the intrigue – undercover people I'm not supposed to admit knowing, not saying anything to the casino manager – I keep feeling I've gotten in over my head . . . in something I'd normally avoid like the plague.'

Beeker allowed himself a small smile.

'If it's any comfort to you, sir, that feeling is not at all uncommon among those employed by Mr. Phule. He has a tendency to get carried away with things, and has the charisma to carry others right along with him. I'm sure you'll do fine once the initial shock has worn off.'

'How do you do it?'

'Sir?'

'You're a fairly ordinary guy, not at all like Mr. Phule or the uniformed fanatics he's associating with. How do you do your job?'

'Very well, sir.'

'Excuse me?'

The butler shook his head. 'Forgive me. It was my effort

at a small joke – something a magician once told me when I asked how he did a particular trick, or "effect", as he called it.'

The manager blinked, then flashed a brief smile. 'Oh. Yes. I see. Very funny.'

'As to your question,' Beeker continued, 'I imagine that my position is not unlike your own, in that since it is not high-profile, headline-quality work, people tend to assume that it's easy. The truth is that our work is extremely difficult. A special type of individual is required to merely survive, much less thrive, on the stressful decisions we must make daily. One must strike a balance between boldness and caution, theatrics and sincerity, all the while maintaining the open-mindedness and creativity necessary to deal with unforeseen situations. As you know, Mr. Bombest, there are no instruction manuals or college curriculums offered for our type of work. We each have to write our own book of rules from our personal experiences, then stand ready to break those rules should circumstances require it.'

'You're right, Beeker,' the manager said thoughtfully. 'I guess I've known that all along, though not in those precise words. I just forget from time to time. Thanks for reminding me.'

He thrust out his hand, and, after the briefest of pauses, the butler accepted it with a firm handshake.

Beeker reflected on his conversation with the hotel manager as he wandered into one of the casino's coffee shops.

It was occasionally difficult to recall, working as closely with his employer as he did, how intimidating most people found the name, much less the presence, of Willard Phule. A special effort had to be made to put such people at their ease before they could function at peak efficiency, and Bombest was a typical example.

Fortunately Phule had a simple formula for dealing with such situations. He sincerely believed that each person was special, though more often than not they were inclined to overlook their own assets. All he had to do was to point out what to him was obvious and express his appreciation, and the individual would respond with puppylike enthusiasm.

The butler helped himself to a cup of coffee, waving at the waitress, who returned his gesture with a smile. He was known here, and by now it was common knowledge among the help that serving himself would not be deducted from his tip.

It had been no major feat for Beeker to provide the necessary strokes for the hotel manager. Though he didn't completely embrace his employer's philosophies about the value of each individual, he was familiar enough with it and had witnessed its application often enough that he could easily play the part when it was necessary. What concerned him at the moment was that it should not have been necessary.

Phule was driving himself hard on this assignment, even harder than was normal. While Beeker had long since resigned himself to his employer's obsessive nature, he found this new pattern disturbing. Lack of sleep was making Phule irritable, particularly when reminded of some minor task or decision he had let slide in the midst of his frenzied, scattered schedule. While it might not be noticeable to the casual observer, it was apparent to those who worked with him normally. From what Beeker had heard and overheard, there was a growing tendency among Phule's subordinates to act independently rather than 'bothering the captain with minor stuff.' Even worse, they were then failing to notify him or deliberately withholding information regarding their activities.

While the butler would not directly betray a confidence or attempt to force advice on his employer, he was aware that if the situation got much worse, he would have to act within his powers to intervene.

Glancing around the coffee shop, Beeker noted with some satisfaction the absence of black uniforms. While he was always ready to listen to the Legionnaires' problems and complaints with a sympathetic ear, he also relished the occasional quiet moment to himself.

He was about to select a booth by himself when a lone

figure at a back table caught his eye and he changed his course in that direction.

'Good morning,' he said warmly, pulling out a chair for himself. 'Mind if I join you?'

Dark eyes rose from the book they had been reading and stared coldly at him from a chiseled ebony face.

'Excuse me? Do you know me?'

The chill in the voice surpassed that in the look, presupposing the answer for the question even as it was being asked.

'Only by reputation,' the butler said, easing into the chair. 'I simply thought I'd take this opportunity to meet you in person. Unless I'm mistaken, you're Laverna, currently in the employment of Maxine Pruet.'

The slender woman leaned back in her chair, crossing her ankles and folding her arms across her chest.

'And who does that make you?'

'Ah. Apparently I lack your notoriety.' The butler smiled, unruffled by Laverna's closed body language or the implied challenge in her voice. 'Allow me to introduce myself. My name is Beeker. I am employed by Willard Phule – or Captain Jester, if you prefer – in a capacity not unlike your own, though I imagine with substantially less input in financial matters.'

'You're what?'

'I'm his butler,' Beeker said. 'I buttle.'

The temperature at the table dropped even further.

'So you're going to sit here at *my* table and try to pump me for information about Mrs. Pruet?' Her tone made it a statement rather than a question. 'Look, Mr. Beeker, I don't get much time to myself, and *this is it*. I don't want to waste it playing twenty questions with some fool . . . *or* his butler.'

Beeker stared at her levelly for a moment, then stood up, gathering his coffee as he did.

'Forgive me for intruding on your privacy Ms. Laverna,' he said. 'It seems I was mistaken.'

'Don't go away mad,' Laverna said with a sneer, and reached for her book once more.

'Not mad. Simply annoyed,' the butler corrected. 'More with myself than with you.'

'How's that?'

'I pride myself in my judgment of people, Ms. Laverna,' Beeker explained. 'In fact, my effectiveness depends on it. I therefore find it annoying when it turns out I misjudged someone, particularly in a case of overestimation.'

'Mr. Beeker, I've been awake nearly thirty hours running now,' Laverna said. 'If you've got something to say to me, you'll have to say it straight out – and in plain words. I'm not tracking things too well.'

The butler paused, then drew a deep, ragged breath.

'Forgive me,' he said. 'I'm rather tired myself. All I meant was, I had assumed that from what I had heard and considering your position, you would be a highly intelligent person – intelligent enough to realize that I would not expect you to divulge any information about your employer any more than I would volunteer information about mine. People in our position don't last long if they are careless with confidences. The trust required has to be earned and maintained, so when dealing with someone of a similar standing to my own, I assumed trustworthiness and expected it would be assumed in return.'

Laverna weighed his words in silence for a few moments.

'So why *did* you come over, then?' she said finally.

Beeker gave a rueful smile.

'Strange as it may seem, considering the constant demands on our time, I was feeling lonely and thought perhaps you felt the same. In our positions as aides-de-camp to rather strong-willed people, it occurred to me that we probably have more in common with each other than we do with our respective employers.'

A sudden smile split Laverna's face, uncharacteristic to anyone who knew her.

'Sit down, Mr. Beeker,' she said, pulling out the chair next to her. 'We may have things to talk about, after all. Nonspecific things, of course.'

'Of course,' the butler said, accepting the offered seat. 'And it's "Beeker" . . . not "Mr. Beeker".'

My first conversation with Laverna was pleasant, though tinged with irony.

I, of course, said nothing to indicate that my employer was aware of her employer's planned computerized assault on the casino, nor gave any hint that Albert and his Bug Squad were working frantically to counter it even as we spoke.

She, in turn, never let it slip that there was a disruptive incident in progress . . . again, even as we spoke.

It was expected that Maxine would order a certain number of diversionary incidents during this period. If nothing else, they served, or so she thought, to draw my employer's attention away from her real attack as well as convince him he had the situation well in hand. In turn, to convince her that her strategy was working, my employer and his force were required to play along with each scenario as it unfolded.

It is worth noting, however, for both the casual reader and the student of military behavior, that however minor or token a diversion might be, for the direct participants the action is very real.

'You'd think they'd have caught on by now,' Kong King said, glancing at the door next to the loading dock as the electric delivery van pulled away. 'That's the third shipment we've turned away.'

'They'll figure it out soon enough.' Stilman didn't even turn his head. 'Restaurants need fresh food to operate. You're sure you've got your orders straight?'

Kong knew his orders, as did his four confederates. They had heard them often enough: no fewer than a dozen times even before they took up their station at the casino's delivery entrance. If anything, it was a bit insulting that the headman felt it was necessary to repeat things to them so often. He kept his annoyance to himself, however. He had worked with Stilman several times before and knew the ex-astroball player wasn't someone you mouthed off to.

'We go through the motions of shutting down deliveries to the kitchen until a security guard shows up,' he said as if for the first time. 'Then we let him run us off. No rough stuff beyond harsh words and maybe a little shoving.'

'That's right,' Stilman said with a minute nod. 'Remember. No rough stuff.'

'These security guards . . . all they have is tranquilizer darts in their guns. Right?'

Stilman turned slowly until he was facing the thug who raised the question.

'That's what I told you,' he said. 'Do you have a problem with that?'

Normally the man would have been cowed by this direct attention, but instead he simply shrugged his shoulders and looked away.

'I just want to be sure this "no rough stuff" rule works both ways,' the thug grumbled. 'I don't want to be no clay pigeon in a shooting gallery for nervous guards.'

'They aren't regular guards,' one of the others supplied. 'They're some kind of army types.'

'Yeah?' The original questioner fixed Stilman with an accusing gaze. 'You didn't say nothing about that when you was briefing us.'

'It's been all over the media,' Stilman said levelly. 'I assumed you knew. All it means is that they shouldn't rattle as easily as normal guards would.'

'Well, I don't like it.'

'You aren't supposed to like it. If you did, we wouldn't have to pay you to do it.'

Kong tensed, waiting for Stilman to quell the rebellion physically as well as verbally. To his surprise, however, the headman simply turned his back on the complainer.

'If it makes you feel any better,' he muttered, 'I don't like it, either. It's Max's orders, though, and while I'm taking her pay, she calls the shots.'

Kong tried to think of another time when he had heard Stilman speak out openly against an order from Max, but couldn't bring one to mind. Coming from him, the casual complaint was of monumental significance.

'Here comes another one.'

One of the small electric vans that were the mainstay of the space station's delivery network was pulling off the main drag into the loading area, a meat wagon this time.

The men waited in silence as it backed into position, then uncoiled from where they had been lounging against the wall and moved forward as the driver came around to open the back of the vehicle.

'*Hey!* You can't unload here!'

'Who says I . . .'

The driver's words died in his throat as he turned and took in the six musclemen between him and the door.

'Hey, I don't want any trouble,' he said, holding up his hands as he backed away.

'No trouble, friend,' Stilman said easily. 'You just got the wrong address is all.'

The driver frowned. 'This is the Fat Chance Casino, isn't it?'

'Maybe you don't hear so good,' Kong said, moving forward slightly. 'The man said you have the wrong address! Something wrong with your ears? Something we should maybe try to fix for you?'

'*What the hell's going on here?*'

Kong managed to keep a straight face as the men turned to confront the white-aproned cook who had come charging out of the kitchen door. It was about time someone inside had noticed the activity on their loading dock. Security should be close behind him.

The urge to smile faded as he recalled their 'no rough stuff' orders.

'Nobody unloads here until you hire some union help,' Stilman was saying, moving to confront the cook directly.

'What are you talkin' about?' the cook said. 'There aren't any unions on Lorelei!'

Kong was distracted from the conversation by a small, dark-skinned figure who emerged from the kitchen behind the original cook. Completely ignoring the raging argument, the little man strode over to the open delivery van and shouldered a quarter side of beef, then turned back toward the kitchen.

It occurred to the thug that he should stop the unloading, or at least call it to Stilman's attention, but he was loath to intrude on the verbal brawl or take individual action while

147

the headman was right there. Fortunately the decision was taken out of his hands. The laden figure passed close by the two arguing men on his way back to the kitchen, and Stilman spotted him.

'*Hey!* What do you think *you're* doing?' the headman demanded, breaking off the debate.

The little man stopped and turned to face him, regarding him levelly with dark eyes.

'Must get meat inside,' he said. 'Not good to leave out here. Too warm. Might go bad.'

'Maybe you didn't get the drift of what I was saying,' Stilman challenged, moving closer. 'You can't unload that stuff while we're around.'

The little man bobbed his head.

'Good. You take.'

With that, he half tossed, half thrust the meat at Stilman, shoving it forward as the balance came off his shoulder. The headman was unprepared for the weighty mass suddenly launched at him, but he managed to catch it – more from surprise than intent.

The little man ignored Stilman's reaction, stepping past him to address the stunned thugs.

'You . . . and you,' he said, stabbing a finger at the two largest musclemen. 'Get meat from there and follow me.'

At this point, Stilman recovered his wits.

'To hell with this!' he roared, throwing the meat down and brushing at the front of his suit.

With his back turned, he couldn't see what happened next, much less have a chance to counter it. Kong was facing in the right direction, but even he had trouble later describing exactly what happened.

With a pantherlike bound the little man was close behind Stilman. There was a flash of metal, which resolved itself into a long butcher's knife – only visible when it came to rest pressed against the headman's throat.

'You do not throw meat on the ground!' the little man hissed, eyes slit in anger. 'Now it ruined! No good! *Understand?*'

Kong and the other thugs stood rooted to the ground in

frozen tableau. They could see that the knife was pressed against Stilman's neck so tightly that the flesh was indented, and knew without being told that the slightest move from the knife or Stilman would lay his throat open.

'Please do not move, gentlemen.'

Their attention was drawn to a new figure who had entered the scene.

'What the hell is *that?*' one of the thugs said, though he echoed the thoughts of the entire group.

'Do not be fooled by my appearance, gentlemen,' the singsong, musical voice continued, though they could see now that the sound was actually coming from a mechanical box hung around the neck of the intruder. 'I assure you that though my form is not the human standard you are accustomed to, I am a member of the casino security force and authorized to deal with disturbances as I see fit.'

The speaker was a sluglike creature with spindly arms and eyestalks. Balanced on a kid's glide board and encased in a tube of black fabric which suggested rather than imitated the familiar Space Legion uniforms, the creature looked more like some bizarre advertising display than an authority figure.

'No, I meant what is that you're holding?' the thug corrected. 'That doesn't look like a tranquilizer gun.'

The Sinthian had a sinister-looking mechanism tucked under his arm. The tubelike barrel, which was pointing at the thugs, appeared to be a good inch in diameter, though they knew from experience that the muzzle of a weapon always looks bigger when it's pointed at *you*.

'This?' the Legionnaire chirped, bending one eyestalk to look at his implement. 'You are correct that it is a weapon. It is magazine-loaded, however, which enables me to change the loads depending on the situation at hand.'

He suddenly pointed the weapon at the fallen side of beef, and it erupted with a soft stutter of air.

The thugs could see a line of impacts on the meat, but no appreciable damage. Then they noticed the surface start to bubble, and a sharp *hiss* reached their ears.

'As you can see,' the Sinthian was saying, 'I neglected to

bring my tranquilizer darts on duty with me today, an omission which will surely earn me a reprimand if reported. All I have with me are acid balls – and, of course, a few high explosives.'

He realigned the weapon with the motionless men.

'Now, if your curiosity is settled, gentlemen, I suggest you begin unloading the van as requested. I'm afraid it may ruin your clothes, but you should have come dressed for the occasion.'

The thugs glanced at Stilman.

'Do as he says,' the headman croaked, still under the knife.

'And pay for ruined meat before you go,' his captor added.

'But I didn't . . .'

'You throw meat on the ground, you pay for it!' the little man growled, tightening his grip. 'Yes?'

'Okay, okay!' Stilman gasped. 'Pay the man . . . Now!'

In my privileged position, I was able to hear not one, but two accounts of the loading dock incident: the one which constituted the official report, and the one passed among the Legionnaires over drinks and coffee. As such, I could not help but note that in the account rendered to my employer, both Escrima's role and the use of the acid balls were diplomatically omitted.

Far more important to me, however, was the evidence of growing bad blood between the forces led by my employer and those reporting to Laverna's employer. This concerned me since, to the best of my knowledge, both leaders seemed unaware of the tensions building in the levels under them.

Chapter Eleven

Journal #234

There is much made of the satisfaction felt by a commander when a plan comes together.

Obviously I cannot comment on the conduct of all, or even the majority of, military commanders under these circumstances, but the behavior of my employer on the opening day of the Fat Chance Casino showed little of this passive enjoyment. Rather, he was more like an insecure party hostess, hurrying here and there and busying himself with countless details, dealing with both important and minor chores with equal intensity.

Huey Martin was in the middle of getting dressed when he was interrupted by an insistent hammering on the door of his suite. This was both annoying and puzzling, as people rarely visited his room, and never without calling in advance.

'Who is it?' he called, hurrying to button his shirt.

Instead of an answer, he heard the sound of a key in his lock. Before he could protest, the door slammed open and the commander of the casino's security force strode into the room, followed closely by two guards . . . and Gunther Rafael himself!

A sudden pang of fear stabbed at the casino manager's gut, but gambler's reflex kept him from showing his emotions openly.

'What's going on?' he demanded indignantly. 'I'm trying to get ready for the opening.'

'That won't be necessary,' the commander said levelly.

'You're being relieved of your duties. Effective immediately.'

'I . . . I don't understand,' Huey said, looking at the casino owner in feigned bewilderment.

'It won't work, Huey,' Gunther said tersely.. 'We know all about your working for Max *and* about the dealers you've been hiring.'

'We have some interesting tapes from the eye-in-the-sky cameras,' Phule said. 'Your pet dealers have provided us with a catalog of skims and scams, often while you were standing on camera watching them. They're being met as they report for duty, incidentally. We felt it was best that they *not* work the opening. In fact, they're being given the entire week off without pay. After that, we'll interview them again to see if they're willing to work for us *without* the skims and perks.'

'But that won't leave you with enough dealers to open!' the manager said, then realized he was admitting the extent of his treachery.

The commander smiled humorlessly. 'That would be true if we hadn't arranged in advance for replacements for them . . . *and* you.'

Huey was stunned by the admission that this action against him was not spontaneous, but rather the result of foreknowledge and substantial planning.

'So what does this mean for me?' he said, both from curiosity and to cover his confusion.

Gunther looked at the commander.

'You will be held here,' Phule said, 'incommunicado.'

As he spoke, he nodded at the Legionnaires, who responded by moving through the suite pulling the phone in each room out of the wall.

'Once the opening is over,' the commander continued, 'you'll be free to go. Your employment here is, to say the least, terminated.'

'You can't do that,' the manager said, shaking his head. 'I have a contract that guarantees me due notice as well as a share of the casino.'

Phule scowled and shot a sidelong glance at the casino owner.

'Do you have a copy of that contract?' he said. 'I'd like to see it.'

Huey produced the document from a drawer in his desk and passed it to the commander, who moved closer to a light to study it.

'Why did you do it, Huey?' Gunther said, the hurt showing in his voice. 'Wasn't the deal we had between us enough for you?'

'Hey, nothing personal, kid,' the manager said. 'It's just that my mom raised me greedy. The way it was, it looked like I could collect on our deal *and* from Max, and by my addition, two paychecks are better than one. Like I say, nothing personal.'

'Excuse me,' Phule interrupted, turning back to the conversation, 'but I don't find anything in here about termination notice or about your having a share in the casino.'

'Of course it's there,' Huey said, snatching the contract back. 'Look, I'll show you. It's right . . .'

He began paging through the document, then scowled and flipped back a few pages to study it closer.

'I don't understand,' he murmured. 'I know they're in here.'

'Believe me, Mr. Martin,' the commander said, 'I just reviewed the contract, and they're not.'

An image flashed across the manager's mind. The image of Phule turning away to look at the contract.

'You switched it!' he accused with sudden realization. 'This isn't the contract I handed you!'

'Nonsense,' Phule said. 'That's your signature on the last page, isn't it?'

Huey barely glanced at the indicated page.

'It may be . . . More likely a forgery,' he spat. 'Either that or you pulled the last page and attached it to a new contract. Don't think you're going to get away with this!'

'That's an interesting accusation,' the commander said, unruffled. 'Though I suspect it would be hard to prove in court. Of course, if you *did* try to take this to court, we'd be forced to make our tapes a part of the public record to defend the position that you were fired with cause. That might make it a little hard for you to find another position, since I doubt the media would let the story die until they had broadcast the footage several dozen times.'

The room seemed to reel around the manager as he had a sudden vision of his face and misdeeds being publicized stellarwide.

'You . . . you wouldn't,' he said.

'We wouldn't unless we felt it was necessary to protect our interests,' Phule corrected. 'Personally I'd suggest you take the more salvageable alternative of a quiet dismissal. Then again, perhaps you can convince Mr. Gunther here to reinstate you. After the opening, of course.'

'Is . . . is there any chance of that?' Huey said, looking to the casino owner.

Gunther shrugged. 'Maybe. But only if – how did you put that again, Willie?'

'Only if you succeeded in convincing Mr. Rafael that your loyalties were now properly aligned,' the commander supplied.

'How could I do that?'

'Well, for starters you could tell us everything you know about Max's plans, beginning with the "special guests" that have been invited to the grand opening,' Phule said. 'If nothing else, that should burn the bridge between you and your old cronies. By the way, you might as well tell us directly. We've pieced together enough on our own that I'm afraid Max will assume you've sold her out, whether you do or not. I suggest you see what information is left to bargain for some protection.'

'Here's your key, Mr. Shuman – room 2339 – and welcome to the Fat Chance Casino. *Front!*'

With the deftness born from many years' practice, the clerk slapped the small bell on the registration desk, summoning a valet before the guests could stop him.

'Elevators are this way, sir,' the valet said, materializing between the elderly couple and their only piece of luggage.

Snatching up the bag with ease, he led the way, leaving the twosome to trail along behind him.

'Well, Mother, we're here!' the portly gentleman declared, giving his wife a hug and one arm as they walked.

'Henry . . . how old would you say that young man at the front desk is?' the frumpy woman at his side inquired.

'Oh, I don't know,' the man said, glancing back. 'Late twenties, early thirties, I'd guess. It's hard to tell with kids these days. Why do you ask?'

'Just curious,' his wife said with a shrug. 'He struck me as being a bit young to be wearing a hearing aid.'

Shuman had also noticed the device in the desk clerk's ear, although, at the time, he had tried to convince himself it was inconsequential.

'I don't think it was a hearing aid,' he said. 'More likely some kind of paging radio or a hookup with the phones. I haven't been keeping up with all the electronic gizmos they've developed lately.'

'I suppose you're right,' the woman said, then returned his hug as if he had just given it. 'It *is* hard to believe we're here, isn't it? After all these years?'

Though the implication was that the couple had been working and saving for years planning for a once-in-a-lifetime vacation, the real truth was hidden in this statement.

In actuality, they had been banned from nearly all casinos for close to five years now. Their guise of retired, unsophisticated grandparents was as complete as it was disarming, allowing them to pull off numerous forms of cheating requiring anything from sleight of hand to complex systems which, to the casual eye, would be assumed to be well beyond their abilities. They had, in fact, relieved most of the major gambling centers of sizable amounts of money before the casinos managed to compare notes and realized that they were not the harmless tourists they seemed to be.

They had been lured from 'retirement' by a promise that they would not be recognized at this particular casino, as well as by a hefty bankroll to fund their charade. Though they were excited at the possibility of once more being able to dust off their long-practiced performance, they still had to fight off the nervousness that at any moment they might be recognized.

'This place really is something, isn't it?' Henry said, making a show of rubbernecking around as they were escorted into one of the elevators.

'Hold the elevator!' The bellman caught the door with his hand in response to the call, and a broad-shouldered, chisel-featured young man in a black uniform burst into the car.

'Sorry for the inconvenience,' he announced in an off-hand tone that didn't sound apologetic at all, 'but I have to commandeer the elevator for a moment.'

As he spoke, he used a key to override the control panel and punched a button. The door closed, and the car began to move – downward instead of up.

Shuman suppressed a quick feeling of irritation, fearing that to protest would be out of character.

'Is something wrong?' he said instead.

'No. Everything's under control,' the man assured him, sparing him only the briefest of glances before returning his gaze to the floor indicator.

'I didn't know this place *had* a basement,' his wife said, tightening her grip on Henry's arm slightly. 'Aren't we on a space station?'

Realizing she was making small talk to cover her nervousness, Henry nonetheless played along.

'I imagine it's some kind of storage area,' he said. 'All the rooms are . . .'

He broke off as the elevator stopped and the doors slid open. Framed in the doorway was another black-garbed figure, an older man with a bald head and a theatric handlebar moustache.

'Got two more for you, Sergeant,' their fellow passenger announced, nodding at the bellman, who unceremoniously tossed their bag out of the elevator.

'Very good, sahr!' the bald man said, barely sparing the couple a glance as he consulted the clipboard he was holding. 'Let's see, you would be Henry and Louise Shuman . . . or should I call you Mr. and Mrs. Welling?'

156

The use of their correct names eliminated any hope Henry might have had of bluffing their way out of the situation with bewildered indignation.

'Whatever,' he said, taking his wife's arm and ushering her out of the elevator with as much dignity as he could muster as the doors slid shut behind them.

'I don't suppose *you're* hard of hearing, are you, Sergeant?' his wife asked their captor.

'Excuse me, mum? Oh, you mean this?' Moustache tapped the device he was wearing in his ear. 'No, this is a direct hookup with the folks at the front desk. Mr. Bascom has one, too. He's watching on a closed circuit camera, and when he spots a familiar face, he tells the clerk and they get relayed down here to us.'

'Bascom?' Henry frowned. 'You mean *Tullie* Bascom? I thought he retired.'

'That's right, sir,' the sergeant confirmed. 'Seems you two aren't the only old war-horses being reactivated for this skirmish.'

'I see,' Henry said. 'Well, tell him we said hello, if you get the chance.'

'I'll do that, sir,' Moustache said, flashing a quick smile. 'Now, if you'll both join the others, it shouldn't be long now.'

As he spoke, he gestured toward a cluster of chairs and sofas which had been set up in the service corridor. There was an unusual assortment of individuals sprawled across the furnishings, ranging in appearance from businessmen to young married couples to little old ladies and obvious blue-collar workers. While Henry did not recognize any of them, the studied casualness of their postures and the uniform flat, noncommittal looks that were directed at himself and his wife marked them all as being cut from the same bolt of cloth. These were grifters and con artists who, like the Wellings, had been caught in the security net. While the setting was pleasant enough considering the situation, and there was no indication of rough treatment among the captives, Henry could not escape the momentary illusion of a prisoner-of-war compound, possibly due to the black-uniformed armed guards spaced pointedly along the wall.

'What are you going to do with us, Sergeant?' Henry said, eyeing the assemblage.

'Nothing to worry about, sir,' Moustache said, flashing another quick smile. 'After we've collected a few more, you'll all be loaded into a shuttle bus and given a lift back to the space terminal.'

'You mean, we're being forcibly deported?'

'Not at all,' the sergeant said. 'It's more a courtesy service . . . assuming, of course, that you're planning to leave. If you'd prefer to stay on Lorelei, that's your prerogative. As long as you stay out of the Fat Chance.'

A vision flashed through Henry's mind, of he and his wife accepting tickets and seed money from Maxine Pruet, then trying to work their scams at one of her casinos instead of the one they had been instructed to hit. He quickly brought the mental picture to a halt before it reached its graphically unpleasant conclusion.

'No, we'll take the ride,' he said hastily. 'I suspect our reception at the other casinos would be roughly the same as here . . . except, perhaps, less polite. My compliments, by the way. Of all the times we've been barred from or asked to leave a casino, this is far and away the most civilized handling of an awkward situation we've encountered . . . wouldn't you say, dear?'

His wife nodded brusquely, but failed to smile or otherwise join him in his enthusiasm.

'It's the captain's idea, really,' Moustache said, 'but I'll be sure to tell him you appreciate it. Now, if you'll just have a seat. There are drinks and doughnuts available while you wait, or, if you're interested, there's a blackjack table set up in back so you can at least do a little playing before you go.'

'At normal house odds?' the wife snapped, breaking her silence. 'Don't be silly, young man. We weren't *gamblers*. Do we *look* stupid?'

'No, ma'am. Sorry, ma'am.'

*

'Lieutenant Armstrong!'

Emerging from the elevator, Armstrong glanced around at the hail to find the company commander walking toward him. Without hesitation, he snapped into a stiff, parade-ground position of attention and fired off his best salute.

'Yes, *sir!*'

When the captain had taken over the company, one of his main projects had been to get Armstrong to 'loosen up' a little, to be more human and less a recruiting-poster caricature. Now it had become a standing joke between the two men. This time, however, the commander seemed distracted, simply returning the salute with a vague wave rather than either smiling or rolling his eyes as had become the norm.

'Anything to report?' he said, scanning the lobby uneasily. 'How is everything going so far?'

'No problems, sir,' the lieutenant said, relaxing on his own now that his attempt at humor had been ignored. 'We've sent four busloads back to the space terminal so far and are just about ready to wave goodbye to a fifth.'

'Good,' Phule said, walking slowly with his head canted slightly down, staring at the floor as he concentrated on his junior officer's report. 'How about the showroom? Should I be expecting another visit from Ms. Watkins?'

'The first show went off without a hitch,' Armstrong said, falling in step beside his captain. 'In fact, word is she got a standing ovation and three encores.'

'No problems at all, then,' the commander said. 'That's a relief.'

'Well . . . not with the show itself, anyway.'

Phule's head came up with a snap.

'What's *that* supposed to mean?' he challenged.

The lieutenant swallowed nervously.

'Umm . . . there was one report that concerned me a bit,' he said. 'It seems that during one of the curtain calls, Dee Dee dragged Lex out of the wings and introduced him to the audience as the show's stage manager and an old friend of hers from her theater days, now on temporary duty with the Space Legion.'

159

'Oh, swell,' the commander growled. 'As if I didn't already have enough to worry about.'

'To be fair, sir, we can't really say it was her fault. Nobody told her not to put the spotlight on our decoy associates.'

'It never occurred to me that she might do it,' Phule said. 'Oh well . . . it's done now, and we can't change it. Let's just hope none of the opposition was at the first show . . . or that if they were, they don't find it unusual that we have an actor in our company. Pass the word to Lex, though, to ask her not to do it again.'

'I'll do that,' Armstrong said.

'Just a moment, Lieutenant . . .'

The commander veered slightly to pass by the hotel's registration desk.

'Mr. Bombest,' he called, beckoning the manager over for a quick consultation. 'I hear things are going fine. Do you have enough rooms now?'

'Yes, Mr. Phule.' Bombest looked a bit haggard, but managed to rally enough to smile at his benefactor. 'The winnowing of the guest list should provide the rooms necessary. I've got a few people I've had to delay check-in for until some of the "special guests" who arrived early can be evicted from their rooms, but nothing I can't handle.'

'Good . . . good,' Phule said, and started to turn away. 'Lieutenant Armstrong has told me you're doing a fine job. Just keep up the good work and we'll get through this opening yet.'

The manager beamed. 'Thank you, Mr. Phule. I trust my handling of the reporter was satisfactory?'

The commander paused and cocked his head curiously. 'The what?'

'The reporter,' Bombest repeated. 'The one from Haskin's Planet that you used to date when you were stationed there.'

'Jennie Higgens? *She's* here?'

Phule's interest was no longer casual.

'Why, yes . . . I thought you knew,' the manager said. 'I recognized her when she was checking in along with her cameraman, and it occurred to me that she could identify

160

some of your troops – the ones under cover, I mean – so I repeated it to your communications person with my wrist communicator. I . . . I assumed you had been informed.'

'No . . . but I think I'm *about* to be,' the commander said grimly, looking hard at Armstrong, who was avoiding meeting his eye. 'Lieutenant Armstrong . . . if I might have a word with you?'

'Is there something wrong?' Bombest said in a worried tone.

'Not that I know of.' Phule smiled. 'Why do you ask?'

'Well . . . for a moment there, you seemed upset . . . and I thought I had done something wrong.'

'Quite the contrary,' the commander insisted, his smile growing even broader. 'I couldn't be happier with your work. Lieutenant, why don't *you* tell Mr. Bombest what a fine job he's doing?'

'You're doing a fine job, Mr. Bombest,' Armstrong recited obediently. 'In fact, the whole company owes you a debt for what you've done.'

The manager frowned. 'Excuse me?'

'I don't think you were quite clear enough on that last part, Lieutenant,' Phule observed.

'A debt of *gratitude*,' the Legionnaire corrected. 'We wouldn't be where we are now if it weren't for you.'

'Oh. Uh . . . thank you,' Bombest said with a hesitant smile.

'Now that that's taken care of, Lieutenant,' Phule said, the grin still on his face, 'I believe we were about to have a little talk?'

'Umm . . . actually sir, I thought I'd . . .'

'*Now*, Lieutenant.'

'Yes, sir!'

With the eager step of a man on his way to the gallows, Armstrong followed his commander into one of the lobby's more secluded nooks.

'Now them, Lieutenant,' Phule said with a tight smile, 'it seems there's at least one item that was omitted in your "no problems" report. What do you know about this reporter thing?'

161

'The incident occurred during Lieutenant Rembrandt's shift, sir,' Armstrong said. 'In fact, she's probably the best person to fill you in on –'

'I didn't ask *when* it happened,' the commander interrupted. 'I asked what *you* know about it.'

Though maintaining his deadpan expression for armor, Armstrong winced internally. There was a tradition in the Space Legion that while it was acknowledged that the Legionnaires would, and did, play fast and loose with the truth when dealing with those outside the Legion, within their own ranks, they were required to tell the truth. In reaction to this, Legionnaires had also become masters at the art of evasive answers and shamelessly diverting the subject of a conversation, which usually worked except for times, like this, when confronted insistently with a direct question.

'Umm . . . a call came in, as you just heard, from Bombest that a reporter and a cameraman from Haskin's Planet were checking into the hotel,' the lieutenant recited in a monotone. 'Lieutenant Rembrandt decided, and I agreed with her, that –'

'Wait a minute. When did all this happen?'

Armstrong studied his watch carefully before answering. 'Approximately fifteen hours ago, sir.'

'*Fifteen hours?* Why wasn't I informed?'

'I suggested that at the time, sir. When we tried to get through to you, however, Mother informed us that you had gone off the air less than an hour before to get some sleep, and Remmie said . . . excuse me, Lieutenant Rembrandt mentioned that you had encouraged her to make more command decisions on her own, so she decided to deal with the matter herself without disturbing you . . . sir.'

'I see,' Phule said, grimacing a bit himself. Then he cocked an eyebrow at the lieutenant. 'It sounds like you were there for the whole thing. Didn't you say that it was Lieutenant Rembrandt's shift?'

'Yes, sir. I . . . I was sort of hanging around before taking my formal shift. I was awake, anyway, sir, and thought I'd

162

give her a hand while I was up. She's done the same for me several times.'

'You're supposed to be using your time off to get some sleep and otherwise relax, Lieutenant. That's why we set up the schedules the way we did. Otherwise, you'll be functioning at less than peak efficiency if something happens while you're on duty.'

'Yes, sir. I'll remember that, sir.'

'Now, tell me . . .'

'Of course, it would help if the captain set an example for us . . . sir.'

The commander eyed him for a moment.

'Lieutenant Armstrong,' he said at last, 'are you trying to change the subject?'

'Yes, sir.'

'Well, forget it. I want to know what happened to the reporter.'

'She's being held in her room under guard, sir. Also her cameraman. In adjoining rooms, that is, sir.'

'*What?*'

Even though Phule had been half expecting the answer, he was nonetheless stunned.

'It was all we could think of to keep her from – '

'*You kidnapped a member of the interstellar press? Against her will?*'

'It seemed impractical to wait until we could do it *with* her will, sir.'

The commander shot a hard look at his junior officer, but Armstrong never cracked a smile.

'All right, Lieutenant. While you're coming up with clever answers, perhaps you can explain to me why I wasn't informed of this when I woke up and came back on the floor. I believe it was *your* shift then?'

'I started to tell you, sir,' Armstrong said, still holding his deadpan expression. 'At the time, however, you were getting ready to lead the expedition to confine the casino manager in his room against his will. If the captain will recall, I asked for a moment of his time, and was asked if it was important.'

Phule frowned, vaguely recalling the brief exchange. 'And you didn't think this was important?'

'I assumed the captain was asking if my question was time sensitive, and in my best judgment, it wasn't. The captain should recall that at that point, the reporter had already been confined for several hours, and I did not think that a few more hours would significantly change the situation, or her mood . . . sir.'

'I suppose there's a certain logic there . . . even if it is a little twisted.'

'Thank you, sir.'

'There's still the question, though, of why you didn't mention it just now when I asked for your report.'

'I . . . I was working my way up to it, sir,' Armstrong said, letting a small grimace flicker across his face.

Phule glared at him for a moment, then heaved a big sigh.

'Well, what's done is done,' he said. 'In the future, however, I want it understood by you *and* Lieutenant Rembrandt that any incident of importance, particularly one involving the press, is to be brought to my attention immediately. That's *immediately*, as in *at the time it occurs*, whether I'm asleep or not. Do I make myself clear?'

'Yes, sir. I'll keep that in mind, sir.'

'All right. Now, are there any other little incidents that I should be aware of?'

'Excuse me, sir, but there's one more thing you should know about Jennie.'

'What's that?'

'When we were informing her that she was to be confined to her quarters, she said . . . well . . . *among* the things she had to say, she indicated that she already knew that we had substitutes standing in for some of our troops.'

'She did?' Phule said with a frown. 'I wonder how she figured that out. Probably too many unfamiliar faces in that news coverage we got when we arrived. Oh well. I'll have to remember to ask her when I get around to talking to her.'

'Is that to say you won't be dealing with the matter right away . . . sir?'

The commander grimaced. 'As you so logically put it, whatever damage has been done won't change significantly if she has to wait a few more hours. Right now, we have matters to deal with that *are* time sensitive.'

Maxine loved casinos.

There was a rhythm to them, almost like the pulse and breathing of a huge animal, a predator on the prowl. Small white balls rattled in the silently spinning roulette wheels and cards were slapped from shoes to the accompaniment of the monotone chants of the pit crews, the repetition of words giving an almost ritualistic, religious air to the proceedings, interrupted only by the occasional yips of glee or curses of the players. Every twenty minutes the pit crews would be pulled for a break, their replacements stepping in without missing a beat in the tables' rhythm. When the rested crews returned, they would be inserted into another pit, so that someone who had been dealing blackjack would now be working a roulette wheel, while the pit bosses watched with flat eyes to see if anyone was following a particular dealer from post to post.

Yes, a well-functioning casino was a living, breathing predator . . . and it fed on money.

Maxine surveyed the casino floor, drinking in the almost electric flow of excitement that radiated from the tables. She was dressed elegantly in an evening gown as befitted a grand opening, but if she had been wearing rags and tatters – or nothing at all, for that matter – no one would have noticed. Lady Luck was a cruel coquette who demanded the total attention and concentration of her suitors.

There was no sign of anything amiss, but that wasn't surprising. If the various imported cheats were half as expert as their reputations would indicate, their actions would go undetected, especially with the assistance of the crooked dealers seeded through the pit crews. If the casino was an animal, then they were leeches, quietly bleeding it of the money that was its sustenance until it wobbled and fell. The

165

casino might think of itself as a predator, but this time the Fat Chance was, in actuality, a fatted calf.

'I don't see any big winners,' Stilman said, breaking his silence as he stood at her side. 'Are you sure this is going to work?'

Maxine shot a distasteful glance at him.

Stilman's tuxedo was tailor-made and fit him superbly, but he wore it like a warm-up suit. Even to the casual observer, he showed all the grace and style of a penguin on steroids.

'I keep telling you, Mr. Stilman,' Max said, 'this is supposed to be a subtle operation. Subtle as opposed to obvious. You should know by now that's my style of operating. While I can appreciate the skill and conditioning required by your speciality of physical action, I prefer to only use it for diversions or as a last resort.'

That settled, Maxine turned her attention to the casino floor once more. Unfortunately, however, Stilman's grumbles had planted a worm of worry in her mind, and she found herself straining to detect any big winners or steady trends at the tables within her immediate sight.

'What do *you* think, Laverna?' she said finally, turning literally as well as figuratively to her financial advisor and confidante, who was also accompanying her this evening.

Laverna had ignored the formality of the opening and was dressed in one of her normal jumpsuits, a pair of diamond earrings her only concession that there was anything special about the occasion. Though her manner was relaxed to the point of appearing bored, her eyes were busy, constantly gathering and analyzing data as was her habit whenever they were actually on the floor of a casino.

'Hard to tell,' she said with a slight shrug, her eyes still moving across the casino. 'It looks pretty normal . . . maybe a bit more flow to the customers than usual, but I'd have to watch for a while to get a real feel for it. Of course, you can't say for sure without moving in close to see which chips are moving in which direction.'

What was she referring to was that experienced gamblers rarely settled for making the same bet over and over. If you

166

did that, the house odds would catch up to you in the long run and you'd lose. Instead, they tended to stagger their bets, betting low for long stretches, then raising their bets dramatically when they felt the odds were in their favor or a run was in effect. As a result, a player could win and lose an equal number of hands, but end up ahead or behind depending on whether or not their larger bets paid off.

'So we really don't know if this grand plan is working or not,' Stilman said crossly.

Surprised at the surliness in his tone, Maxine glanced at him and noticed for the first time that he was looking around nervously and fidgeting ... something totally out of character from his normal aloof manner.

'You seem uneasy, Mr. Stilman,' she observed. 'Is something bothering you?'

The muscleman glanced around again before answering.

'I'm just not sure how happy the staff is going to be to see me here is all,' he said. 'After that fiasco on the loading dock, I wouldn't be surprised if they tried to throw me out - tuxedo or no.'

'I think Mr. Phule's security team has Stilman a bit spooked, Max,' Laverna said with a wink and a grin.

Stilman fixed a cold, level gaze on her.

'It's not funny,' he said. 'These soldier boys of yours haven't shown me much so far, but I'll tell you, this casino has some of the toughest *employee's* I've ever seen. Where did Huey find them, anyway?'

'You'll have to ask him the next time you talk,' Max said, suppressing a smile of her own. 'Not tonight, though. While I don't think there will be any trouble as long as you're just here as a guest, it probably wouldn't be prudent if Mr. Martin were seen conversing with us or any of our known associates this evening.'

'Yeah ... well ... it's all nice and easy for you to say "Don't worry,"' Stilman growled, glancing around once more, 'but *you* aren't the one they'll be coming after if you're wrong. I don't know why I had to be here, anyway.'

'You don't, really,' Maxine said. 'Realizing, though, that you and your men have had to put up with being roughed up and humiliated due to my policy of no rough stuff during our various diversionary probes, I thought you might enjoy being around "for the kill," as it were.'

'What? For this?' Stilman made a small gesture at the casino floor. 'I suppose it was a nice thought, but this is about as exciting as watching grass grow.'

Maxine cocked a regal eyebrow at him. 'I know you sometimes think me dull, Mr. Stilman, and perhaps in comparison to the excitement of the astroball circuit, I am. You should recall, however, that I also have a love of the dramatic. Rest assured that things will get much more lively soon – in fact, in about fifteen minutes, I'd say.'

'Lively like how?'

Maxine returned her gaze to the casino floor. 'Do you ever play the slots, Mr. Stilman?'

'Not since I first got here,' Stilman responded. 'I tried them once, just because it seemed the thing to do at a casino, but they always seemed to be pretty much a sucker bet to me.'

'That's quite correct,' Max said with a nod. 'They're popular with the tourists, and because of that they provide a surprisingly high income for any casino. Even the lure of a high jackpot, however, doesn't offset the fact that the odds are depressingly high against the player.'

'Yeah. So?' Stilman pressed, but Maxine was not about to be rushed.

'Take that island of machines over there, for example,' she said, indicating a cluster of slots with a nod of her head. 'They only accept fifty-dollar tokens to play, but there's a progressive jackpot attached to them, with a guaranteed minimum of ten million dollars. Of course, if you read the fine print on the machine, you have to bet the maximum of five tokens *and* hit a very rare combination of images to qualify for the big jackpot.'

'Are you saying that someone's going to win the jackpot tonight? Ten million dollars?'

Stilman craned his neck to peer at the machines, obviously impressed.

Maxine smiled. 'I know I've said it before, Mr. Stilman,

168

but you habitually think too small. You'll notice that, like all casinos today, Mr. Gunther is using the video-image slot machines as opposed to the old models that mechanically match the various images. This both reduces the maintenance necessary, since there are fewer moving parts, *and* lets the house control the odds more closely, as the payout rate is controlled by the central computer which all the machines are tied into – the computer, if you'll recall, that we've paid substantially to gain access to.'

She paused to check her watch again.

'Now, in about thirteen minutes, a sleeping program we've had planted in that computer is going to cut in and change the odds for that cluster of slots down to one in fifty. *Then* I think we'll see some excitement.'

'You mean they're *all* going to start paying out? At ten million dollars a pop?' Even Stilman's legendary calm was shattered as he gaped openly at Maxine.

'Realistically I'm afraid it will only work a few times before they pull the plug,' she said. 'The way I see it, the first jackpot will cause a stir, and the management will try to play it up big for the publicity. The second will startle them, but they'll still try to maintain a generous front.'

Her eyes narrowed slightly.

'When the third jackpot hits, however, they'll know there's something wrong and shut down the system. Of course, that decision takes time, both to make and to initiate. If we're lucky, we should hit one, maybe two more jackpots before they can put a stop it it.'

'Thirty to fifty million dollars,' Stilman said, saying the words in a soft, almost reverent voice.

'Before you ask,' Max added with a smile, 'those are, of course, *our* people manning the key machines right now. No sense letting all that money fall into the wrong hands.'

'At ten thousand dollars a minute,' Laverna put in.

Max blinked. 'What's that, Laverna?'

'Five fifty-dollar tokens per pull, times ten machines, times at least four pulls a minute, is ten thousand dollars a minute they're pumping into those machines by my count,' her aide clarified. 'I assume they're only playing minimum bets until the right time comes, but even if they only play for ten minutes after the flag goes up, that's one hundred thousand dollars they'll be going through.'

'The end profits more than justify the investment,' Maxine said flatly, annoyed at having her explanation interrupted. 'Now then, Mr. Stilman, as I was saying . . . As you can tell, that many high jackpots will put a severe drain on Mr. Rafael's funds. He doesn't dare not pay off the jackpots, or the negative publicity would drive him out of business. Combined with the losses we've planned for him at the tables, however, it should keep him from making the necessary payment on his loan. What's more, word of the multiple jackpots should get sufficient media coverage that I doubt he'll be able to find anyone willing to let him borrow the money.'

Maxine was smiling again. A sweet, grandmotherly smile.

'In short, Mr. Stilman, when those jackpot bells start to sound, what you'll be hearing is the Fat Chance Casino sliding into our cash drawer.'

'Max?'

'Yes, Laverna?'

'We've got a problem.'

Maxine followed her aide's gaze and saw the unmistakable figure of Willard Phule, the security force commander, pausing to watch the activity at their targeted cluster of slot machines.

'I thought Huey was supposed to come up with something to keep him busy when the program was scheduled to cut in.'

'He was,' Maxine said through tight lips, 'but obviously he hasn't. Well, there's only one thing to do.'

'What's that?' Laverna said as Max started forward.

'Provide the distraction myself,' the crime leader explained, flashing a quick smile. 'Besides, I think it's about time the two of us talked directly.'

'Good evening, Captain Jester.'

The Legionnaire commander turned and smiled vaguely at being addressed by name.

170

'Good evening,' he said with reflective politeness.

'I was wondering if I might buy you a drink?' the woman continued.

The Legionnaire smiled. 'Thank you, but I'm on duty.'

'I see. I thought you might be able to make an exception this time. My name is Maxine Pruet.'

As expected, that caught Phule's entire attention, though he made a deliberate effort to remain outwardly casual.

'Of course,' he said. 'Forgive me for not recognizing you from your picture.'

'What picture was that, Captain?'

'Well, it was two pictures, actually,' Phule said. 'One profile, one full face.'

For a moment Maxine's eyes narrowed dangerously, then she caught herself and smiled again, though a little forced this time.

'No need to be insulting, Mr. Phule,' she said levelly. 'You probably know as well as I do that I've never been arrested.'

'Quite right.' The commander nodded, and for a moment a flash of weariness showed on his face. 'I'm sorry . . . that was a cheap shot. You just caught me a bit by surprise, is all. Here, let me take you up on that drink.'

As he spoke, Phule stopped one of the cocktail waitresses with a gesture and plucked two glasses from the tray of complimentary champagne she was distributing.

'Here,' he said, passing one to Maxine. 'What shall we drink to? Somehow I don't imagine you're eager to drink to the success of the Fat Chance.'

'Not for a while, anyway,' Max purred. 'How about "To honorable enemies and dishonorable friends"?'

'I think I can accept that.' The commander chuckled, raising his glass in mock salute. 'We seem to have at least that much in common.'

Maxine hid her irritation as she returned his gesture. She had hoped to lead Phule off to one of the cocktail lounges, but instead they were standing near the targeted island of slots . . . too near for her comfort.

'I was wondering if you could answer a question for me,

171

Captain?' she said, drifting slowly along the aisle as if to get a better view of the tables.

'Depends on the question,' Phule answered, but followed along, apparently unaware that they were moving.

'Why exactly did you join the Space Legion, anyway?'

The commander gave a slow smile.

'Within the Legion,' he said, 'it's generally considered impolite to ask that question.'

'How very interesting,' Maxine drawled. 'However, I'm not *in* the Legion, nor have I ever been overly concerned with being polite.'

Phule hesitated, then shrugged.

'Oh, just call it a rich boy's whim,' he said dismissively.

'I find that very hard to believe,' Max pressed, unwilling to let the subject drop.

'How so?'

'In the simplest terms, Mr. Phule, I doubt that anyone in your position has gotten where they are by whimsical or casual thinking. No, I believe you have a specific purpose behind nearly everything you do, *including* joining the Space Legion.'

The commander glanced at her sharply.

'How very perceptive of you,' he said. 'You're right, of course. I'll admit that much. I'm afraid, however, my reasons will have to remain my own. While I can't fault you for asking, you must also be aware that people in my position don't *stay* on top by sharing their plans with others, particularly not with the opposition.'

'Opposition,' Maxine repeated, wrinkling her nose. 'Really, Mr. Phule. You have such a delicate way of phrasing things. You *must* meet Laverna sometime. Perhaps it's a result of your common background in financial maneuverings, but you both tend to walk around a subject verbally rather than acknowledging it for what it is.'

Again Phule was forced to smile. Despite himself, he found himself liking Maxine more and more.

'Old habits die hard, I guess,' he said. 'Of course, the Legion itself tends to feed the pattern by encouraging, if not requiring, double talk. For my own information, how would *you* describe our relationship?'

'Why, we're rival commanders in a gang war for control of this casino, of course,' Max said with an easy shrug, then, noting his frown, she continued, 'Come now, Mr. Phule. Surely you don't see this as a conflict between the forces of light and darkness . . . with yourself on the side of the angels?'

'Actually I was thinking that you're the second person who's recently described me as the leader of a band of criminals,' the commander explained with a wry smile. 'While it's no secret that Legionnaires often have spotted pasts, I'd rather hoped for a better public image.'

'Spotted pasts,' Max exclaimed with a quick bark of laughter. 'There you go again, Mr. Phule, trying to verbally tie a ribbon around the neck of a hardworking mule. We provide the brains and direction for a pack of criminals and live off the profits. There's no other way to accurately describe it.'

'I'm sorry, but I can't agree,' the Legionnaire said, shaking his head, 'though I'm sure you intend it as a compliment to view me as an equal. I prefer to think of what I'm doing as assisting certain individuals in finding constructive, beneficial applications for their talents. For proof, let me remind you that we were *assigned* to protect this casino at the request of the *proper* owner, and that we don't stand to profit from our efforts beyond our normal wages.'

'I suppose you have a point, Captain,' Maxine returned easily. 'I can't honestly say, however, that I see your position as an improvement on my own. I've always found that people work harder for direct benefits than for a straight wage.'

The commander nodded. 'We're in agreement there. However, sometime you might consider whether or not there are direct benefits to the individual that can outweigh monetary gain. In the meantime, if you'll excuse me, I must return to my duties. It's been a pleasure talking to you.'

Realizing both that Phule was about to break off the conversation and that there had been no sign that the expected run on the slots had begun yet, Maxine cast about quickly for something to prolong the discussion.

'Just a moment, Captain,' she said, laying a restraining hand on his arm. 'There's someone I'd like you to meet.'

Without further explanation, she led the Legionnaire commander over to the line by the cashier's window, which was, of course, another half dozen yards farther away from the slot machines.

'Excuse me . . . Jonesy?' she said, lightly touching the shoulder of one of the men waiting for more chips.

The young Oriental turned with a smile, then started visibly when he saw the black-uniformed figure who was accompanying Max.

'I don't believe you two have met,' she continued, as smoothly as a society hostess at a reception. 'Jonesy, this is Captain Jester, commander of the security force for this casino. Captain Jester, this is Jonesy.' She bared a few extra teeth in a smile. 'Of course, that isn't his real name, obviously, but that's what he's asked us to call him.'

'Captain Jester.'

'Jonesy.'

The two men eyed each other with open wariness. Neither offered to shake hands.

'Jonesy, here, is visiting us from . . . I guess you'd call it one of our sister organizations.' Maxine smiled. 'His superiors have expressed an extreme interest in how you and I manage to work out our differences.'

The Oriental gave a small movement of his shoulders. 'I'm afraid, Captain, that curiosity is only natural for those in our line of work. Should we ever find ourselves . . . how should I put this? . . . in a similar relation to you that Mrs. Pruet is, I trust you will accept that there would be no personal rancor involved. I'm sure that, if anyone, *you* would understand that business is business.'

'Of course,' Phule answered through tight lips. 'In return, might I suggest that you inform your superiors, from me, that if they choose to visit Lorelei to witness our methods firsthand, I will do my best to see they are treated with the

174

same hospitality as we have shown Mrs. Pruet and her organization?'

Jonesy's eyes flickered slightly.

'I'll be sure to do that, Captain,' he said with a small bow. 'Now, if you'll excuse me, they're holding a seat for me at one of the tables.'

'I don't think he likes you, Captain,' Max said softly as they watched the Oriental walk away.

Phule smiled humorlessly. 'I think I can live with that. Then again, I don't think he was particularly happy with you, either, for singling him out that way.'

Maxine gave an unladylike snort.

'Believe it out not, Mr. Phule, the possibility of Jonesy's associates appearing on Lorelei is even less appealing to me than it is to you. Besides, as I said earlier, "honorable enemies and dishonorable friends." I considered it a matter of courtesy to make you aware of what you might be up against someday.'

'I see,' the commander said, looking at her thoughtfully. 'All right, I guess it's up to me to return the favor. Do you see that man sitting at the far right on the end blackjack table? The pale one?'

Maxine craned her neck slightly, then nodded.

'Well, realizing your interest in collecting casinos, he's someone you might want to watch out for in the future.'

'Really?' Max said, studying the indicated individual. 'What is he? A card cheat?'

'Not hardly,' Phule said easily. 'In fact, we've taken steps to screen out as many known cheats as possible – part of our job as security, you know. It might be of interest to you that we've already sent over a hundred of them back to the spaceport so far today.'

Maxine digested this news in silence for a few moments.

'That's quite a claim, Captain,' she said at last, speaking slowly and carefully. 'Might I inquire as to how you managed to detect them?'

'It wasn't that difficult,' the commander said. 'We had spotted most of them during the past week, along with the dealers who were feeding them bad deals and extra chips.

175

Tullie Bascom, the new casino manager, helped us pick out the rest. It seems he knows most of them on sight. Once they were identified, it was just a matter of picking the right time to weed them out without disrupting the legitimate guests, and I felt today was the right time.'

'Tullie Bascom.' Max said the name as if it tasted bad. 'I thought he had retired. For that matter, I was under the impression that Huey Martin was the manager.'

'He was,' Phule confirmed. 'Unfortunately he was also weeded out today. Some question as to whether he was working *for* the house or against it, if I understand correctly.'

'I see.'

'However, I was about to tell you about the gentleman at the blackjack table,' the commander continued, as if unaware of Maxine's reaction to his disclosure. 'His name is Albert, and he heads a team of computer auditors – some of the best I've ever worked with.'

'Computer auditors,' Maxine echoed tonelessly.

'Yes. I highly recommend him if you ever feel the need to have your central computer's programming checked.' Phule locked eyes momentarily with his rival. 'I know you'll find this hard to believe, but Albert there discovered that someone had been tampering with the Fat Chance computer. According to him, someone had put in a time-triggered program which would have drastically changed the payment odds on the progressive slot machines at midnight tonight.' He made a show of looking at his watch. 'We had him correct it, of course, but I was curious to see who might be watching those slots at midnight and what their reactions would be when the machines simply continued to eat the money instead of paying out millions like they expected. Now, here it is nearly half past and all I've done was talk to you. *C'est la guerre*, I guess. I really must be going now, but it *has* been a real pleasure spending time with you, Mrs Pruet.'

With that, he gave her a mock salute with his index finger, then turned and walked away, smiling.

Watching him go, Maxine did not share his smile. Rather,

the look she focused on him was not unlike that of a snake watching a supposedly flightless meal disappear into the clouds.

'Max . . . I think we've got problems,' Laverna hissed, materializing at her side.

'What's that, Laverna?' Maxine blinked, tearing her eyes away from Phule's retreating back.

'I said we've got problems,' her aide repeated. 'It's been nearly half an hour since midnight, and those damn machines aren't – '

'I know,' Max snapped, cutting her off. 'Tell those idiots to stop feeding *our* money into the house's coffers. And don't bother being subtle. The gambit has been blown and countered.'

'It has?'

'Just *go*,' Maxine said. 'Come up to the room when you're done and I'll fill you in on the details. Right now, as you pointed out earlier, every minute's delay is costing us money.'

'On the way,' Laverna said, and headed for the slots with a speed quite unlike her characteristic amble.

'*Mr. Stilman!* A moment, if you please?'

At her summons, the ex-astroball player floated over to her.

'Yes, Mrs. Pruet?'

'I want you to take over the floor operations for a while,' she said. 'See if you can arrange some sort of incident to remind Mr. Phule's troops that we haven't forgotten them completely. I need some time to rethink things.'

'Is something wrong?'

'It seems I've underestimated our Mr. Phule . . . Rather badly, at that,' Max admitted, shaking her head. 'I'll be in my suite with Laverna trying to figure where we go from here.'

Preoccupied as she was with her own thoughts as she headed for the elevators, Maxine failed to look directly at her violence specialist after she spoke. If she had, her usually alert warning signals might have been triggered by the rare, slow smile that spread across Stilman's face.

177

Chapter Twelve

Journal #236

One would think that the key turning point of this particular assignment was the event chronicled in the last chapter, the grand opening of the Fat Chance Casino, when my employer's forces successfully prevented the implementation of Maxine Pruet's multifaceted assault on Gunther Rafael's financial resources.

While there is no denying the importance of that skirmish, viewing the conflict from ground zero, as is my privilege, I would have to say that the events immediately following the opening were in many ways far more crucial to the eventual outcome of the confrontation.

Nicknames tended to abound among gamblers. What was more, certain nicknames were recurring almost to the point of being traditional. Thus it was that anyone in the gambling circles named Edward would invariably be hailed as 'Fast Eddie.'

Lucas, however, had managed to avoid the obvious title of 'Lucky Luke' and was known to his associates simply as 'Lucas.' This was, in part, because he strove for, and achieved, a certain degree of anonymity in the casinos, dressing and acting the part of an accountant or an actuarial on vacation. Mostly, however, the nickname was avoided because Lucas didn't think of himself as a gambler. He thought of himself as a crook, and luck had nothing to do with his success.

He was a meticulous planner, which was fortunate

because the type of theft he favored required careful attention to detail and timing. In fact, he had been scouting the Fat Chance for nearly a week before he decided that a score was possible, and passed the word to the other members of his team who were scattered through the other Lorelei casinos.

The plan Lucas used required five people working in close cooperation, though, of course, great care was taken to be sure the pit bosses and casino security would not be able to spot that they even knew each other, much less were functioning as a unit. Their target was the craps table, where the odds were nearest to favorable to the player, and even more favorable with their system. It was a complicated system which involved the shooter palming one of the die as he threw while another player dropped a loaded die onto the table as if it were one of the original pair. A third player would snatch up the dice and throw them back to the shooter, covertly switching them for a pair of honest dice as he did it, so that even if the house got suspicious and examined the dice, they would be clean. Two other players were at the table solely to create a diversion at the crucial moment, while the fifth, Lucas, placed the bet.

The beauty of the system was that the very number of players necessary to work it would make the pit bosses reluctant to believe they were being taken. The one placing the big bet wasn't the shooter, who would be betting the table minimum, and the shooter himself would never be vulnerable to being caught with the crooked die. While they could only work a gag a couple of times in a given casino without drawing undue attention, at the 'adjusted odds' a few times was usually enough.

The other necessary ingredient to the scam was a sloppy croupier, which was much of what Lucas had been watching for the last week. It was also why he had chosen this time for the team to assemble for work.

The crowds from the opening-night festivities had thinned to a point where there were several seats available at the various tables. More important, the pit crews were tired from the crush and were openly glancing at their watches as if they could speed the end of their shift by willpower alone.

Lucas had been sitting at the target table for nearly an hour, carefully building the pattern of a slow loser who would bet heavily occasionally in an apparent effort to recoup his losses. The croupier was behaving as he had for the last several nights, splitting his attention between the table and a shapely cocktail waitress who winked at him in passing with increasing frequency as the end of their shift neared. Whether they were flirting or lovers, Lucas neither knew nor cared. What was important was that the croupier wasn't paying attention to what was happening at his table.

One by one, his team had drifted in and eased into their places with apparent casualness, until they were only lacking one member before they could swing into action. In spite of his confidence and control, Lucas felt his excitement starting to build. In another fifteen minutes, they'd either have scored their hit or scattered, looking for another target.

'Your dice, sir.'

Lucas gathered up the dice and began shaking them slowly in preparation for his throw. This wasn't the big score, of course. He'd be the bettor, not the shooter, when they were ready for that. He was simply marking time and taking his turn in the rotation of shooters until the team was assembled.

Out of the corner of his eye, he saw the last team member drifting toward their table, pausing to watch the action at the other tables in his show of indifference. They were just about ready to go.

'Come on, *seven*,' Lucas said almost automatically as he raised his hand to throw the dice and . . .

'Just a moment, sir!'

A vicelike grip closed on his wrist. Startled, Lucas glanced around and discovered he was held by a black-uniformed security guard, flanked by two others.

'What . . .'

'Let's have a look at those dice . . . Hold all bets!'

Genuinely puzzled, Lucas surrendered up the dice he was holding to the guard with the red handlebar moustache.

He had no idea what had prompted this interruption, since he had done nothing to cause any suspicion, justified or not.

The guard barely glanced at the dice.

'Just as I thought,' he declared. 'Check his pocket, Do-Wop . . . the left-hand jacket pocket.'

Before Lucas could gather his wits to protest, the greasy-looking guard next to him had plunged a hand into the indicated pocket and emerged with . . .

'Here they are, Sarge. Just like you thought.'

Lucas gaped at the pair of dice the guard was holding aloft. *There hadn't been any dice in that pocket . . . or anywhere else on his person, for that matter!*

'But . . .'

'Thought you'd pull a little switcheroo, eh, sir?' The moustached guard smiled. 'I think it's time you moved along . . . if you'll follow me. No harm done, folks! Just keeping the Fat Chance tables honest. Reclaim your bets and pass the dice to the next shooter!'

Lucas barely noticed the shocked faces of the other team members as they faded back into the casino crowd. His entire attention was arrested by the firm hands gripping his arms as he was propelled gently but steadily toward the casino entrance.

'But I'm a guest at this hotel!' he managed at last, still trying to make sense of what had happened.

'Not anymore, you aren't, sir,' the sergeant informed him. 'You'll find your luggage waiting for you outside.'

'But I didn't do anything! Honest!'

While he might have accepted the risks of his chosen profession, Lucas shared everyman's belief and indignation at being found guilty of a crime when he was, in fact, innocent.

'I know that, sir.' The sergeant winked. 'We just got tired of waiting for you is all. Now, if you'll step this way?'

Things suddenly snapped into focus in Lucas's mind.

'Wait a minute,' he said. 'If my luggage is waiting, then somebody had to have packed it before you . . .'

Wrenching his arms free from his captors, he stopped

181

dead in his tracks and pointed an accusing finger at the sergeant.

'You set me up!' he proclaimed. 'There wasn't anything wrong with the dice I was holding! And he . . . he *planted* that extra pair in my pocket!'

'Quite right, sir,' Moustache said smoothly. 'The dice *were* yours, though. We just took the liberty of moving them from your room into your pocket is all.'

'My room?'

'Yes, sir. If I might suggest, sir, it's unwise to keep an extra couple dozen pairs of dice in your luggage when staying at a casino. It tends to make nasty blokes like us suspicious, and not everybody's as nice and understanding as we are.'

'What . . . you searched my luggage? *Before* I did anything?'

'Just looking out for the owner's interests, sir,' the sergeant said.

'But that's . . . that's . . .'

'Illegal? Quite right, sir. It would seem that you're not the only crook on Lorelei, but, of course, you already knew that. The *real* trick, sir, is not getting caught. Now, if you'll step this way?'

Sprawled at a table near the open front of one of the casino's cocktail lounges, Doc and Tiffany watched the procession march past.

'You know,' Doc said, 'that actually looks like it would be fun. Maybe I should put in a request to stand regular duty once in a while. If nothing else, it would justify wearing these uniforms all the time.'

The actress made a face as she sipped her drink.

'It's *got* to be more fun than troweling makeup onto Dee Dee the Dip five times a day,' she said. 'Wouldn't you know that, after making that big fuss about not wanting a live stage crew, now the computer's been dry-cleaned, she's insisting we keep working the shows?'

'All I have to do is work the curtains,' Doc said, 'but I know what you mean. Still, I suppose it's closer to show business than standing around watching drunks lose money day in and day out.'

'Maybe for you, Doc, but you're used to working behind the scenes. For someone like me who's used to being in view in some capacity or other, working support is a real comedown. At least standing guard would be role-playing of sorts.'

The stuntman cocked an eyebrow at her. 'You sound kinda down, Tiff. Anything bothering you?'

'This just isn't what I expected when I signed on is all,' she said with a grimace. '*Or* after our surprise briefing, either.'

'I see,' Doc said, then shifted in his seat to stare pointedly at the ceiling. 'This wouldn't have anything to do with your efforts to charm our captain, would it?'

Tiffany glared at him for a moment, then broke into a rueful smile.

'Bingo.' She laughed. 'You know, when we were on the ship on the way here, I thought that he was just busy planning this operation, and that I'd see more of him once we got settled in. The way it's worked out, though, what with us working the showroom, I see even less of him than I did on shipboard.'

Smiling, Doc signaled the bartender for another round.

'To be honest with you, Tiffany,' he said, 'I don't think it would make much difference. From all I can tell, our Fearless Leader is pretty much married to his work. Everyone I've talked to says pretty much the same thing – that they don't get as much time with the captain as they would like, while at the same time muttering that they're afraid he's pushing himself too hard. All in all, I don't figure him as being much for play, no matter how tempting the bait is or how often you wave it at him.'

The actress smiled and laid a hand on his arm.

'Thanks, Doc,' she said. 'That helps a little. Maybe it's because I'm spending so much time in front of a makeup table these days, but more and more I catch myself staring in the mirror and wondering, "Have you lost it? Has time finally run out?" I guess a bit of insecurity goes with the job . . . or with being a woman, for that matter.'

'Well, for what it's worth, *I* don't think you've lost it,' the stuntman said with a wink. 'That's not just *my* opinion, either. In case you haven't noticed, Junior has a real thing for you.'

'I *know!*' Tiffany exclaimed, rolling her eyes. 'I'll tell you, Doc, I don't know what to do about him. It seems like every time I turn around he's there offering to run an errand for me or just staring at me like I just stepped off a half-shell or something. I mean, he's a nice enough kid and all that, but he's just that – a kid!'

Doc grinned. 'He's not *that* young. You should talk to him sometime. He's really quite mature mentally. And it might help him to see you more as a person than as a goddess.'

'I might give that a try. You know, when it comes right down to it, he's really kind of . . .'

'Excuse me?'

The two broke off their conversation as a young woman in a short, tight skirt, possibly one of the show girls, stepped up to their table.

'I thought you should know . . . there's a man hurt outside.'

'What?' Doc frowned, momentarily confused by the change in focus.

'In the alley beside the casino,' the woman said, 'there's a man lying on the ground.'

'What makes you think he's hurt?'

'I don't know . . . He's not moving. He may just be drunk. I didn't get that close. I just thought I should tell someone, and you're the first people I've seen in a uniform.'

'Thanks,' Doc said. 'We'll look into it.'

'We will?' Tiffany said, cocking her head as the woman marched away.

'Sure. Why not?' the stuntman said, rising to his feet and digging out some money for their bill. 'Weren't we both just complaining about being stuck backstage? Besides, remember that as far as the guests are concerned, we're as much security guards as anyone else in a black uniform. It would be out of character for us to try to find someone else to send instead of going ourselves.'

The actress glanced around the casino, but none of the regular troops were in sight.

'I suppose you're right,' she said, gathering up her purse. 'I guess we can handle it.'

'Sure we can,' Doc assured her. 'There's two of us and only one of him, and it sounds like he's drunk, to boot. Besides, if he gives us any trouble, we're armed, remember?'

He patted the tranquilizer pistol in the holster at his hip.

Tiffany rolled her eyes.

'*Please* don't start going macho on me, Doc. One of the things I like about you is that you don't strut.'

'Sorry,' the stuntman apologized easily. 'Hanging around with both actors and military types seems to bring out the melodramatic in me. Seriously, Tiff, I figure all we have to do is check to see what the problem is, then use our wrist radios to call for the appropriate help – if it's needed at all, that is. *That* much we should be able to do.'

Even though it was still technically 'indoors,' the open air along the Strip was a pleasant relief for the mock Legionnaires after days of close confinement in the casino showroom. Because of the size of the Fat Chance, it was a several-minute stroll to reach the alley – a service access for the loading docks, really – and they took advantage of it, moving at an unhurried pace as they drank in the sights and sounds of Lorelei.

'You know, this place is really something,' Doc commented as he shifted his gaze from the soaring light shows to watch the stream of people walking along the Strip. 'I can't remember how long it's been since I've been outside. I guess working backstage, it's easy to forget just where the stage is located.'

'Take away all the lights and glitz, and what you have left is more lights and glitz,' Tiffany agreed, then frowned. 'Say, speaking of being outside, didn't the captain say something about out jurisdiction only being *inside* the complex?'

185

The stuntman thought for a few moments.

'You know, you may be right,' he said finally. 'It seems to me there was something in one of those briefings. There were so many of them, though, I can't recall for sure. Oh well, we've come this far, we might as well take a look before we head back.'

The light dimmed radically a bare dozen steps into the alley. The casino light shows were designed to impress and lure the tourists on the Strip, not the hired help, and there was little point in wasting wattage on areas traveled only by residents and employees. Walking down the alley was like entering another world, a land filled with shadows and blind angles giving it such an air of gloom and menace that it was hard to realize there were lights and teeming humanity a stone's throw away.

'I don't see anybody,' Tiffany said nervously, peering into the almost impenetrable shadows that lined the access.

'Maybe he woke up and moved on,' Doc said. 'We'll just check a little further, then – uh-oh.'

'What is it Doc?'

'Just keep walking, Tiffany. Don't look back.'

Too startled to think clearly, the actress immediately shot a look behind them toward the mouth of the alley.

There were three men, faceless in the gloom but unmistakably heavyset, following the mock Legionnaires. When they saw Tiffany had spotted them, they quickened their pace as if to close the gap separating them from the pair.

'Doc . . .'

'Just keep moving, Tiff.'

'Shouldn't we call for help?'

'It may be nothing,' the stuntman said, though his tone said he didn't believe it himself. 'If it is, though, I don't think they'd give us time to use our wrist radios. No, I figure our best bet is to try to make it to the loading dock, then – *shit!*'

A lone figure appeared ahead, blocking their path . . . a figure that was noticeably larger than any of the three following them. It was as if the man had materialized out of the

186

shadows, though he stood so motionlessly that he might have been there all along and simply escaped their attention.

'Okay, listen close, Tiff. We don't have time to argue,' Doc murmured. 'The odds ahead of us are still better than what's behind us. I'm going to brace this character, and you're going to keep going. Got that? Don't stop, don't look back until you get to the loading dock. Once you're inside, get on the radio and tell them where I am and what's going on – but only *after* you're inside.'

'But . . .'

'*Just do it!*' the stuntman hissed, then started angling away from her.

'*Hold it right there, fellah!*' he called to the figure ahead, who was now moving toward them in a curious, floating stride. 'I *said* hold it!'

The figure kept coming, and Doc reached for his tranquilizer pistol . . . far, far too late.

The stuntman's work had given him experience in fight scenes and falls that looked quite impressive in the holos, but in actuality were planned and choreographed to minimize the risk of serious injury. The few real fights he had been in were of the barroom variety, and even those were far behind him since he had become much more of a homebody after his marriage. Nothing in his past, however, had prepared him to deal with, or even recognize the speed and agility of, a professional athlete . . . even a retired one.

His hand had barely touched the grip of his tranquilizer pistol when the oncoming figure accelerated with bewildering speed. Unable to even sidestep, Doc felt the air rush out of his lungs as the man slammed a massive shoulder into his midsection, then he was lifted and carried backward as the monster continued to drive forward, paying no more attention to the stuntman's weight than a bull would give notice to a towel dropped across its horns. Something smashed into Doc's back, and he thankfully lost consciousness.

Tiffany watched in horror, her orders to run forgotten, as the attacker stepped back from the wall, still carrying Doc's now-limp body, then flung it to the ground. Breathing heavily in what could only be described as animal growls, the man stared at her fallen companion for a moment, then kicked the still form savagely in the side.

That broke her trance.

Snatching her own tranquilizer pistol from its holster, the actress fired at the hulking menace.

There was a soft *pfutt* of compressed air when she pulled the trigger, but aside from that there was no indication that she had done anything at all.

She fired again . . . and again . . .

No effect.

In frustration, she hurled the weapon away and launched herself at the man's back.

He turned at the sound of her approach, then backhanded her lazily out of the air like a troublesome insect.

Tiffany hit the ground in a boneless heap and lay still.

'Big bad soldier boys, huh?' one of the men who had been trailing the twosome said, stepping out of the shadows where he had been waiting. 'They aren't so tough.'

Still coming down from the adrenaline high of battle, Stilman only grunted in response.

'Hey! This babe's a real looker,' one of the other men called, turning Tiffany over with his foot. 'Guess we're going to get a little pleasure with our business.'

Stilman's head came up with a snap.

'None of that,' he said sharply. 'We mess 'em up a bit to remind them they're playing out of their league, but that's *all.*'

'I thought Max said we could take the gloves off,' the man said sullenly.

In reality, Stilman wasn't even sure that Max would approve of what they *were* doing. He had put this ambush together on the strength of her *not* giving him his usual order to 'lay off the rough stuff.' Taking a couple of the security guards out of action should be okay, and it was certainly a welcome change for the boys not to have to keep their hands in their pockets during a brawl. Still, Max was a woman, and Stilman was almost certain that she'd get upset if the crew got *too* frisky with the female Legionnaire.

'Never mind what Max says,' he snapped. '*I'm* telling you to keep it impersonal. We're sending these guys a message to back off, and I don't want to confuse the issue with anything else. We're going to mess them up *period!* Got that?'

'Yeah. Sure.'

Turning back to his original victim, Stilman raised his foot and brought his heel down sharply on the fallen man's leg.

The sound of the bone breaking echoed briefly off the alley walls.

'Do something to her face,' he called back over his shoulder. 'Women are sensitive about stuff like that.'

'Beeker here.'

'Yo, Beeker! It's me ... Chocolate Harry.'

Leaning against the bar's back wall next to the public phone, Harry grinned as if the butler were standing in front of him instead of on the other end of the line.

'Hello, C.H. Sorry, but Captain Jester isn't in at the moment. If you'll just hold on, I'll have Mother patch you through to him.'

'Whoa! Hold on there, hoss! I was callin' for you, not the cap'n.'

The big man shot a glance around the bar to be sure no one was in hearing range, but the place was empty except for one couple sharing a late sandwich and beers.

'I see. Well then, what can I do for you, Harry?'

'I hear tell how you've been makin' a play for the Ice Bitch and thought I'd give you a call with a friendly warning. That's a real Stone Fox you're messin' with, bwana. Now, don't get me wrong ... you're one hell of a man, but that gal will eat you alive, manners and all.'

There was a slight pause on the other end of the line.

'Are you, by any chance, referring to Ms. Laverna?'

'That's the one.'

'Well then, I appreciate your concern and advice, Harry, but the truth of the matter is that Laverna and I are getting

189

along rather well. In fact, I find her one of the warmest, kindest people I've met for some time.'

'No foolin'?' The ex-biker was genuinely impressed. 'Beeker, either we're talkin' about different women, or I'd be greatly obliged if you'd give me a few pointers on technique sometime over a few brews.'

'I'd be glad to,' the butler's voice came back. 'But I'm sure how much help I can be. I've never really considered my conduct with women as being "technique." In fact, I make a point of being myself rather than trying to impress them, and the response has been favorable, for the most part.'

'Hmmm. I dunno. There's got to be more to it than that,' Harry said. 'Every time I've tried bein' myself with the ladies, they tend to look around for a cop.'

That got a laugh from Beeker.

'Of course, Harry, you should remember that when it comes to being oneself, you and I are notably different people. Still, I'll be willing to chat with you on the subject sometime, if you'd like.'

'All right, my man, it's a date. Just say when and where, and I'll be there with a notepad.'

'It will probably have to wait until this assignment is over,' Beeker said. 'I'm of the impression that while it's on, we're to avoid each other's company publicly, for the sake of secrecy.'

'Yeah, I know.' Harry sighed heavily. 'Well, let me know when you think it'll be all right.'

There was another moment's pause.

'Are you all right, Harry?' the butler said at last, a note of concern creeping into his voice. 'Forgive me if I'm prying, but you sound a little down.'

'I guess I am . . . a bit,' the ex-biker admitted.

'What's wrong? Is it anything you'd like to talk about?'

'I dunno . . . It's just that . . .' Harry struggled for a second, then the floodgates went down and the words came in a rush. 'I just feel kinda cut off out here . . . out of the information loop, you know? One of the things I've always liked about the cap'n is that he always made sure I knew what was goin' on, even when it didn't involve me direct. Now I only hear about some of the things that are happenin', and even then it's after the action is over. For the most part, I just stand around here and polish glasses and wonder what's goin' on with the crew. I'll tell you, Beeker, it's gettin' to me. You know, it seems like more and more often I see somethin' or think of somethin' and turn to point it out to the guy next to me, only there's no one there. I mean, there're folks here and all, but no one I can talk to. Know what I mean?'

'If it's not pointing out the obvious, Harry,' the butler observed once the ex-biker had run out of words, 'it sounds to me like you're lonely.'

Harry thought for a few beats, then his face split in a wide smile.

'Damn! You know, I think you're right, Beeker! Son of a gun! That never occurred to me . . . I guess 'cause I've never been lonely before.'

'Excuse me, Harry' – Beeker's voice was gentle – 'but don't you mean that until recently, you've *always* been lonely?'

If it was from anyone else, Harry would have simply laughed at the suggestion, but he had a great deal of respect for Beeker, so he gave the idea serious thought.

'I never thought of it that way,' he said slowly, 'but . . . you know, it's funny. When I first heard about this assignment, I was really lookin' forward to bein' out on my own again . . . gettin' away from uniforms, and maybe mixin' with a few of the folks like I used to hang around with. The way it is, though, I just can't get into it. There's even another biker here who keeps wantin' to talk about old times, but I have trouble gettin' fired up to brag about how bad the old club used to be. In fact, the more I think about it, the more it seems we ran on bullshit – all the time tryin' to impress each other with how tough we was so's nobody would think we was afraid. The fact is, the only place I've felt comfortable just bein' *me* is with the cap'n and the troops.'

'I can't say I'm surprised, Harry,' the butler said. 'Of course, I've been with Mr. Phule for a long time now and watched the effect he has on those around him. Let me assure you that you're not alone in your reactions. After a lifetime of feeling one has to pretend to be something he's not, finally meeting someone who can not only accept but appreciate people as they are tends to generate – '

'Excuse me, Beeker,' Harry interrupted. 'Hang on just a sec.'

A flurry of activity at the door had caught the ex-biker's attention. Four men had just trooped in, Stilman the obvious leader. Paying no attention to Harry, they took seats at a table and noisily called for a round of drinks.

'It's okay, Beeker,' Harry said. 'Just a little movement in the enemy troops. What was that you were sayin'?'

'Just that many people who had long since resigned themselves to being alone or the oddball in any given group, find that . . .'

Harry was only listening with half an ear, the rest of his attention focused idly on the table of heavies.

They seemed to be in a good mood, shaking hands and patting each other on the back, and he caught the flash of Stilman passing out thick envelopes, presumably full of money, to the other three men.

'Hold on, Beeker,' Harry said, still eyeing the table of men. 'There may be something goin' on here. You might want to pass the word that . . .'

He broke off in midsentence, his blood suddenly turning ice cold.

Stilman had produced two objects from his pocket and was holding them up for inspection. From the back of the room, the ex-biker couldn't see too clearly, but he didn't have to. He'd know those things from a mile away. He should . . . he'd issued enough of them.

Stilman was holding two of the company's wrist radios.

'Harry?' came Beeker's voice in his ear. 'Are you there? What is it?'

'Listen close, Beeker,' Harry growled into the phone, barely recognizing his own voice. 'I may not have time to say this twice . . . got me? Tell the cap'n to run a body count on the company. Fast. I think someone's in trouble.

Only . . . listen up. Beek . . . be sure to tell him not to use the wrist radios for the check. In fact, tell him to pass the word to be careful what gets said over the radios *period*! It looks like the opposition has gotten hold of a couple of 'em, so there's a good chance they'll be listenin' in . . . for a while, anyway. You got that?'

'Got it, Harry,' the butler shot back. 'Do you want him to get back to you when he's done?'

'Tell him not to bother. I'll get back to him later if I can.'

'Harry, are you in trouble? You sound –'

'Just tell the cap'n,' the ex-biker said hurriedly, and broke the connection.

Stilman had just gotten to his feet and, after one last round of handshakes, was heading for the door.

Forcing himself to move casually, Harry strolled behind the bar.

'Can you cover for me for a few, Willie my man?' he said. 'I gots to slip out for a minute.'

'I suppose so,' the other bartender said. 'It's not like it's real busy, or – hey! What's up?'

Harry had been fishing around under the bar, but now he straightened up holding a sawed-off pool cue loosely in one hand. Effectively a lead-weighted club, it was kept to break up fights and happened to be one of Harry's favorite weapons.

'You really don't want to know,' he said with a wink. 'In fact, you haven't seen a thing, right?'

'If you say so.' Willie shrugged, and pointedly turned his back.

Holding the weapon close to his side so it would not be noticed easily, Harry headed out of the bar, hurrying slightly to make up for the lead Stilman had on him.

Tiffany looked smaller stretched out in the clinic bed, the sight tugging at Phule's heart and conscience as he had known it would. He had been stalling making this visit since he heard the doctor's appraisal of the extent of the actress's injuries, even to the point of prolonging his conversation with Doc. The stuntman had been in surprisingly good spirits, remarkably good considering his two broken legs, and had even succeeded in putting the Legionnaire commander relatively at ease over the incident. That feeling had fled, though, upon first viewing Tiffany's bandaged face, draining away as if someone had pulled a plug in his mind and let his hastily constructed defenses run out like so much water.

She seemed to be asleep, and after a few silent moments Phule started to leave.

'Hi, Captain.'

'Hello, Tiffany,' he said, forcing a smile as he turned back.

'I don't suppose you know anyone who's casting for *The Mummy's Bride*, do you?'

The actress's hand came up to touch her bandages.

'I . . . I don't know what to say, Tiffany,' Phule stammered. ' "I'm sorry" doesn't start to express what I'm feeling.'

'Sorry about what?' Tiffany said, raising herself slightly on her pillow. 'You warned us it might be dangerous when you gave us that first briefing, and you gave us a chance to back out then. If anything, it's *our* fault, because we went against your set procedures. We were the ones who decided to play soldier on our own, going outside the hotel and not bringing one of your regular troops along.'

The commander shook his head.

'I never imagined it would come to this,' he said. 'If I had, I never would have – '

'Listen to me, Captain,' the actress interrupted. 'It's *our* fault, not yours. Okay? If *I* don't blame you, don't go blaming yourself. I never should have let Doc talk me into tagging along.'

'I'm sure Doc didn't think that – '

'Hey! I'm not trying to hang this on Doc, either,' Tiffany said hurriedly. 'I've been making my own decisions for a long time and living with the consequences, good or bad. I'm a big girl now, in case you haven't noticed.'

'Oh, I've noticed, all right,' Phule said, smiling in spite of himself. 'Don't think that I'm *totally* insensitive or blind.

It's just that running this outfit is taking a lot more of my time and attention than I had expected, and I really can't afford any distractions right now.'

'A distraction, eh? Well, that's something,' the actress murmured.

'Excuse me?'

'What? Oh, nothing.' She managed to let him see her close one eyelid in a broad wink. 'At least *now* I know what it takes for a girl to get you into her bedroom.'

The smile disappeared from Phule's face as if someone had turned out the light.

'Since you're awake, Tiffany, I wanted to tell you not to worry about . . . about the damage to your face. I've already put in a call for a plastic surgeon, and we'll be covering all the expenses *and* continuing your salary for however long it takes to erase any trace of what's happened.'

'I know. The doctor told me, except . . .' The actress turned her face toward the commander. 'You know, it's funny. I was still groggy from the painkillers he gave me, but I think he said something about Maxine Pruet covering all the expenses.'

Phule's expression tightened slightly.

'I know,' he said. 'I was told the same thing. We'll see about that. You just get some rest and concentrate on getting better and don't worry about where the money is coming from. *I'll* take care of dealing with Mrs. Pruet.'

He started to ease toward the door.

'In the meantime,' he continued, forcing a lighter tone into his voice, 'be sure to let me know if there's anything I can do.'

'Well . . . there *is* one thing, Captain.'

'What's that?'

'When you talk to the surgeon . . . Is there any chance he could do a little work on my nose at the same time? I've always thought it was too big, and since he'll be operating, anyway . . .' She let her voice trail off.

'Consider it done.' Phule smiled, more confident now that Tiffany hadn't been merely putting on an act for his benefit. 'I'll be sure he confers with you on what the final result should be, and you can make any adjustments you want.'

'Thanks, Captain,' she said. 'I suppose it sounds silly, but – '

'Excuse me, Captain?'

They looked around to find Doc's son standing in the doorway to the room.

Tiffany waved. 'Hiya, kid! Welcome to the horror show.'

'Hello, Tiffany.'

'Hi, Junior,' Phule said. 'Your father's right down the hall. He was awake a little while ago when I talked to him.'

'I know, Captain,' the youth said. 'I've already been to see him, thanks. You're the one I was looking for.'

'Oh?' The commander glanced quickly at Tiffany. 'I was just finishing here, if you'd like to step into the hall.'

'No, here is fine. In fact, I want Tiffany to hear this, too.'

'Okay. What's on your mind?'

'Well . . . the others asked me to talk with you, since I was coming over anyway to visit Dad.' The youth seemed suddenly uneasy. 'What it is, is . . . well, we all appreciate what you told us, about paying off our contracts and sending us back to Jewell, but – '

'What? Wait a minute!' Tiffany broke in. 'You didn't tell me anything about *this*, Captain.'

'It didn't concern you,' the commander said tersely. 'Not for a while, anyway. You were saying, Junior?'

'Well, sir,' the youth continued, squaring his shoulders, 'we'd like you to reconsider your decision. We want to stay on until this thing is finished. As far as we're concerned, nothing has changed from the original agreement.'

'Nothing?' Phule scowled. 'That isn't how *I'd* describe what's happened to your father and Tiffany.'

'I can't speak for Tiffany,' the youth said. 'But my father's had broken bones before. It goes with the job. As for the rest of us, we were warned of the possible danger involved in this deal, and we accepted it. Just because it's become a reality hasn't changed the terms of our contract. We're all ready to go on working for you if you'll let us.'

'All of you?'

196

'Well, we haven't had a chance to check with Tiffany,' the boy admitted. 'That's why I wanted to discuss this in front of her.'

'You can add my vote to that, kid,' the actress said firmly. 'It looks like I'll be stuck here for a while, anyway, but . . .' She pulled herself up into a sitting position, hugging her knees to steady herself. 'Let me tell you something, *Mister* Phule. You may be some kind of hotshot in the business world, or even the military, but it seems you have a lot to learn about show business.'

'I guess I do,' the commander said, shaking his head slightly. 'Would either of you care to enlighten me?'

Tiffany gave an unladylike snort.

'It appears you have the common misconception that entertainers are hothouse flowers that have to be babied and protected. Well, nothing could be further from the truth. Our profession has never really been socially acceptable, and anyone who makes a living at it has had to put up with physical and mental abuse as a norm, not as an exception. You may think of the theater as being sophisticated and artsy, but our roots are in traveling troupes that were closer to carnivals and snake-oil shows than any black-tie opening night.'

'We're *used* to butting heads with the locals,' Doc's son supplied calmly. 'It's almost like we're gypsies, and being hassled or exploited – *or* blamed for whatever goes wrong in the near vicinity – gets to be *expected* after a while. Usually we have to knuckle under and go along with things or risk being run out of town. *This time*, though, we've got the forces of authority on our side for a change. Heck, we *are* the forces of authority.'

'What the kid's trying to say, Captain,' the actress added, 'is that we may be temperamental and sometimes quit a job in a huff, but *nobody* runs us off a stage . . . except maybe the director or stage manager. In this case, that's *you*. Now, if you tell us that we're not performing up to snuff or that you have to make some budget cuts, that's one thing. But *don't* tell us we're being pulled from the cast for our own good. You hired us because we're all pros . . . "real troop-

197

ers" as the phrase goes. These yokels can't even *imagine* a situation bad enough to close us down if *you* say it's all right to keep working.'

'The show must go on, eh?' Phule smiled wryly.

'That's about it,' the youth said.

'All right.' The commander sighed, reaching a decision. 'Pass the word that any of the actors who want to stay on, can. Oh, and son . . . ?'

'Yes, sir?'

'There's a tradition in the Space Legion that lets a recruit choose his own name when he signs on, and suddenly I don't feel comfortable thinking of you as "Junior". Is there anything else you'd like to be called?'

The youth's face split in a sudden smile.

'Well, sir,' he said, 'I think I'll take my cue from the lovely lady here. Why don't you just call me "Trooper"?'

'Consider it done,' Phule said. 'Pass the word on that as well, and be sure to give everyone my personal thanks.'

'Thank you, sir!'

The youth drew himself up and gave a snappy salute.

'Thank *you*, Trooper,' the commander corrected with a smile, returning the salute.

'That was nice, Captain,' the actress said after the youth had departed. 'Would it be a horrible imposition to ask if I could give you a kiss before you left?'

'Tiffany,' Phule said with mock solemnity, 'it would be a pleasure.'

The phone rang on the bedside table.

'*Damn!*' the actress snarled, then caught herself and smiled again. 'Don't go away, Captain. I'm going to hold you to that kiss.'

'I'll be right here,' the commander promised.

The phone rang again, and the actress reached for it.

'Hello? . . . Who? . . . Oh . . . No, I'm fine, thank you. It's nice of you to ask.'

Catching Phule's eye, she covered the phone's mouthpiece with one hand while silently mouthing a name.

Maxine Pruet.

The commander's face hardened, and he held out his hand for the phone.

'Mrs. Pruet?' he said. 'Captain Jester here.'

'Good evening, Captain.' Max's voice came after only the slightest pause. 'I was going to call you next, but I should have known you would be there.'

'Yes . . . Well, I just wanted to tell you that while we appreciate the gesture of your offering to cover the medical costs, they're being paid by the Space Legion. We take care of our own.'

'I'm aware of that, Captain . . . now more than before, I'm afraid.'

'Excuse me?'

'I was going to extend my personal apologies for what happened tonight, as well as my assurances that it was not done at my orders. It seems, however, my apologies would have been a bit premature . . . all things considered.'

'Forgive me, Mrs. Pruet, but I don't know what you're talking about.'

'Oh, come now, Captain. I'm sure neither of us believes in coincidence. Do you really expect me to accept that it was sheer chance that Mr. Stilman was brutally beaten so soon after his attack on your members?'

'You can believe what you like,' Phule said tersely, 'but whatever happened, I'm unaware of it.'

'I see.' Max's voice was thoughtful. 'Very well, Captain, I'll believe you . . . if for no other reason than I can't think of why you would claim ignorance if you *were* responsible, since there has clearly been provocation. I'll admit that it struck me as strange that you'd use outside help rather than your own troops. For your information, however, the person responsible for the attack on your people tonight, Mr. Stilman – I believe you're familiar with the name, if not the person – is currently receiving medical attention for a shattered kneecap as well as multiple breakage to his jawbone. As I said, the coincidence is a bit too much for credibility, so I suggest you make inquiries within your own forces as to who ordered the attack.'

'Excuse me, did you say that he's here? At this clinic?'

'No, Captain. He's at another facility. We have several clinics here on Lorelei, though it's not highly publicized. I felt it would create an unnecessarily messy situation if he were treated at the same location as your people. In fact, I'll be having him shipped off-station for intensive care on the next available ship. While I am far from pleased with his independent action, we take care of *our* own, too.'

'I see.' Phule frowned. 'I was hoping I could speak with him directly about who it was who attacked him.'

'His injuries make it impossible for him to talk, Mr. Phule.' Maxine's voice was momentarily cold. 'But he can write. I suggest that you confine your investigation to your own people to determine who ordered the attack. We already know who *executed* it.'

'Who was it?'

'I already said that it was not one of your Legionnaires, Captain, and as the attack did not take place on the premises of the Fat Chance, I don't believe it's any of your concern. Now, if you'll forgive me, there are things which require my immediate attention.'

With that, she broke the connection.

Phule frowned at the receiver for several moments before gently placing it back on its cradle.

'What is it, Captain?' Tiffany said, noting the expression on his face.

'I'm not sure,' the commander admitted. 'It seems that the person who attacked you and Doc has been . . .'

A shrill beep from his wrist communicator interrupted him. Despite the urgency of the sound, Phule stared at it for a few moments before answering the signal. There were only a few of the command communicators such as he was wearing, so the radio silence order did not preclude the use of the exclusive channels. Still, he had left orders with Mother that he was to be disturbed only for an emergency while he was visiting the clinic.

'Phule here,' he said, finally opening the line.

'Sorry to bother you, Captain,' came Mother's voice without any of her usual banter, 'but things are popping back here at the casino and I thought you should know about it.

First of all, we've got the two missing communicators back, and – '

'Wait a minute. Who got them back?'

'It was the sergeant . . . Chocolate Harry, I mean.'

'Harry! I should have known.' Phule grimaced. 'Listen, Mother. Pass the word: I want Harry pulled in *fast!* The opposition's looking for him. I don't care if it means sending out a team to escort him in, we've got to – '

'That's what I'm trying to tell you, Captain,' Mother broke in. 'He's already in. We've got him up in your suite. He's hurt, but he won't let us call a doctor. You'd better get back here pronto.'

The supply sergeant was stretched out on the suite's's sofa attended by Beeker and a small group of hovering Legionnaires when Phule arrived back at his room. He was stripped to the waist, and even from the doorway the commander could see the massive purple bruise that showed even against his dark skin, stretching from armpit to hip and across a large part of his rib cage.

'Hello, C.H.,' he said. 'It's good to see you again.'

'Hey, Cap'n,' came the weak response. 'How's it goin'?'

The sergeant shifted his huge form, and Phule realized with a start that he was trying to rise.

'Just stay where you are,' he said, moving quickly to Harry's side. 'Well, I hear you've been busy tonight.'

'You heard that, huh?' C.H. grinned, sinking back into his pillows. 'Busier'n I expected, that's for sure. Man, that dude was fast! If I hadn't gotten his kneecap with my first shot, he would have cleaned my clock. Even as it was, he got me a good lick before I put him to sleep.'

He gestured vaguely at his bruise with the opposite hand.

'So I see,' Phule said sternly. 'I want a doctor to look at that, Harry. No arguments.'

'Don't do it, Cap'n,' Harry wheezed, shaking his head. 'I've been knocked around before, and this's nothin' more'n a few cracked ribs. I'm pretty sure the Max has the local medics in her pocket, and you bring one of 'em up here, she's gonna *know* I'm with you, and maybe start lookin' around to see who else might be Legionnaires in civilian clothes.'

The commander hesitated.

'*Please*, Cap'n,' the sergeant pressed. 'I'll be all right . . . really. Just let me get some sleep, and I'll be good as new.'

Phule pursed his lips, then nodded.

'Beeker,' he said, 'I want you to stay close to Harry tonight. Watch him close. If there's any indication he's hurt worse than he's telling us, I want you to call me . . . cancel that. Call a doctor, *then* call me.'

'Certainly, sir.'

'The rest of you, clear out of here and let the man get some rest. We'll keep you posted as to his condition.'

'One more thing, Cap'n,' the prone sergeant said, raising his head painfully.

'What is it, Harry?'

'The bulletproof material our uniforms are made of? Well, Stilman's outfit was made of the same stuff, probably standard issue for their troops as well. I don't think our tranquilizer guns will work against it.'

'Don't worry, C.H.,' Phule said grimly. 'I already planned to have heavier armaments issued to everyone and to put an around-the-clock guard on Gunther. It looks like things are starting to get rough.'

'Yeah, well, you might want to find that salesman and see about gettin' some of your money back.' Harry grinned humorlessly as he let his head ease back down. 'That stuff may stop penetration, but it ain't much good against impact. If he wants to argue, I bet there are four people who will be glad to give him a demonstration that he's wrong!'

Chapter Thirteen

Journal #244

Despite the ominous turn events had taken, the next several days passed without incident. Although this proved to be merely the quiet before the storm, it nonetheless gave my employer the opportunity to indulge in a few of the more civilized elements of life.

I refer here to eating, which to me requires specifically sitting down to eat rather than simply wolfing down a sandwich, a hamburger, or some other form of 'energy pellet' fast food while continuing with one's duties. This was a luxury I noticed my employer allowed himself less and less of late.

I had long since abandoned any effort to convince him that it might be desirable for him to sleep more than one or two hours at a time.

'I've *really* got to get going soon,' Phule declared, glancing at his watch again. 'I'm overdue to check on the troops.'

'Relax, Captain,' Sydney said, reaching for the wine bottle once more. 'Those roughnecks of yours are more than capable of taking care of themselves without you hovering over them . . . or they *should* be. Besides, I thought the whole point of those snazzy communicators you wear was so they could get in touch with you if anything important happened.'

'I suppose you're right,' the commander said, though he glanced involuntarily at the restaurant door even as he spoke. 'I guess I've been edgy ever since Tiffany and Doc got jumped, and I'm not particularly confident that the troops will always check with me before they swing into action, as you well know.'

'Don't remind us, Willard,' Jennie Higgens said, wrinkling her nose slightly as she held her own glass out to her cameraman for a refill. 'I mean, we've accepted your apology and all, but don't push your luck. You know, I can't help but feel we'd *still* be cooling our heels under guard if you hadn't remembered I had been to nursing school before signing onto the glamorous world of broadcast news. How is Harry, by the way?'

'He seems to be coming along fine,' Phule said. 'At least, it's getting more and more difficult to keep him horizontal while he's mending. Fortunately I think he's met his match in Beeker. Incidentally I want to thank you again for taping him up.'

'I've had a lot of practice with that, though I'm better on bone bruises,' the reporter said. 'In case the subject ever comes up, don't ever let anyone con you into thinking that field hockey is a ladylike game. It can be as rough or rougher than lacrosse – at least the way *we* used to play it.' She paused and cocked an eyebrow at the Legionnaire commander. 'Maybe I shouldn't mention it, but you *are* aware, aren't you, that that's the fifth or sixth time you've thanked me for patching up the sergeant?'

'Is it?' Phule frowned, rubbing his forehead with one finger. 'Sorry. I don't mean to be redundant. I seem to be a bit forgetful lately. I guess I'm a little tired.'

The reporter and the cameraman exchanged glances. It had been impossible not to notice the lines of fatigue etched into Phule's face, though they had both been careful not to comment on it.

'Oh well.' The Legionnaire commander shrugged and forced a smile. 'The one thing I *can't* thank you enough for is your willingness to sit on this story – for a while, anyway. I know how much it must mean to you.'

'No, you don't,' Sydney muttered, glancing away as he took another sip of his wine.'

Jennie shot him a dark glare, then turned back to the conversation.

'It's nice of you to thank us,' she said easily, 'but really, Willard, reporters aren't *totally* insensitive, no matter what you've heard – the good ones, anyway. It's easy to see that publicizing what you're doing would endanger your undercover operatives, so it's no big thing for us to hold off for a while.'

'Well, Jennie,' Phule said carefully, 'contrary to popular belief, *I'm* not totally insensitive, either. What was that you were saying about my not really knowing how much this story means to you, Sydney?'

'What?' The cameraman blinked in surprise at suddenly being the focus of the conversation. 'Oh . . . nothing.'

The Legionnaire commander leaned back in his seat, his arms folded across his chest, as he looked back and forth between his two dinner companions.

'Now, look,' he said. 'I've been up-front and candid with you two in this whole deal – probably more than I should have been. I don't think it's asking too much for you to return the favor. Now, what is it that I don't know about your involvement with this story?'

Uncomfortable silence hung in the air for a moment. Then the reporter shrugged her shoulders.

'Tell him, Sydney,' she said.

The cameraman grimaced before he spoke.

'I guess loose lips really *do* sink ships,' he said. 'All right, Captain. What I was so carelessly referring to is that both our jobs are on the line for this assignment. The news director wasn't particularly convinced that there was a story here, but Jennie kept leaning on him until he agreed to send us, but on the proviso that if we didn't come up with something to justify the cost of the trip, we needn't bother coming back, and whatever benefits or severance pay we had coming would be applied against the cost of the wild-goose chase.'

'Why, Jennie?' Phule said.

'Oh, he just made me mad,' the reporter admitted. 'He acted like I was making the whole thing up to get the news

205

service to pay for a passion-filled vacation on Lorelei for Sydney and me. I kept trying to convince him it was a legitimate story and . . . well, when he got around to making his 'take it or leave it' offer, I couldn't refuse or it would look like he was right all along.'

'Interesting,' the commander said. 'But what I meant was, why didn't you want to tell me about this?'

Jennie shrugged. 'I don't know. I guess I didn't want it to seem like you were under any obligation to us. You have a habit of taking responsibility for everything and everybody around you, Willard, and I was afraid it would come across like we were trying to play on your generosity . . . or your guilt.'

'Well, this assignment has aged me a bit,' Phule said, a ghost of a smile flitting across his face. 'As somebody told me not too long ago, I figure you're both adults and capable of making your own decisions *and* living with the consequences. You two made the deal, and I assume you did it taking into account how much you were willing to risk against what potential losses. That makes it your business, not mine.'

The reporter smiled. 'Thank you, Willard. I appreciate that.'

'Of course,' the commander added carefully, 'if it turns out that you *do* end up in the ranks of the unemployed, I hope you won't hesitate to let me help you find a new position. That much I'd be willing to do whether or not the story in question involved me and mine.'

'We'll see.' Jennie grinned impishly. 'We're not dead yet.'

'Just one thing, Sydney,' Phule said, 'if you don't mind my asking. I notice you had your holo-camera gear along, and that's fairly expensive equipment. Is it your own, or does it belong to the news service? Would you have to send it back if things went bad?'

'Oh, it's mine,' the cameraman acknowledged. 'It's not the newest stuff available, mind you, but I've pieced together an adequate rig over the years. I figured that just in case the time had come for me to finally strike out on my own,

206

I should . . . Excuse me, but is this someone you know, Captain? She seems to be coming this way.'

The commander followed Sydney's gaze and saw a matronly woman in a loose-fitting almost bat-wing black dress approaching their table. While she seemed somehow familiar, he couldn't quite place her in his memory. As their eyes met, however, the woman smiled her own recognition.

'Good evening, Captain Jester. May I join you?'

The voice swept away any uncertainty.

'*Colonel Battleax?*' Phule gaped, rising reflexively to his feet. 'What are . . . Please . . . have a seat.'

The colonel graciously accepted the chair he held for her as if it was what she had been expecting all along.

'I . . . Excuse me, I don't think you've met,' the commander managed, still trying to recover from the shock of Battleax's presence in the middle of an assignment. 'This is Jennie Higgens and Sydney Nolan.'

'Ah yes, the reporter,' Battleax said, smiling sweetly as the two women shook hands. 'I believe we met briefly on Haskin's Planet.'

'That's right,' Jennie acknowledged. 'Back during the . . . investigation of Willard's handling of the alien invasion.'

'Well, I don't think *we* ever met. Not to talk, anyway,' Sydney interrupted, extending his own hand. 'I was behind the camera that day.'

'Of course,' the colonel said. 'I never did get a chance to thank you both for the coverage you provided. It made our job so much easier to have half the galaxy looking over our shoulder.'

'Umm . . . what brings you to Lorelei, Colonel?' Phule interjected, trying desperately to change the subject before things got bloody.

'Actually, you do, Captain.' Battleax smiled, showing a few extra teeth. 'You and your merry band of cutthroats. I think, however, our discussion of that should wait for another time – sometime, shall we say, more private? I wouldn't want to bore your guests with Legion chitchat.'

'We..uh . . . were just leaving, weren't we, Sydney?' Jennie said, rising abruptly to her feet.

'That's right,' the cameraman echoed, following her example. 'Thanks for the dinner, Captain. Nice seeing you again, Colonel.'

'That was really unnecessary, Colonel,' Phule murmured as the two left. 'Jennie and Sydney are okay.'

'Forgive me if I don't share your love of the media, Captain,' Battleax growled, her pasted-on smile slipping away, 'but my own experiences with members of the fifth estate have been less than pleasant.'

'So, to return to my original question,' the commander said, 'what are you doing on Lorelei? Forgive me, but I hadn't expected to see you – or anyone else from head-quarters, for that matter.'

'I was on Brookston when I caught the media coverage of your arrival here,' the colonel explained, 'and realized why Blitzkrieg was so eager for me to take my vacation. Since I was having trouble figuring out what to do with my off time, anyway, I thought I'd drop by to see how things were going.'

Phule made a few mental calculations and realized that to make the trip from Brookston to Lorelei by commercial transport, Battleax would have had to start her journey almost immediately upon seeing the newscast. Despite his surprise at her appearance, he was nonetheless touched by her obvious concern for himself and his troops.

'It was good of you to come,' he said, 'but we pretty much have things under control. I can probably get you a complimentary room, though, for the balance of your vacation. I have an 'in' with the management here, and Lorelei really is a spectacular place.'

He smiled warmly, but Battleax didn't return it.

'Uh-huh,' she said. 'Now, tell me the rest of it, Captain. *All* of it. What exactly is going on here?'

Phule hesitated for a moment, then heaved a heavy sigh.

'You've heard, huh? Well, let's just say that it's been a far cry from the easy duty in paradise that the general billed this assignment as.'

'Could you be a bit more specific, Captain?' Battleax said,

helping herself to some of the remaining wine. 'Remember, I just got here.'

'Well . . . how much do you know so far?'

'Not a thing,' the colonel said.

'But then how did you know . . .'

'That things were rough?' Battleax finished. 'Give me credit for a *little* intelligence at least, Captain Jester. It really wasn't all that hard to figure out. First, there's the fact that Blitzkrieg wouldn't give you a drink of water in a desert unless there was poison in it. That coupled with the timing of the assignment – waiting until he could deal with you without going through me – made the whole thing suspect from the beginning.'

She paused to take another sip of wine.

'Second . . . frankly, Captain, you look like hell. While I know you have a tendency to push yourself, you usually take better care of yourself than this – or, at least, that butler of yours does. It looks like you haven't slept in a week, and I'd be willing to bet it's because things are bad enough that you feel you have to oversee things *personally*, to a point where it takes priority over your own well-being. An admirable stance, perhaps, but still an indication that something's desperately wrong with this assignment. And finally . . .' The colonel fixed the commander with a steely gaze. 'I've made a point of keeping up on the Legionnaires under your command, Captain. I review their records and your reports on a regular basis. Even in the short time I've been here, I've noticed that there are several unfamiliar faces wearing Space Legion uniforms and I've recognized a few of your legenerates working as hotel staff. Realizing they all view you as their ringleader and wouldn't say boo to a goose unless they cleared it with you, I thought it best to come straight to the source for my information.' She leaned back in her chair. 'Now it's your turn, Captain. I want to know the truth behind what's happening on this assignment *before* I hear it from the media, for a change.'

Phule made a face and shook his head ruefully. 'It's a long story, Colonel.'

Battleax waved for a waiter and signaled for another bottle of wine.

'I've got time,' she said, settling into her chair.

Again, I am handicapped in my account by a lack of specific knowledge of the details surrounding an event or conversation which took place in my absence.

I do, however, feel I can state with some certainty that some form of the following exchange took place roughly in the time frame I am recording it here. I base this conclusion on the simple fact that Maxine Pruet is said to be a decisive leader, and it is doubtful she would have delayed long before implementing a decision once it had been made.

Shit!' Laverna declared, tossing down her pencil onto the nest of work sheets and notes in front of her. Like many of her profession, she preferred the old, manual form of doodling and numeric experimentation when trying to work out a problem.

'I know you don't want to hear this, Max, but my best recommendation is to throw in the towel and eat our losses on this one.'

'How so?' her employer prompted from the sofa.

Laverna tapped the table repeatedly with her finger, organizing her thoughts for several moments before she spoke.

'The time factor is the killer,' she said at last. 'We might be able to put together something that would hurt Rafael financially, but not in time to keep him from paying off the note to you.'

'Nothing at all?'

'Well, we *could* try to burn the place down to keep him from turning a profit at the tables, but then you'd have to rebuild from scratch once you took over . . . *and* figure out how to offset the bad publicity from the fire. Besides, he's probably got insurance for 'interruption of business,' so even *that* might not stop him.'

'In any case, I don't think we want to go *that* far,' Maxine said with a faint smile. 'No, I tend to agree with you

210

Laverna. In fact, I arrived at much the same conclusion yesterday.'

'You did?' Her advisor made no effort to hide the surprise in her voice. 'Then how come you've been having me—'

'There might have been an option I overlooked,' Max said. 'That, and I guess I've been stalling having to say it out loud. This isn't the first time I've been outmaneuvered, but it doesn't make me any happier about running up the white flag.' She rose and wandered over to the window. 'I think what irritates me the most,' she said, looking down at the inevitable stream of passing tourists, 'is that I can't figure out just how he managed to do it.'

'That's simple enough,' Laverna said as she gathered up her work sheets. 'The man used his money better than you used yours.'

'What do you mean?'

'Well, it's clear that he's been spreading bribe money around the staff pretty good – or, at least, better than we have. There's no way he could have pulled this off without a lot of inside information.'

'You think so? That's interesting. I assumed that Huey Martin provided him with all the information he needed.'

'Uh-uh. He got more information somewhere than what Huey had to sell. There have got to be other folks in this complex serving as his eyes and ears – and I don't mean the security guards.'

'Speaking of that,' Maxine said, 'has there been any word as to the whereabouts of that bartender? The one who so effectively removed Mr. Stilman from the picture?'

'Not yet,' Laverna said. 'I'll tell you, it's like the man vanished into thin air. He hasn't left Lorelei on any ship either as a passenger or as a crew member. We got that much from the watchers at the spaceport. The thing is, though, he hasn't shown up at any hotel on or off the Strip, either.'

'That's strange,' Maxine said thoughtfully. 'If nothing else, it should be hard to hide that hover cycle of his.'

'You'd think so,' her aide said. 'The only thing I can

figure is that he's holed up with someone – someone who's better at hiding things than we are at finding them.'

'Like young Mr. Phule, for example?'

Laverna eyed her employer for a moment.

'Excuse my asking, Max, but is he going to take the blame for *everything* that goes wrong for us from now on?'

'I'm not getting paranoid *or* obsessive – not yet, anyway.' Maxine smiled. 'Think about it for a moment, Laverna. It makes sense. We have a network of spotters all through this space station. We should be able to locate anyone in a relatively short time, yet this one gentleman who is rather memorable in appearance eludes our efforts. Now, where is our current blind spot – or, at least, where our web is the thinnest?'

'Right here at the Fat Chance,' Laverna admitted.

'Correct,' Max said. 'Now, add to that our suspicions that the attack on Mr. Stilman was not entirely coincidental – that there is some link between our fugitive and the forces under Mr. Phule's command.'

'I thought he told you that he didn't have anything to do with it.'

'He may have lied,' Max said, 'though I somehow doubt it. What he specifically said, though, was that he didn't *know* anything about it. It's my guess that one of his subordinates indulged in a little independent action, just as Mr. Stilman arranged the attack on *his* own. Anyway, with those two pieces – our lack of information on the internal workings of the Fat Chance and the possible connection between our missing bartender and someone in the security force – I don't think it's unreasonable to conclude that he might be hiding right here, in this complex.'

Laverna thought about it.

'It's possible,' she said. 'It still bothers me, though, that they used free-lance help instead of going after Stilman themselves. That doesn't make sense.'

'It may have been to keep their own hands clean if anything went wrong,' Max said. 'Besides, young Mr. Phule hasn't been averse to hiring outside specialists before. Look at the computer auditors he sneaked in on us.'

'That's true,' her aide said. 'You know, that's something else that's been bothering me.'

'What's that?'

'Well, for some things, like the computer jockeys, they've been going outside, but for the crew that was working the stage at the showroom, they used their own people. I would have thought that they'd hire some specialists for that, too.' She shook her head. 'Oh well, I guess it's just that he had some show business people in the Legion, but nobody who really knew computers.'

'Just a moment, Laverna.' Max was suddenly alert. 'Say that again.'

'What? You mean about there not being any computer experts in the Space Legion?'

'No, before that. You said he must have some show business people in his force.'

'That's right. So?'

'So what if all the security force *aren't* from the Space Legion? What if some of them are actors?'

'You mean stand-ins?' Laverna frowned. 'That's interesting. I guess if that were the case, I'd be wondering where the soldiers were they were replacing.'

Maxine was staring into the distance. 'I was just recalling something Mr. Stilman said – about how he wasn't impressed by the security force, but that the complex had the toughest *staff* he had ever run into. What if young Mr. Phule decided early on that uniformed guards were of limited value, and that instead he was going to put a portion of his force to work under cover, seeding them through the staff as waitresses or cooks?'

'Or bartenders!' Laverna supplied. 'That would explain the guy who jumped Stilman!'

'Of course that means he hasn't restricted himself to infiltrating the staff for this complex,' Maxine continued thoughtfully. 'He could have people anywhere, including as guests.' She snapped her fingers suddenly. 'Weren't you saying a moment ago that he must have had more information about our plans than Mr. Martin could provide? Who have we shared our plans with recently? In detail?'

'Jonesy!' her aide gasped. 'You mean – damn! Posing as someone from the Yakusa. Now, that takes brass!'

'Audacity seems to be something young Mr. Phule is not lacking in – or his troops, for that matter,' Max said grimly.

The two women lapsed into silence, each analyzing this new hypothesis.

'Well,' Laverna said finally, 'I guess that clinches it. Without knowing how many he's got scattered around or who they are, I don't see any way we can put something together by the deadline.'

'Oh, it's true that we'll probably have to abandon our efforts to gain control of this enterprise,' Maxine said, 'but that doesn't mean I'm ready to quit the field. Not just yet, anyway.'

Her aide frowned. 'I don't think I follow you.'

'There's a fallback, contingency plan I've had in mind for some time now. Something that will at least recoup our investment *and* give us a chance to pay young Mr. Phule back for his interference. Now seems an appropriate time to implement it.'

'What plan is that?'

'It's really simply a matter of shifting our aim from a target which is defended to one which is not. Actually, Laverna, you deserve at least part of the credit for this. You gave me the idea yourself back when Mr. Phule arrived on Lorelei with his troops.'

'I did?'

'Certainly. I recall specifically your pointing out that young Mr. Phule comes from a *very* rich family.'

Beeker was jarred awake by the discordant jangle of the phone next to his bed. Bleary-eyed, he glanced at his watch to see how long he had been asleep, but abandoned the effort when he realized he had no recollection of when it was he had gone to bed. Not for the first time, he found himself annoyed with the Lorelei timetable, or lack thereof, which made any adherence to a schedule next to impossible.

The phone rang again.

Rather than reaching for the instrument immediately, the

butler took a moment to compose himself. Perhaps business tycoons could function while giving the impression of being rushed and harried, but that simply wouldn't do for one in his position.

Again the phone jangled.

'Beeker here.'

'Beeker, what the hell's going on there?'

The voice was a surprise, not so much for its statement as in its identity. Even in its agitated condition, the butler had no difficulty recognizing it as belonging to Paul Phule, his employer's father.

'Unfortunately, sir, I am unable to reply to that query – at least until you have calmed yourself sufficiently to properly identify yourself.'

'Oh. Sorry. This is Paul Phule, Beeker, and–'

'Ah yes. Good evening, Mr. Phule. How may I help you?'

'You can start by telling me what's going on there on Lorelei!'

The butler rolled his eyes in exasperation. He had hoped that by forcing his caller into following formal protocol, the elder Phule would also be coerced into discussing rationally whatever it was that was bothering him. Clearly, however, this was not to be the case.

'Events on Lorelei are meticulously chronicled by the media, sir,' he said. 'Or is there something specific you require information on?'

There was a long pause on the other end of the conversation.

'Look, Beeker,' the voice came at last, grim but in control. 'Are you trying to be cute or do you really not know what's going on? I just got a call from some old dragon who says she's holding Willard, and that unless I pony up a hundred million, they're going to ax him or shove him out an air lock or whatever the hell they do to kill someone out there.'

'I see,' the butler said. 'No, Mr. Phule. I assure you this is the first I've heard about it.'

'Do you think it's on the up-and-up?'

'Yes, sir. I believe I know the parties involved, and they do not strike me as the sort to attempt to bluff on something

215

of this magnitude. I'm afraid the probability is quite high both that they have your son and that they'll kill him if you fail to pay the ransom.'

'Damn it, Beeker! How could this happen? He's supposed to have a whole troop of soldier boys around him. No – scratch that. From what I hear of this Space Legion, I wouldn't trust them to guard a piggy bank. But you! How could you let this happen, Beeker? I always thought you were one of the best in the business.'

'I try, sir,' Beeker said, unruffled. 'We all do. Your son, however, has a mind of his own as well as an unfortunate flair for the unorthodox. Taking that into account, I'm sure you'll realize the difficulties involved in watching over him.'

'I know all about his independence,' the elder Phule growled darkly. 'I guess I knew this was bound to happen sooner or later.'

'Excuse my asking, Mr. Phule,' the butler said, seizing the pause in the conversation, 'but is it still the policy of Phule-Proof Munitions and yourself that no extortion payments are to be made under any circumstances, regardless of who or what is being threatened?'

'That's right,' the voice confirmed. 'Once you start paying, there's no end to it. We pay taxes to the government for protection, and that should be the end of it. If more people were willing to stand up to criminals and terrorists –'

'Yes, I'm familiar with the argument,' Beeker interrupted. 'Tell me, Mr. Phule, would it be too much of a compromise of your principles to withhold your refusal for a while – say for forty-eight hours?'

'No. They said they'd call back and broke the connection before I could say much of anything. If they call back, I can try to stall them, but – '

'Fine,' the butler said, cutting the elder Phule short again. 'Then if you'll be so good as to clear the line, sir, I'll see if anything can be done to bring the situation to a satisfactory conclusion from this end.'

'Right . . . and Beeker?'

'Yes, Mr. Phule?'

The voice on the other end of the line was suddenly very

weary, as if anger had been the only thing giving it strength and now that that emotion had been vented there was nothing left.

'Be careful not to . . . I mean . . . I know he and I have had our differences, but he's still my son, and . . .'

'I understand. I'll try, sir.'

As soon as the connection was broken, the butler abandoned any pretense of nonchalance.

His face set in a grim mask, he hurried through the door that connected his bedroom with the suite's main living area. Chocolate Harry was asleep on the sofa, having stubbornly refused to move into one of the beds normally used by the suite's residents, and Beeker moved quietly so as not to wake him. It was his intention to check his employer's bedroom in the vain hope that this was all some sort of ghastly prank, but before he reached the other bedroom door something caught his eye. There, on the chair next to the door into the corridor, were the sidearm the Legionnaire commander normally wore and his wrist communications command unit.

The butler stared at the items for a few moments, then sank into a chair and turned on a lamp.

'Hey, Beeker!' Harry said, awakened by the light. 'What's up?'

Beeker ignored him, bending over his own wrist communicator as he depressed the Call button.

'That you, Beeker?' came Mother's voice. 'What are you doing up at this hour? I thought—'

'Give me an open channel to Lieutenants Armstrong and Rembrandt,' the butler said tersely. 'And Mother? I want you to listen in as well. We have an emergency situation, and there's no point wasting time going over the information twice.'

Chapter Fourteen

Journal #245

As near as I can determine, Maxine Pruet was either ignoring the presence of the Space Legion company under my employer's command or operating under the old assumption that if you cut off the head, the body dies.

To say the least, this was an error in judgment.

The removed of my employer from his position of leadership did not cause the company to wither and die, but rather unified and intensified their already substantial energies. That is, it had the effect of removing the emergency brakes from a locomotive and putting it on a straight, downhill stretch of tracks.

One of the Fat Chance's conference rooms had been hastily commandeered for the company's emergency war council, but even that was growing crowded. In an effort to keep the meeting manageable, the room had been cleared of everyone except cadre and officers, which is to say those holding the rank of corporal or higher, and a few concerned individuals, like the Voltron, Tusk-anini, who refused to budge and whom no one had the energy or courage to chase out. A large crowd of Legionnaires loitered and hovered in the hall just outside, however, muttering darkly to each other as they waited for a course of action to be decided upon.

All the undercover Legionnaires had been recalled, though not all had taken time to change into their Legion uniforms, giving the assemblage the appearance of being a catered party rather than a planning session. This impression would be shattered, however, upon viewing the faces of the participants. The expressions ranged from worried to grim, without a single smile in evidence.

The focus of the group was on the company's two lieutenants, who stood on either side of the conference table reviewing a stack of floor plans, stoically ignoring the faces that peered anxiously over their shoulders from time to time.

'I still don't see what this is supposed to accomplish, Remmie,' Armstrong grumbled, picking up another sheet from the stack. 'We don't even know for sure that he's still *in* the complex.'

Though he was from a military family and had consequently had more experience with planning, the same background had also made Armstrong a stickler for protocol and chain of command. Lieutenant Rembrandt's commission predated his, making her the senior officer and his superior, and he deferred to her as much from ingrained habit as from courtesy.

'It's a starting point, okay?' Rembrandt snapped back at him. 'I just don't think we should start tearing the whole space station apart, dividing our forces in the process, until we're sure they aren't holding him right here. It's our best bet that he's being held here somewhere, since I don't see them running the risk of being spotted while trying to move him out of the complex. That means we've got to take the time to check out all the out-of-the-way nooks and crannies in this place before we go barging around outside – and there are a lot of them.'

'You can say that again,' Armstrong said, scowling at the sheet he was holding. 'As long as we've been here, I never realized how many access corridors and service areas there were in this place.'

'Hey! Look who's here!'

'C.H.! How's it goin', man?'

The officers looked up as the company's supply sergeant made his way into the room through the waiting crowd,

219

smiling and waving his response to the greetings that marked his arrival.

'Come on in, Harry!' Rembrandt called. 'Good to see you back in uniform.'

Indeed, Chocolate Harry was decked out in his Legionnaire uniform, complete with – or incomplete, as the case may be – the torn-off sleeves that were his personal trademark.

'Good to *be* back, Lieutenant,' the massive sergeant said. 'Hey, Top! Lookin' good!'

He waved across the room at Brandy, still in her housekeeping uniform, who interrupted her conversation with Moustache long enough to give him a grin and a wink.

'Excuse me, Sergeant,' Armstrong said, 'but the last thing I heard you were on the inactive list. Aren't you supposed to be convalescing?'

'What? For this?' Harry gestured at the bandages around his torso that peeked through the armholes of his uniform. 'Heck, I hardly remember that I got hit . . .'cept if someone should happen to want to give me a good ole hug.'

He dropped his voice, but maintained his grin, though his eyes glittered darkly as he met Armstrong's gaze with a hard stare.

'Besides, there ain't no way I'm gonna sit this one out – not with the cap'n in trouble – and with all due respect, Lieutenant, I'd advise you not to try to change my mind. You ain't nearly big enough – or mean enough.'

He waited until Armstrong gave a small, reluctant nod of agreement, then raised his voice again.

''Sides, I brought along a few goodies just to be sure I'd be welcome. That is, they should be along any – *there they are! Bring 'em on in, boys!*'

Half a dozen of Harry's team of supply clerks, also known to be the biggest thieves, scroungers, and con artists in the company, were coming into the room, towing or pushing a small caravan of float crates. From their appearance, even while still sealed, it was apparent what they contained, and a small cheer went up from the crowd.

'Just line 'em up along this wall here!' the supply sergeant instructed, grabbing the first long crate himself and manipulating the float dial until it settled on the carpet. With a flourish, he punched a combination into the lock's keyboard, and the crate lid hissed open.

'Help yourself!' he declared, then thought better of it. 'No . . . cancel that. Form a line! Jason! I want 'em to sign for whatever they take! We gotta be sure we know who's got what so's we can go after 'em if it don't come back in good shape.'

As expected, the long, flat cases held the rifles and other long arms that had been packed away when the company was pulled from their old duty as swamp guards. The square crates held ammunition.

'Well, I guess that solves our firepower question,' Rembrandt said, frowning at weapons being passed out, but making no move to object or interfere as the Legionnaires seized the armaments and scattered through the room, each of them clearing, checking and loading his or her weapon of choice.

'I just figured that whatever goes down, it don't hurt to have a few extra persuaders close to hand.' Harry winked, then his face sobered. 'All right, what have we got so far?'

'Not much,' the senior lieutenant admitted. 'Until we can figure out where they're holding him, there's not much we can do. The trouble is, everyone wants to be here. It's all we've been able to do to keep the duty crew at their posts while we're working this out . . . Which reminds me . . .'

She raised her wrist communicator to her lips and pressed the Call button.

'You got Mother!' came the quick response.

'Rembrandt here, Mother,' the lieutenant said. 'How are you holding up?'

'I'll tell you, if it wasn't for every mother's son and daughter in this outfit wanting personal updates every fifteen minutes, it'd be a real breeze.'

The lieutenant smiled despite the pressure she was feeling. 'You want some help?'

'Oh, don't you mind my carping. I got it covered – for the time being, anyway. You just keep working on figuring out where the captain is and let me worry about keeping the wolves at bay.'

'All right, Mother. But holler if it gets too much for you. Rembrandt out.'

She turned her attention to the floor plans once more.

'Now, the way I see it, the most likely places are here and here.' She indicated two points with her finger. 'We need to have someone run a quick check . . . Brandy?'

'Here, Lieutenant,' the top sergeant said, stepping forward.

'Do you think we could–'

'*Pardon* me!'

The commander's butler was standing in the doorway.

'What is it, Beeker?'

'I . . . I don't mean to intrude,' Beeker said, looking uncharacteristically uncomfortable, 'and, as you know, I have no official standing in your organization, but in this instance we share a common interest – namely, the well-being of my employer – and I believe I have some information you might need in your planning.'

'Don't worry about your standing with us, Beek,' Rembrandt said. Like everyone in the company, she had a great deal of respect for the butler – more than most, since he had assisted her when she was recruiting the actors for stand-ins. 'What have you got?'

'I . . . I can tell you where Mr. Phule is being held.'

'You can?'

'Yes. I can say definitely that he's currently in Maxine Pruet's suite – room 4200. At least, he was fifteen minutes ago.'

Rembrandt frowned. 'Hey, Sushi! I thought you said the suite was empty!'

'No one answered the phone when I called,' the Oriental said. 'I didn't actually check it out, though.'

'I see . . . Okay. Brandy? I want you to use your passkey and see if–'

'Excuse me . . . Perhaps I didn't make myself clear,' Beeker interrupted, his voice taking a slight edge. 'I said that my employer is *definitely* being held in that suite. There should be no need for confirmation. In fact, any effort to intrude might endanger the lives of both Mr. Phule *and* whoever was sent to check.'

The lieutenant pursed her lips, then shot a glance at Armstrong, who gave a small shrug.

'All right, Beeker,' she said at last. 'Not to say I don't believe you, but would you mind telling me just how it is you're so certain that's where he is?'

The butler's haughtiness slipped away, and he glanced around at the gathered Legionnaires uneasily.

'It's . . . well, it's a secret technique I've developed to ease my duties in keeping track of my employer's comings and goings. I'd ask that you all keep this in strictest confidence, just as I have respected the secretive nature of the things some of you have shared with *me*.'

He looked around the room again and was answered by an assortment of nods. 'Very well. I've taken the liberty of sewing small homing devices into each item in my employer's wardrobe, both civilian and military. This gives me forewarning of his approach so that I might be prepared to welcome him, and allows me to pinpoint his location at any given moment.'

Armstrong gasped. 'You've bugged the captain's clothes?' Struggling between laughter and incredulity, he spoke for the whole room.

Beeker winced. 'You might say that, sir. I, myself, prefer to think of it as a necessary technique for providing the exceptional service which justifies my salary, which, as you might assume, is well above the scale normal for one in my profession.'

'Whatever!' Rembrandt said, pawing through the scattered floor plans. 'The bottom line is that you're *sure* he's being held in the old dragon's suite.'

'Yes, ma'am,' the butler said. 'If I might add, there seems to be a rather muscular gentleman standing guard outside her door as well. That, at least, is easily confirmed by anyone who bothers to take the time.'

He sent a withering glance toward Sushi, who shrugged apologetically.

'One guard? That one's mine!' Brandy declared. 'Might as well get some use out of this Fifi the Maid outfit before I turn it in for good.'

'You want any help, Top?' Super Gnat offered.

'For *one* guard? From up close when he's not expecting it?' The Amazonian top sergeant flexed her sizable right hand, then clenched it into a fist and smiled broadly. 'I don't think so.'

'All right, then, we have a target area!' Rembrandt declared, studying the sheet of paper which had finally come to hand. 'Let's see . . . we've got a large living room flanked by two bedrooms . . . one door that . . . Heck with this!'

She strode over to the nearest wall and paused for a moment, rummaging through her belt pouch. Producing a tube of lipstick, she began sketching a larger version of the floor plan directly on the wall in long, broad strokes.

'Okay, gather round!' she called back over her shoulder. 'Now, the corridor runs here, parallel to the three rooms. Sushi, do you know if they've moved the furniture at all, or is it like it is here in the plans?'

'Let me see,' the Oriental said, moving to her side for a better view of the floor plans. 'I only saw the living room area, but – '

'What's going on here?'

Colonel Battleax was standing in the doorway. Still dressed in her bat-wing black dress and towering in her anger despite her diminutive size, she might have been a demon from an opera production as she dominated the room with her voice and presence.

The Legionnaires froze in their places. While they had all heard that the colonel was in the complex, no one had expected her to appear at their meeting.

'My God! This looks like an armament trade show! I don't even *recognize* half these weapons!'

While it was well known that Willard Phule was supplementing the company's equipment from his personal fortune, what was not as widely known was that he was also using his connection with his munitions-baron father to obtain new weaponry which was still in the testing stages and not yet known, much less available, to the general market.

'Do I need to remind you all that you're Space Legionnaires and have only *limited* authority for using *reasonable* force on civilians?'

The company exchanged nervous glances, but still no one moved.

'Well, this Wild West show is going to stop *RIGHT NOW*! I'm ordering you to turn in all arms other than sidearms, and – '

'Just a minute, Colonel!'

Lieutenant Rembrandt, her face flushed and her limbs rigid, broke the tableau. Like the Red Sea, the crowd parted to open a corridor with the two women at either end.

Standing against the back wall with Trooper, Lex watched the confrontation with professional curiosity and interest. Though neither Battleax nor Rembrandt was shouting, both were using what could only be called a 'command voice,' which involved a controlled projection from the diaphragm that any stage actor would envy.

'In Captain Jester's absence,' Rembrandt declaimed, '*I'm* the acting company commander of this outfit. What gives *you* the right to try to give orders to *my* troops?'

'Are you *mad?*' Battleax sputtered. 'I'm a colonel and the ranking officer present—'

'—who is on vacation and *not* in the current chain of command!' Rembrandt snarled. 'Our original orders came directly from General Blitzkrieg. You have no authority over us on this assignment! In fact, as far as I'm concerned, you're just another *civilian*.'

'*WHAT?*'

'My general orders state that I am to hold my command *until properly relieved*, and I do not accept you as *proper relief!*'

The colonel gaped at her for a moment, then shut her mouth with a snap.

'Interpreting the Legion's general orders is *not* within your authority, *Lieutenant!*'

'So *court-martial* me!' Rembrandt shot back. 'But until

225

I'm found guilty and *formally* removed, these troops are under *my* command, not yours!'

Battleax recoiled, then glanced around the room. The Legionnaires displayed a variety of expressions ranging from sullen to bemused. It was clear, however, that they stood with Rembrandt, and there was no visible support for her own position.

'I see,' she said through gritted teeth. 'Very well, if you want proper authority, I'll get it! A call to General Blitzkrieg should settle this. I'd advise you all not to do anything rash until I get back.'

She started for the door, but was stopped short as Lieutenant Rembrandt's voice shattered the sudden silence.

'All right! I want you all to bear witness to this! As of *now*, I'm using my authority to declare *martial law!*'

'*What?*' Battleax shrieked, any trace of poise or dignity slipping away at the outrage. 'You can't do that! No one in the Space Legion has ever—'

'I've *done* it,' Rembrandt returned grimly, 'and it stands until someone overrules it. Someone with more available firepower than I have!'

'But . . .'

'Lieutenant Armstrong!' Rembrandt barked suddenly, turning her back on the colonel.

'Sir!'

'There is an *unauthorized civilian* interfering with our operation. Have her removed and held under guard until further notice.'

'Yes, *sir!*'

'Have you all gone—'

'Sergeant Brandy!'

'Got it, sir. Harry?'

'I'm on it, Top.'

The supply sergeant clicked his fingers and pointed. In response, one of the supply clerks tossed him a pump shotgun, which Harry plucked from the air. Against his bulk, the weapon looked almost like a toy.

Battleax stood stunned, sweeping the entire room again with her eyes. This time, no one was smiling.

226

'You're all really quite serious about this, aren't you?' she said.

In answer, Chocolate Harry worked the slide of the shotgun he was holding, racking a live shell into the weapon's chamber with a harsh sound that echoed in the room, and the weapon no longer looked like a toy.

'Easy, Harry,' Rembrandt ordered, her voice still tight with tension. 'Look, Colonel. We're going after the captain, no matter who gets in our way. Now stand back or fall back. It's your choice.'

'You know, don't you, that they're likely to kill him if you try to take him by force?' Battleax's voice was suddenly soft.

'There's that possibility,' the lieutenant acknowledged. 'But there's as much a chance that they'll kill him if we don't. You see, his father won't pay the ransom.'

'It don't make no difference,' Chocolate Harry put in.

'What was that, Sergeant?'

'You folks may know more about the military then me,' C.H. said, 'but let me tell you somethin' about criminals. They're lookin' at some serious charges now that they've moved up to kidnappin'. They're not gonna want to leave any witnesses around, and the biggest witness against them is the cap'n. They *gotta* kill him, whether the money gets paid or not.'

'We're the only chance Captain Jester has of coming out of this alive,' Rembrandt continued quietly. 'We've got to at least try. If we just sit around . . .' She shook her head, letting her voice trail off.

'I see,' Battleax said thoughtfully. 'Tell me, Lieutenant, since you won't let me relieve you of command, would you be willing to accept me as a civilian advisor?'

Lieutenant Rembrandt's face split in a sudden smile.

'I'm always ready to listen to advice, Colonel,' she said. 'I'm still fairly new at this.'

'You'll do,' Battleax said. 'However, there's one thing I think you should consider in your plans – something I get the feeling you've overlooked in your enthusiasm. There are large numbers of civilians in the complex who are legitimate innocent bystanders. I think it would be wisest in the long run if an effort was made to ensure they didn't get caught in your cross fire.'

The two lieutenants exchanged glances.

'She's got a point there, Remmie,' Armstrong acknowledged reluctantly.

'What I would suggest is some sort of diversion,' the colonel continued. 'Something to give you an excuse to evacuate people from the complex, or at least from the vicinity of your action.'

'I suppose,' Rembrandt said, chewing her lower lip subconsciously. 'Maybe we could arrange a bomb threat or a fire alarm . . .'

'Why not a movie?'

The officers looked in the direction of this new voice.

'What was that, Lex?'

'I said, "Why not a movie?" ' Lex grinned, moving to join their discussion. 'Just tell everyone you need to clear the complex for an hour or so because you're shooting some footage for a new holo. Believe me, they'll cooperate. You'd be amazed at how people bend over backward to be helpful if they think it gets them a closer look at the magical mystical world of moviemaking.'

'That has possibilities,' Rembrandt said, looking at Armstrong.

'I know I'd go along with a holo crew if they asked me to get out of their way,' her partner admitted.

'It's better than a bomb scare or a fire alarm,' the actor urged. 'No panic, no bad publicity for the complex. What's more, we have everything we need to pull it off.'

'How so?'

'That cameraman you were holding has a holo-camera rig in his room. It's not the same as they use for the big productions, but we can say it's a low-budget operation or that we're just shooting test footage. We've even got a recognizable holo star we can parade in front of everyone to be sure it all looks legit.'

'You mean Dee Dee Watkins?' Armstrong frowned. 'Do you think she'd go along with it?'

'Leave her to me.' Lex winked. 'Remember, I speak the language. It might cost a little, though.'

'Set it up, Lex,' Rembrandt said, reaching her decision. 'In fact, I'll put the whole diversion in your hands, since you know more about this sort of thing than any of us. If anyone gives you any flak, tell them I've given you a battle-field promotion to the rank of acting sergeant for the duration of this operation.'

She glanced at Battleax, who nodded her approval.

'Yes, *sir*,' Lex said, snapped off a salute, and started to turn away, then hesitated. 'What about the owner . . . whazizname . . . Gunther? Should I clear this with him as well?'

'If you want, Remmie, I'll handle that,' Armstrong offered. 'I've gotten the impression that Mr. Rafael is afraid of me, for some reason.'

'Do that, Lieutenant,' Rembrandt said. 'But remember to ask nice.'

Armstrong frowned. 'I hadn't planned to *ask* . . . just inform him of what we were going to do.'

'That's what I meant' Rembrandt smiled sweetly. 'Carry on, Lieutenant. You, too, Sergeant.'

The actor moved a few steps away and triggered his wrist communicator.

'Lex, you rascal,' came Mother's voice. 'How many times have I got to tell you no before you stop tying up the airwaves? You're a gorgeous hunk of man, but I just ain't interested. Okay?'

The actor flushed slightly at the snickers that erupted from the Legionnaires standing close enough to hear, but pressed on with his new duty.

'This is *Sergeant* Lex, Mother, and this is an *official* call.'

'Come again?'

'I said this is Sergeant – all right, *Acting* Sergeant Lex. I'm down here at the war council, and Lieutenant Rembrandt has just put me on a special assignment. I need your help.'

'Who doesn't?' came the jaunty response. 'Okay, *Acting* Sergeant Lex, what can I do for you?'

229

'Dee Dee Watkins should be finishing her show in the next few minutes,' the actor said. 'Have someone meet her when she comes offstage and bring her over to the war council. Then see if you can find that cameraman and send him along as well. In fact, get the reporter, too, if you can find her. No harm in a little publicity while we're doing this. Also, pass the word to the duty crew that there'll be new orders coming shortly. We're going to be evacuating the complex for a while. Got that?'

'Got it,' Mother echoed. 'Sounds like we're finally on the move.'

'I'll leave that explanation to Lieutenant Rembrandt,' Lex countered. 'Just put those calls through, and give me a confirmation when you're done. Okay?'

'I'm on it. Mother out.'

Glancing around, Lex caught Trooper's eye and beckoned him over.

'I've got to duck out of here for a few minutes,' he said. 'If Dee Dee or the others show up, hang on to them until I get back.'

'Where are you going, Lex?' the youth inquired.

'I don't know about the cameraman,' the actor explained, 'but I *do* know Dee Dee won't powder her nose without a contract. Fortunately I happen to have a couple blanks upstairs in my room.'

'You do?'

'I never leave home without one, kid, even if I only end up using it for a reference.' Lex winked. 'As you can see, there's no telling when your next job might pop up.'

In short order, the meeting had broken down into a number of small groups, each working out the details of their own portion of the operation. Conversation ebbed and swirled as small arguments broke out over one specific or other, but these were quickly smoothed over. Despite their occasional differences, everyone was united behind one objective – to free their captain before any harm came to him – and there was simply no time to indulge in petty bickering.

'I *know* there are holes in it,' Lex was saying to Dee Dee.

'I just thought you'd rather have *some* kind of contract. If you want, we can do this on scout's honor.'

'Not a chance,' the starlet said. 'But *really*, Lex, this contract is for a series, not a movie.'

'It's a fast copy of *my* last contract,' the actor explained, 'which happened to be for a series. We don't have time to put together a new agreement from scratch. Think of it as being for a series of *movies*.'

'At *these* prices? Not bloody likely,' Dee Dee said with a snort.

'I keep *telling* you, love, there's no actual movie involved. We just want to make a bit of noise and clutter so that the tourists will *think* we're making a movie.'

'Even so, I'm worth ten times what's being offered here.'

Lex flashed a wide smile at her.

'Oh, come *on*, ducks. Maybe the *rabble* will believe that, if you plant it in enough columns, but you and I both know that if you could command those kinds of prices, you wouldn't be doing a lounge act right now.'

'You're such a bastard, Lex,' the starlet said, baring her teeth.

'Look, don't think of it as being *underpaid* for a movie, think of it as being vastly *overpaid* for maybe an hour's posturing. Now, do you want in on this or not? We can shove someone else out in front of the camera, you know, but I'd rather it was someone the common folk will recognize.'

'Oh, all *right!*' Dee Dee grumbled, scribbling her name next to Lex's on the document. 'Now, how about wardrobe? What's this thing supposed to be about, anyway?'

'We figured the rough scenario would be the wronged woman – only you're an ex-army type so you're getting even with a machine gun or something. That will explain all the uniforms and lethal hardware we'll have hanging around.'

'Not bad,' the actress said judiciously. 'With the Lorelei backdrop, we could call it *The Long Shot*. Say, does that mean I get one of those uniforms like everyone else is wearing?'

That much of the conversation, at least, caught the attention of several of the Legionnaires in the room. Glancing over to check Lex's reaction, they noted that, to his credit, a quick expression of distaste swept across his features before he caught himself and regained his confident smile.

'And hide those luscious curves of yours in baggy fatigues?' he said smoothly. 'Not a chance, love. We want something that will show off everything the public is paying to see. How about that sexy tight outfit you were wearing at rehearsals?'

'You mean my old leotard?' The starlet frowned. 'It's got a couple tears in it and is worn almost through in spots . . . some rather *revealing* spots.'

'Precisely.' Lex beamed. 'Of course, we'll give you some nasty-looking weaponry and maybe an ammo belt . . . Sergeant Harry?'

'Yo, Lex.'

'Can you fix Dee Dee up with some big, ugly armaments? Something that looks scary, but is light enough for her to handle?'

'Can do,' the supply sergeant said, his eyes darting over the starlet's form. I'll have one of the boys pull the firing pin just to be sure it don't go off accidental.'

'There. You see?'

'But . . .'

'Just scamper along, love, and fetch back that outfit. I think we're going to be moving soon.'

Chocolate Harry, in the meantime, was having problems of his own. A small tug-of-war was escalating between one of his supply clerks and the big Voltron, Tusk-anini.

'Come on, Tusk,' Super Gnat was saying, trying to dissuade her partner. 'We can go with something else.'

'*Give me weapon now!*' the Voltron insisted, ignoring the little Legionnaire as he tugged once more at the armament the supply clerk was clinging to, all but lifting the man's feet from the ground in the process.

'Hold it, tusk-anini!' C.H. said, stepping in. 'What seems to be the problem here, Jason?'

'He wants to use one of the Rolling Thunder belt-fed

shotguns,' the clerk complained, still red-faced from the argument and the exertion, 'but he hasn't ever qualified with it!'

'You really want to use this, Tusk?' the sergeant said, making no effort to hide his surprise. 'It don't really seem to be your style.'

The belt-fed shotguns were some of the deadliest, most vicious weapons in the company's arsenal. To say the least, it was an unlikely choice for the Voltron, whose pacifistic nature was well known.

'Captain need help. *This* will help!' Tusk-anini growled, not releasing his grip on the weapon.

'Give it to him,' C.H. said, turning back to the supply clerk.

'But Sarge . . .'

'*Give it to him*. I'll check him out on it myself.'

With a shrug, the clerk released the weapon and watched as Tusk-anini walked away, cradling the bit of nastiness protectively in his arms.

'*You* tell *me*, hoss,' the sergeant said softly. 'Can you think of anyone in this outfit who could hold down that weapon better'n Tusk? It's got a kick like a sonofabitch.'

'Well, no. But . . .'

''Sides, didn't your mama ever tell you it ain't healthy to argue with somethin' that outweighs you by maybe a ton?' Harry finished. 'I'll tell you, Jase, you still got a lot to learn about survivin'.'

With that he turned to go, only to find his path blocked by Colonel Battleax.

'Tell me, Sergeant,' she said, 'now that we have a moment relatively alone. That little episode we had earlier . . . would you have *really* shot me?'

Harry had the grace to look a bit abashed.

'I'd of had to, Colonel,' he admitted. 'Truth is, I'd rather of just tried to knock you out, but the cap'n says there's a rule against noncoms hitting officers.'

'Excuse me . . . Lieutenant Rembrandt?'

'Yes, Beeker?'

'If I might have a moment of your time?'

The lieutenant glanced around the room to be sure everything was going smoothly – or as smoothly as could be expected – then nodded.

'Sure, Beek. What's up?'

'Am I understanding correctly that you're nearly ready to commence your rescue attempt?'

'Well, I think we're about as ready as we'll ever be,' Rembrandt confirmed.

'I notice that I have not been included in any of your planning,' the butler said, 'and I do appreciate that. I believe my employer would be most distressed if he thought I was attempting to assume a place in the company chain of command.'

The Lieutenant smiled. 'Don't worry. You're considered a civilian for this one – strictly noncombatant.'

'Quite . . . well, not quite.' Beeker frowned. 'That's what I wished to speak to you about. You see, I feel my own course of action in this situation is quite clear, nor is it likely that anyone could dissuade me from it. I thought, however, that you should be made aware of exactly what it is I intend to do, so that you could take it into account in your planning or, perhaps, even interphase with it.'

Leaning close, the butler launched into an explanation of his thoughts. At first, Rembrandt frowned, shaking her head slightly, but as Beeker continued speaking, a slow, broad smile crept across her face.

As I have mentioned throughout this account, my role in this campaign was larger than normal, and never so noticeable as it was for the rescue attempt. I would hasten to clarify, however, that this did not mean I joined the Space Legion, even on a temporary basis, and was therefore never under their command or control. I am a butler, and owe my loyalties to a single, chosen individual, and the idea of accepting assigned authority has always been abhorrent to me. If anything, I prefer to think that the Space Legion temporarily joined me.

*

Max did not share Laverna's taste for holos, preferring instead to read during her occasional leisure time. She was indulging in this pastime now, having a substantial hunk of time to fill, and curled up on the sofa with a lamp shining over her shoulder and onto the book she was reading, Maxine almost gave the suite an air of domestic tranquillity. The effect was ruined, however, by the presence of the two gunmen in the room with her. Wearing their weapons openly in shoulder holsters, they alternately wandered around the room, peered out the window through the crack in the drawn curtains, fidgeted, and idly leafed through the room's small stack of magazines, looking at the pictures rather than actually reading.

Max found the extra movement in the room to be an irritating distraction, but refrained from saying anything. It wouldn't do to have her guards sullen or resentful at this stage of the game.

The truth was that they were all a trifle on edge. The nature of their operation normally allowed Maxine and those under her command free rein to prowl the casinos and walkways of Lorelei at will. Close confinement like this was unusual, and even though she had deliberately kept the contingent of guards down to four, Max found having extra people in her living quarters to be an unexpected trial. In idle moments, she mused over the irony that, as much as their unwilling guest, she and her people were being held prisoner by the current situation.

Max glanced up as Laverna eased into the room through the bedroom door, gently closing it behind her.

'Is he still asleep?' she said, glad for the interruption.

'He sure is,' her aide responded, shaking her head. 'I swear sometimes I think we're doing that child a favor. He hasn't budged since he stretched out.'

Upon arriving, under guard, at Maxine's suite, Phule's first request had been to ask if he could 'lie down for a few minutes,' and he had been sleeping ever since. Seemingly unruffled by his capture, he appeared to be taking advantage of the situation to get some long-overdue rest.

Laverna caught the eye of one of the guards.

'Your buddy in there wants someone to spell him for a while,' she said. 'Says he's going a little buggy sitting in the dark with nothing to do but watch our friend sleep.'

One of the guards shrugged and started for the bedroom door, but Max waved him off.

'That won't be necessary,' she countered. 'I think our guest has slept long enough. Besides, it's about time we had a little chat. Laverna, would you wake Mr. Phule up and ask him to join us?'

'*No, ma'am.*'

The sudden fierceness in her aide's tone startled Max almost as much as the rare refusal.

'What was that, Laverna?' She blinked, more stalling for time to collect her own thoughts than actually requiring a repetition.

'I said, "No, ma'am",' Laverna repeated, shaking her head. 'I usually stay out of this side of the business and just handle the books, and I know you might have to kill him sooner or later' – she fixed Maxine with a hard gaze – 'but I don't ever want to have to tell Beeker that I had any part in mistreating his gentleman while he was in our care. I say if the man wants to sleep, let him sleep! Otherwise, get someone else to wake him up. *I'm* not going to do it.'

Before Maxine had to reach a decision over what to do about this open rebellion, the matter was settled for her. The bedroom door opened and Phule emerged, his uniform slightly disheveled, but aside from that looking relaxed and refreshed.

'No need to fight, ladies.' He smiled, his eyes twinkling with amusement. 'I'm already awake. Thanks, anyway, Laverna. I'll be sure to mention your consideration to Beeker when – or should I say *if* – I see him again.'

He ignored the guard who ghosted through the door behind him to rejoin the others, just as the guards tended to ignore the main conversation in the room.

'Sit down, Mr. Phule,' Maxine said, setting her book aside and gesturing toward a chair. 'I take it you overheard Laverna's unfortunate comment about the possibility of having to eliminate you?'

'I did,' Phule admitted, sinking into the indicated seat, 'but to be honest with you, it was no surprise. I assumed from the beginning I was only being kept alive so that, if necessary, I could speak to my father for you to confirm that I was in good health. Once the ransom is paid . . .'

He shrugged and left the end of the sentence unsaid.

'Then you think he'll pay?' Max pressed. 'Forgive my curiosity, but this is the first time I've dealt with someone of your father's standing.'

'I really don't know,' the Legionnaire said easily. 'Frankly I doubt it, but he's surprised me before.'

'If you don't mind my saying so, Mr. Phule,' Maxine said, 'you seem to be taking this very calmly.'

'I see it as the price of stupidity,' Phule replied, grimacing slightly. 'I got so wrapped up trying to protect the complex, *and* Gunther Rafael, *and* my troops, that I completely overlooked the possibility of my own danger until I opened my door and saw your assistants standing there with their weapons trained on me. They're very good, by the way.'

He paused to nod his compliments to the guards, but they ignored him.

'Anyway,' he continued, 'as I was saying, it was a stupid oversight, and stupidity at my level is unforgivable. It's also usually fatal, either physically or financially. By rights, I should have been dead as soon as I opened the door without checking first, and I tend to view any time I have after that as a bonus rather than brooding, getting bitter, or attempting any hopeless heroics when faced with the possibility of my eventual demise. I mean, everybody dies sometime.'

'True,' Maxine acknowledged thoughtfully, 'though somehow I've never been able to accept it as philosophically as you seem to. However, getting back to your father for a moment . . .'

'Please,' the commander said, holding up a restraining hand, 'if this is going to be a long discussion, I'd like something to drink first. I seem to be a bit dehydrated after my nap. Is there any chance you have any coffee or juice about?'

'I'll get it,' Laverna said, heading for the suite's kitchenette.

'Excuse me,' one of the guards said suddenly. He was standing at the windows and had just parted the curtain slightly with one finger to peek out. 'Did anyone hear a fire alarm?'

'No,' Maxine said, speaking for the whole room. 'Why do you ask?'

'There's a big crowd of people down there, just standing and staring up at the casino. Looks like a fire drill. They've got some of those black uniforms keeping the space in front of the entrance clear.'

'Let me see,' one of the other gunmen said, moving to join him. 'No, it must be a newscast or somethin'. See, those lights . . . and there's a camera!'

Max felt a vague twinge of alarm. She really didn't believe in coincidences, and a news team appearing while they were holding a mega-millionaire hostage . . .

'Hey! Look at the babe! They must be shooting a commercial.'

'Yeah?' the third gunman said, suddenly attentive. So far, he had resisted joining his colleagues, staying at his post on the far side of the room. 'What's she look like?'

'Can't see her too well,' came the response. 'I think she's only wearing body paint, though. C'm'ere and look.'

A sharp rapping at the room door froze everyone into a startled tableau. The guards at the window let the curtain drop back into place and stood, hands on their weapons, waiting for orders.

The knock came again, and the guard closest to the door shot an inquiring glance at Maxine, who answered with a silent nod.

Flattening against the wall beside the door, the guard drew his weapon, then reached out and put his hand over the peephole used to check visitors. It was an old trick, and a normal precaution against someone shooting through the door when they saw the dot of light visible from the other side change as someone looked through.

Nothing happened.

Moving carefully, the guard slowly turned the doorknob, then threw the door open with a jerk.

'Good evening. My name is Beeker. Forgive the intrusion, but I'm with – oh! There you are, sir.'

The guard gaped helplessly as the butler strode past him and into the suite.

'Hey, Beek!' Phule called in greeting. 'I was wondering how long it would take you to show up.'

'It's good to see you, sir.' Beeker said unemotionally. 'If I might say so, you're looking well.'

'Beeker, what are you doing here?' Laverna demanded, emerging from the kitchenette.

'Oh, hello, Laverna.' The butler flashed a quick smile. 'I was simply–'

'If I might interrupt,' Maxine broke in, her voice dripping with cold sarcasm, 'could somebody search this man for weapons, if it's not too much trouble, and *shut that door!*'

Her words broke the spell, and the guards galvanized into action. The door to the corridor was quickly closed, and one guard patted the butler down in a careful search while another stood by, weapon at the ready.

'He's clean,' the searcher said, but missed the withering glare his victim gave in answer to this report.

'Now then, Mr. Beeker,' Maxine purred, 'I believe you were about to explain what you're doing here.'

'Ah, you must be Mrs. Pruet.' Beeker smiled. 'I've heard so much about you, it's a real pleasure to meet you at last. And it's just "Beeker," if you please.'

He gave a small half-bow in Max's direction.

'As to my presence,' he continued, 'I should think that would be obvious – to Ms. Laverna, at least. I am Mr. Phule's butler, ma'am, and my place is with him, regardless of circumstances. Simply put, when you acquired the company of my employer, you acquired us both. While I apologize if this presents an unexpected inconvenience for you, I'm afraid I must insist. It's a package deal.'

'I . . . umm . . . think you've gone a little overboard with your conscientiousness, Beek,' Phule said, smiling in spite of his concern. 'Your presence really isn't required – or appropriate. I suggest you leave.'

'Nonsense, sir,' the butler chided. 'As you are aware, under the terms of our contract you may define my duties for me, but the method by which I execute them is left to *my* discretion.'

'I *could* fire you,' the commander suggested, but again the butler shook his head.

'Quite impossible, I'm afraid. That would require giving written notice, not to mention—'

'It's too late, anyway,' Maxine said, cutting the exchange short. 'You see, Mr. Phule, now that ... Beeker ... has seen fit to join us, I'm afraid that ...'

Another knock at the door interrupted them.

It was an indication of how rattled the guard was that he simply opened the door without taking any of his earlier precautions.

'Room service!'

'I'm afraid you're mistaken,' the guard said. 'We haven't ordered anything.'

He glanced back over his shoulder for confirmation.

'I'm afraid *I* did,' Beeker declared. 'Forgive me, but I took the liberty of ordering a meal for Mr. Phule. Over here, please!'

The short, dark, white-coated waiter wheeled the table-cloth-covered service cart into the room past the hapless guard.

Laverna frowned. 'What's the matter, Beeker? Didn't you think we'd feed him?'

'Did you?' the butler asked, arching an eyebrow.

'Well, as a matter of fact ... I mean, he's been sleeping ...' she stammered, but the butler came to her rescue.

'No need to apologize,' he said. 'I'm aware of Mr. Phule's eating habits, such as they are. That is, in fact, what prompted me to order a meal without bothering to check first. Certain things can almost be taken as assumed.'

'Well, can *I* assume that someone is going to search the

waiter?' Maxine prompted, making no effort now to hide her annoyance. 'And will you please *shut that door!*'

The guards hastened to carry out her bidding.

'And while you're at it, check to see if there's anything besides food on those covered plates.'

The guard who had just finished searching the waiter started to reach for one of the metal covers on the cart, but the waiter knocked his hand away in a sudden show of anger.

'Do not touch the food,' he snarled. 'I fix myself for the captain. Here . . . *I* show you plates.'

Startled by this abrupt display, the guard stepped back.

'Just a moment!' Maxine said, rising to her feet. 'Did you say that *you* prepared the food? And how did you know . . .'

Her eyes darted to the door to the corridor.

'For that matter,' she said, 'isn't there supposed to be a guard outside that door? Would somebody *please* check to see . . .'

A shrill noise interrupted her.

All eyes turned toward Beeker, as the butler glanced at his wrist communicator, from which the sound was emanating.

'I'm afraid it's too late for that,' he said calmly, carefully hitching up his trouser legs before sitting abruptly on the floor. 'In fact, I would strongly suggest that no one in the room have any portion of their persons above the height of waist level when the sound stops. If you'd care to join me, sir?'

Without hesitation, Phule slid off his chair to lie beside the waiter, who was already squatting next to the service cart.

'What in the world . . . ?'

'The man's saying *get down, Max!*' Laverna cried, throwing herself to the floor.

'Oh, very well,' Maxine grumbled, lowering herself gingerly.

The guards lost no time diving to the carpet as the room seemed to explode.

BA-AM-BAM-BAM-AM-BAM-BAM-AM-AM–

Salesmen for Phule-Proof Munitions claimed, with some

241

justification, that merely the *sound* of one of their Rolling Thunder belt-fed shotguns was sufficient to intimidate most opponents. However, few, if any, attempted to convey, or even consider, the effect of *three* of these same weapons being fired simultaneously in a close space.

AM-BAM-AM-AM-BAM-AM-BAM–

Large chunks were being blasted from the wall separating the living room from the corridor outside. Through the holes, if anyone dared to raise their head to look, could be seen Tusk-anini, Moustache, and Brandy, standing abreast as they swept their murderous weapons across the wall.

BAM-BAM-AM-BAM-AM-AM–

Not content with the holes, the quartet continued to fire, opening a long, ragged slot in the wall. Within the room, pictures fell and lamps exploded as more and more of the blast-driven shot poured in unhindered by the rapidly disintegrating wall. In the teeth of the carnage, Super Gnat and the Sinthian, Louie, the two smallest Legionnaires in the company, emerged from where they had been hiding on the lower shelf of the covered room-service cart, rolling sideways into a firing position with their weapons covering the prone criminals.

AM-BAM-BAM-AM-AM-BAM!!

The firing ceased abruptly, but before the echoes had fully died, a row of Legionnaires who had been lying against the wall outside while the shotguns did their work over their heads rose into view, thrusting their weapons through the ruined wall to menace the entire room.

'*Nobody move!*'

Rembrandt's voice cracked slightly, and seemed pitifully weak in the wake of the senses-shattering din, but no one chose to challenge her.

Ironically, considering the gaping hole in the wall, someone had to open the door from the inside to let the troops in.

As some disarmed the shaken criminals, including relieving Maxine of her sleeve pistol, others opened the drapes and waved at the crowd below.

'*We got him! He's okay!*' they called, and a faint cheer answered them from below.

Maxine tipped some debris off one of the chairs, then sat down on it, resting her arms on the table as a host of Legionnaires watched her carefully.

'Well, Captain,' she said, 'it looks like I underestimated you again.'

'Actually I believe you underestimated my troops,' Phule corrected, winking at the Legionnaires, who grinned back at him. 'Them . . . and Beeker, of course.'

'Of course,' Max said, sending a dark look toward the butler. 'I certainly shan't forget his role in this. Well, I'll know better next time.'

'Next time?' The Legionnaire commander frowned. 'I really don't think there'll be a next time, Mrs. Pruet. I believe the charges against you will keep you out of circulation for quite a while.'

'Nonsense, Captain,' Maxine said, favoring him with a superior smirk. 'Do you think it's accidental that I've never been arrested? Laverna! Please fetch me some paper and a pen.'

'Do you really think you can just walk away from this?' Phule said, shaking his head in disbelief. 'There's no one you can write to with enough authority to keep you from going to jail.'

'And just what would that accomplish, Mr. Phule?' Max said, accepting the pen and paper from Laverna and beginning to write as she spoke. 'The potential for crime on Lorelei is far too great to go unexploited. If I'm removed from my position of control, all that will happen is that another person or group will take my place – someone, perhaps, like that organization your man posed as a member of. Believe me, Captain, there are those who would be far less genteel than I in running things. As to there not being anyone who can prevent me from going to jail, you're wrong. There *is* one person, Mr. Phule. *You!*'

'Me?'

'Certainly. If you should choose not to press charges or

243

bring my activities to the attention of the authorities or the media, I shall be free to continue my operation as normal.'

'You expect me to turn a blind eye to what you've tried to do? Just because you're more civilized than most about running your syndicate?'

'No, Captain. I expect you to seriously consider a proposition of mutual advantage to both of us – a bribe, if you will. First, however, let me remind you that your *stated* objective was *not* to put me out of business, but rather to stop me from attempting to gain control of the Fat Chance. I'm prepared to offer that in exchange for my freedom.'

'That's a surprisingly weak offer, coming from you, Mrs. Pruet,' Phule said stiffly. 'In exchange for my letting you go, you're proposing to give me a promise in writing that you won't try to gain control of the Fat Chance – something you haven't been able to do so far and would find doubly difficult to attempt from jail?'

'Don't be crass, Mr. Phule,' Maxine said, signing the paper in front of her with a flourish and setting the pen aside. 'What I have here is a document assigning Mr. Rafael's loan agreement with me over to you, or more specifically, your Space Legion company. *That* will negate my interest, not to mention my primary weapon, in taking over this facility. Allow me to walk away from this, and you can renegotiate more favorable payment terms for Mr. Rafael, accept the scheduled payment, or eliminate the debt completely.'

She picked up the paper and extended it toward the commander.

'Well, Captain?' She smiled. 'What do you say? Do we have a deal?'

Chapter Fifteen

Journal #250

Maxine Pruet's capitulation effectively ended the challenging portion of this assignment. All that remained was the cleaning up of a few details, and, of course, normal guard duty.

Anyone who believes that a cease-fire, surrender, or treaty automatically means the end of hostilities, however, lacks even the shallowest awareness of military history . . . or even a general history of mankind . . .

The meeting in Phule's suite was originally intended as an informal debriefing with his officers. Colonel Battleax came calling, however, with a large bottle of excellent brandy, and the gathering soon took on a more relaxed, social atmosphere.

'One thing I'll grant you, Captain Jester,' the colonel said as she raised her glass, the most recent of several, in a mock toast. 'Things are certainly never dull around you.'

'Hear, hear!' Lieutenant Rembrandt agreed, raising her own glass. She was finally starting to relax from her brief stint as acting company commander, and the combination of the brandy and relief was making her a little owlish.

'Of all the possible outcomes of this debacle,' Battleax continued, shaking her head, 'the one thing I never thought I'd see was Maxine Pruet presenting you with a unit commendation – on stellarwide network, no less – "with the gratitude of the Lorelei Casino Owners Association for successfully preventing organized crime from taking over the Fat Chance Casino"!'

She let out a sudden bark of laughter, nearly spilling her drink.

'I thought she handled it rather well . . . all things considered,' Phule said, grinning. 'Actually, though, it was a logical move for her, if you stop to think about it. I mean, she *is* the president of the association, which isn't surprising considering that she owns the lion's share of all the casinos on the space station *except* the Fat Chance. By making a big thing of organized crime being repelled from the Fat Chance, she implies that it's not anywhere else on Lorelei. Basically she got a lot of favorable free publicity out of a bad situation. She's a sharp old bird, I'll give her that. Oh well, at least Jennie got her exclusive story.'

'True,' the colonel said. 'Of course, the way she glossed things over with half-truths and distortions, there might be a bigger future for her as a popular-fiction writer. I had trouble sorting out exactly what happened, and I was *there* – for most of it, anyway.'

'Just one thing puzzles me, Captain,' Armstrong said from his seat on the sofa. 'What was that bit she was saying about welcoming you to the Casino Owners Association?'

The company commander made a face, then took another sip of brandy before answering.

'I was going to sit on this for a while,' he said, 'but we might be stuck with part ownership of the Fat Chance for a while.'

The lieutenant frowned. 'How so? I thought our share was going back to Rafael once he paid off the loan.'

'That's the problem,' Phule said. 'I had a meeting with Gunther earlier today, and it seems he might not be able to pay off the loan.'

'Why not?' Battleax demanded. 'I thought you and your hard cases pretty much eliminated the cheats that were going to bleed off the profits.'

'We did,' Phule said. 'The trouble is, there wasn't that much profit to start with. Gunther's big plan was to draw customers by giving better odds than the other casinos on Lorelei. Unfortunately the odds he gave were so favorable to the guests that his profit margin was next to nothing.

The reason I haven't said anything is that I'm still trying to make up my mind as to where to go from here. Do we give him an extension of the loan, or do we go ahead and accumulate forty-nine percent of the ownership?'

'Something you might want to consider, Captain,' the colonel said, staring into her glass as she twirled it between her hands. 'Mr. Rafael may not want to buy back your shares. I can see certain advantages to him in keeping you as a silent partner, with a vested interest in the continued success of the Fat Chance.'

'It's funny you should say that.' The commander smiled wryly. 'Beeker raised the same point. I may want to make a quick audit of Gunther's books at some point. At the very least, I want him to ease his payout odds down until they're more in line with the other casinos.'

'By the way, where *is* Beeker?' Rembrandt said, peering around the room as if expecting to discover the butler hiding behind the furniture. 'I'd like to buy him a drink sometime now that things have eased up a little.'

'He has the night off,' Phule said. 'In fact, I believe he has a date.'

'You mean with the Ice Bitch again?' Rembrandt scowled. 'I don't know why you don't try harder to discourage that, Captain. That woman gives me the creepy-crawlies.'

'I figure who Beeker sees is his own business,' the commander said. 'Since you asked, though, I believe he's seeing Dee Dee Watkins tonight.'

'Now, *there's* a mismatch,' the lieutenant growled, refilling her glass.

'You see something wrong with a starlet showing interest in a lowly butler?' Phule said, his voice chilling slightly.

'No . . . I mean I don't know what *he* sees in *her*.'

'*I* do,' Armstrong smirked.

Rembrandt stuck her tongue out at him.

'Speaking of Ms. Watkins,' Armstrong said, 'there *is* a situation that's come up that you should be aware of, Captain.'

'Now what?'

'Well, sir' – Armstrong sneaked a wink at Rembrandt,

who grinned in return – 'you know that fake holo-movie we threw together as an excuse to evacuate the complex? It seems we've gotten a raft of calls both from people who want to invest in the film as backers and from outfits that want to bid on exclusive distribution rights. So far Mother's just been taking names and messages, but eventually someone is going to have to call them back and let them all know there's no movie. Remmie and I have talked it over, and we agree that you're the logical person to handle that . . . sir.'

The commander frowned. 'Why?'

'Well, aside from the fact that you have more experience dealing with money people, there's the fact that–'

'No,' Phule interrupted. 'I meant why tell them that there's no movie?'

'Sir?'

'Why not just form a film company and make the movie? Between the backers and the distributors, you already have the main necessary ingredient: money. If anything, it sounds like it might be a worthwhile investment for the company fund.'

'But we don't know anything abut making movies!' Armstrong protested.

'So hire people that do to run it for us,' the commander said. 'People like . . . say, actors and stuntmen? Maybe even a cameraman? I'll bet that any aspect of the industry they can't cover, they'll know someone who can.'

'My God!' Battleax said, starting to giggle uncontrollably. 'That's so outrageous, it just might work!'

'No reason why it shouldn't,' Phule said. 'It's got a lot more going for it than most of the companies I bought or founded when I was first starting out. Heck, we even have Dee Dee Watkins signed to a multiple-movie contract.'

'She's going to scream bloody murder when she finds out,' Rembrandt said. 'Can I be the one to tell her, Captain? Please?'

'First, let me review the contract with Lex,' the commander insisted. 'I think we're going to have to renegotiate it with fairer terms. It doesn't really pay in the long run to have your contract help sullen and bitter because they think they're being exploited.'

'Oh, *that's* no fun!' Rembrandt said, dropping into a mock sulk.

Phule grinned. 'You'd be surprised, Lieutenant. I didn't say we were going to give her a super offer – just something a bit fairer than what she's already signed. If anything, it can be a real hoot negotiating a new contract with someone who's already signed off on a bad deal, especially if they know that if they don't agree to the new terms, the old deal stands. If you'd like, you can handle the first rounds on *that* discussion.'

'Thank you, sir!' The lieutenant beamed, and blew him a kiss, to boot.

'You know, Captain Jester,' Battleax said, 'the more I hear about this, the more I find myself thinking about investing some of my own money in it, if there's still openings for new backers. Perhaps we can discuss it over dinner – that and a few other things.'

'A few other things like what, Colonel?' Phule said warily.

Battleax hesitated, glanced at the lieutenants, then shrugged.

'I suppose there's no harm in at least *mentioning* this in the current company.' She smiled. 'After seeing your junior officers in action, I think it's time we discussed their next promotion. If you agree with me, I think they're just about ready for commands of their own.'

Startled by this unexpected turn in the conversation, the lieutenants exchanged glances.

'I. . . That really isn't necessary, Colonel,' Rembrandt stammered. 'I can't speak for Lieutenant Armstrong, but I'm quite happy right where I am.'

'If given a choice, sir,' Armstrong said, 'I'd prefer to continue my training under Captain Jester.'

'We'll see,' the colonel said. 'In the meantime . . .'

She broke off with a frown as Phule's wrist communicator began to beep insistently.

'Really, Captain. Isn't there any way you can put a Do Not Disturb sign on that thing?'

'As a matter of fact, I did,' Phule said as he opened the channel. 'Jester here!'

'Hey, Big Daddy!' Mother's voice chirped at him. 'Sorry to bother you, but I got General Blitzkrieg on the line. You up to talking to him, or should I tell him you're in jail overnight?'

'I'll take it,' the commander said. 'Hang on a second.'

'Shall we leave, Captain?' Armstrong offered, starting to rise to his feet.

'Don't bother,' Phule said. 'But it might be better if you could all move to the far side of the room, so the holo cameras can't pick you up.'

He waited for a moment while his visitors gathered up their drinks and moved over against the wall, then opened communications again.

'All right, Mother,' he said. 'Patch him through on the regular communications gear.'

'You got it. Here he comes.'

Phule stepped in front of the communications console that was a part of the furnishing of his quarters and/or office wherever he went, and a few seconds later the image of General Blitzkrieg materialized before him.

'Good evening, General,' he said.

'I caught your showboating for the media, Captain Jester,' Blitzkrieg growled without greeting or preamble. 'Looks like you came out smelling like a rose . . . again.'

'Thank you, sir,' Phule said gravely. 'It was—'

'Of course,' the general continued, ignoring the response, 'I *also* saw some preliminary footage from what's supposed to be a new holo-movie being shot there on Lorelei . . . except that it has some of *your* troops in it, and they're doing an incredible amount of damage to the very complex they're supposed to be guarding!'

'Nothing to worry about there, General,' the commander said smoothly. 'The occupant of the room in question has agreed to pay for the necessary repairs and renovations.'

'Why would he do that?' Blitzkrieg scowled. 'It's clear that it's *your* pack of hell-raisers who are doing the damage.'

'Well, there's the fact that legally whoever rents a room

is responsible for any damages to the facility,' Phule explained. 'As to my troops actually causing the damage, the truth is they were sort of *invited* to take that action, by the room's occupant – and it's a she, sir, not a he. In fact, it's the same woman you saw presenting me and my unit with the commendation.'

'*Sort of* invited?' the general growled, catching the careful phrasing. 'I'd like to hear some more details on *that*, if you don't mind. First, though, I want to know what your troops are doing appearing in a holo-movie *in Space Legion uniforms.*'

'That's easy enough to explain, sir,' the commander said. 'As you yourself just said, sir, that was preliminary footage only. My troops were simply standing in while the camera angles were being blocked out. I can assure the general that they will not be present in the final version when it's released.'

'I see,' Blitzkrieg said grimly. 'Well, Captain, while I have you on the line, there are a few other matters I want to know about. For example . . .'

'Good evening, General,' Battleax said, leaving her place by the wall and stepping in front of the cameras.'

The general gaped. 'Colonel Battleax! What are *you* doing there? I thought you were—'

'On vacation?' the colonel purred. 'I was . . . as you very well know. It just so happens that my itinerary included a stop on Lorelei. You can imagine my surprise when I ran into Captain Jester and his troops here, especially since I hadn't heard a thing about this assignment before I left Headquarters.'

'Ummm . . . yes, of course,' Blitzkrieg mumbled, obviously uncomfortable. 'So you were in charge when all this was happening?'

'Not at all.' Battleax smiled. 'I'm merely a tourist while I'm on vacation. In fact, great pains were taken to be sure everyone knew I wasn't in the chain of command here.'

'I . . .'

'No need to apologize, General,' the colonel continued. 'I can understand your concern that I might have inadvertently

251

usurped your power, but I can assure you that *you're* still responsible for everything that Captain Jester and his troops do on this assignment.'

'*What's that?*' The general looked stricken.

'I'm simply reminding you that as the one who gave this assignment to Captain Jester, you are his immediate superior officer for the duration, and as such are ultimately responsible for anything he might do or order while under your direct command,' Battleax explained. 'Of course, if no inquiries are convened and no one of civil or *Legion* authority openly questions his activities, then nothing out of the ordinary will ever show in the records and the entire assignment will be filed as being routine. Do you see my point, General?'

'Yes, I see,' Blitzkrieg growled.

'I thought you would. Now, unless there's anything else of an urgent nature, do you mind if we conclude this interview? Captain Jester and I were just enjoying a quiet drink *in his room.*'

The general looked startled.

'Oh . . . I didn't realize . . . of course. Anything else I have can wait until a more convenient time. Good night, Colonel . . . Captain. Be sure to let me know when the new recruits arrive.'

'Wait a minute. New recruits?' Phule was suddenly alert. 'Excuse me, General Blitzkrieg, but I thought you agreed to hold off on any new recruits or transfers until I had a chance to get my outfit into shape.'

'I did,' Blitzkrieg said with an evil grin. 'But I don't think you object to these – most of them, anyway. The others, you *can't* object to.'

'Could you explain that a little more, sir?'

'Well . . . I don't want to intrude, so I'll keep this short. You're getting a trio of Gambolts . . . you know, the Cats? They're the first Gambolts to ever enlist in the Space Legion instead of joining their own unit in the Regular Army – which is a feather in our cap – but they signed on under the express condition that they be assigned to *your* unit. It seems your showboating for the media is finally paying some dividends.'

'I suppose that if—'

'The next one isn't really a recruit,' the general continued. 'He's an observer, sent by the Zenobians to study our tactics *and ethics* prior to their signing a treaty with us. You remember the Zenobians, don't you, Captain? Those little lizards you tangled with back on Haskin's Planet?'

'Of course, sir. I . . .'

'Since you were the first human to make contact with them, the government felt, and I agreed with them, that you would be the logical choice to deal with their observer. He remembers you, by the way. Even asked for you by name . . . except he remembers it as "Captain Clown".'

'I see.' Phule scowled. 'Is that all, sir?'

'Not quite.' The general grinned. 'The last one we're sending you is in response to *your* request.'

'My request, sir?'

'Yes. I have it right here.' Blitzkrieg held up a sheet of paper. 'It took me a while to find just the right Legionnaire to fit your needs, Captain, knowing as I do how selective you are, but I think I've got what you need. You requested a chaplain for your company, and I'm sending you one. Don't ever say that Headquarters doesn't give you the support you deserve. Blitzkrieg out.'

For several moments the four officers stared silently at the empty space left by the general's image after he broke the connection.

'Sir?' Armstrong said at last. 'A chaplain?'

'It's a long story, Lieutenant,' Phule said, rubbing his forehead with one hand. 'To be honest with you, I had forgotten completely about making the request.'

'I'd watch my step if I were you, Captain,' Colonel Battleax advised. 'The general's dislike for you doesn't seem to be mellowing with time.'

'We'll manage,' the commander said. 'However, in honor of the general *and* to celebrate the assignment, I'd like to propose a toast. I'm blatantly stealing it, but it somehow seems appropriate.'

He raised his glass toward his colleagues.

'To honorable enemies and dishonorable friends!'

In a casino restaurant elsewhere on Lorelei, another discussion of a totally different nature was taking place.

'I've got to admit, Max,' Laverna was saying, 'you're taking this a lot better than I thought you would.'

Maxine frowned. 'Taking what?'

'You know . . . having to back off from Willard Phule and his crew. I know it goes against the grain for you to throw in the towel.'

'Don't be silly, Laverna.' Max smiled. 'We're far from done with young Mr. Phule. I thought you realized that.'

Laverna cocked her head in surprise.

'You're going back on your word? I've never known you to do that, Max.'

'Who said I was going back on my word?' the crime kingpin said. 'All I promised was to abandon my efforts to gain control of the Fat Chance – a plan which, you'll recall, we had already all but given up on. Of course, you and I know that just because the Fat Chance is safe from *me* doesn't mean it's safe. What's more, as far as "safe" goes, I said nothing about leaving Mr. Phule and his force alone.'

'That's true,' Laverna admitted.

'It occurs to me that a lot of people saw that transmission today, when I effectively announced to one and all that the Fat Chance was outside my sphere of influence.'

'You mean you think some of the other families might have seen it?'

'Or the Yakusa,' Max acknowledged. 'Remember, we both found the tale our fraudulent Jonesy told to be possible enough to take him seriously. As a matter of fact, just in case they missed it, I'm sending them a copy of the tape, along with a personal note. Even if they aren't interested in the Fat Chance, I'm sure they'll be fascinated by the news that someone was posing as their representative. I'm also making inquiries as to whether or not a certain bartender did indeed ever ride with the Outlaws Hover Cycle Club,

254

and if he did, under what circumstances he left their company.'

Laverna leaned back in her chair and stared at her employer.

'You're really pulling out the stops on this one, aren't you?'

'As you pointed out, Laverna, I don't like to lose. However, you seem to have missed completely the most dubious maneuver I've pulled. It's not surprising, really. Young Mr. Phule seems to have missed it as well.'

'What was that?'

Maxine's eyes narrowed as she looked into the distance.

'Think for a moment, Laverna,' she said. 'If anyone, *you* would know about the disproportionate interest and suspicion the tax people level at casinos and their owners. Well, this afternoon's broadcast not only alerted *our* colleagues as to the opportunity now available at the Fat Chance, it also made some of our traditional adversaries aware that Mr. Phule is now among the ranks of casino owners ... and I don't think he's even *begun* to realize what's in store for him there.'